The
GIRL
FROM THE
RESISTANCE

BOOKS BY IMOGEN MATTHEWS

IMOGEN MATTHEWS

The
GIRL
FROM THE
RESISTANCE

bookouture

Published by Bookouture in 2023

An imprint of Storyfire Ltd.
Carmelite House
50 Victoria Embankment
London EC4Y 0DZ

www.bookouture.com

ISBN: 978-1-83790-172-2
eBook ISBN: 978-1-83790-171-5

ONE

HAARLEM, THE NETHERLANDS, MAY 1941

Trudi tiptoed down the narrow wooden staircase, trying to avoid putting her foot down on the parts of the treads that always creaked. She knew it was pointless really, for the two little girls following on behind took no notice of the clattering noise their shoes made as they concentrated hard on not tumbling down the steep stairs that rose almost vertically to the attic.

'Rosy, give me your hand,' Trudi said quietly and turned to help the three-year-old, who had stopped suddenly with a look of fear on her face as she stared intently at the drop.

'Keep going,' whispered her big sister, Louisa, from behind.

From two flights down, Trudi could hear her mother moving about in the kitchen. She liked to rise early and get her household chores done before the family was up and about. Trudi's sister Frida often worked a late shift at the hospital, never rising much before ten, and their father... Trudi pursed her lips as she listened out and failed to hear any sounds that he was at home. He often stayed out late, never saying where he went, though she suspected that drink was involved.

Today, Trudi wondered if her mother had got up early on purpose so she could rebuke her for taking the girls out before daylight. Her mother had tried to deter Trudi when she'd told her of her intentions the night before, saying it was foolhardy to expose children so young to danger. But it had been weeks since the Friedman family had gone into hiding in her family's attic and Trudi knew it would be good for the girls to get outside into the fresh morning air and to run around. She promised to be careful. After all, she had never seen any German soldiers out on the street this early. Surely a short trip to the river couldn't do any harm?

Rosy slipped her hand into Trudi's and they continued down the remaining treads, across the landing and down the wider, altogether less daunting staircase leading to the red and black tiled hall. When they reached the bottom, Rosy jumped off the last step and skipped into the kitchen and over to Trudi's mother. The little girl held up her grey, rather moth-eaten, toy rabbit for her to admire. Trudi caught sight of her mother's disapproving expression as she turned to face Rosy, but was relieved to see it soften into a smile.

'Happy bunny,' lisped Rosy, her face open and trusting as she presented her toy.

'Good morning, happy bunny. How are you today?' said Trudi's mother, crouching down to Rosy's height and wiggling the toy's long ears.

Rosy giggled. She grabbed her bunny and ran back to Trudi, who enveloped her in a warm hug.

Trudi waited for her mother to say something. She always did.

'It's been raining all night. Is it wise to take the children out in this?' she said, straightening up. Frowning, she glanced out of the kitchen window, which was peppered with raindrops.

Trudi wasn't to be deterred. 'I can see it's stopped. And we won't be gone long. We're only going down to the canal to feed the ducks.' A five-minute walk away, that was all.

'Hmm. You know what I think about that, don't you?' Her mother glanced quickly at the children, then back to Trudi with a meaningful look. Neither of them liked to say too much in front of the children and Trudi was grateful for it.

Trudi pretended to be distracted by straightening the collar of Rosy's coat, though it didn't need it. 'Mother, you worry too much,' she murmured. Then her eye was caught by Louisa, who, quiet as a mouse, had come to stand beside her.

'Louisa,' Trudi said with a bright smile, hoping Louisa would return it, but the older girl simply stared back, her large dark eyes watchful.

Trudi went to the breadbin and filled a small paper bag with a few crusts from the remains of yesterday's loaf of bread. 'Louisa, will you carry the duck bread?' she said softly and pressed the bag into her hand. Finally, Louisa's solemn face broke into a smile.

Trudi felt on edge as she pulled the door behind her and led the children out of the gate. She blamed her mood on her mother, who had made her feel bad at what she was doing. She looked quickly up at the house opposite in case the young man who lived there was standing at the upstairs window. She'd never bothered to look before, and the thought occurred to her that he might have been watching her movements without her knowing whenever she left the house. *Of course he wasn't. You're just imagining it,* Trudi told herself crossly, stepping round the puddles as she hurried the children away along the deserted street. It was barely six thirty and the neighbours never stirred much before seven, but her mother's words had unnerved her. Turning the corner, she gave a start as she noticed something she hadn't seen the day before. It was a poster stuck to a lamp post, showing the Dutch red, white and blue flag beneath the words, 'A new Netherlands in a new Europe' written in bold alongside the unmistakable emblem of the Dutch Nazi party. Trudi looked away and shook her head as she attempted to erase the image from her mind. Perhaps what she was doing could be construed as reckless... but just seeing the change in the children's mood and the colour in their cheeks convinced her it was worth it.

She remained on her guard as they arrived at the main road, looking around her to make sure no one was observing her who might have bad intentions. All it took was for a neighbour or a loose acquaintance to report her movements to the authorities... Trudi did her best to push the thought from her mind. Her mood lightened when they reached the footpath leading to the canal and could already hear the ducks quacking in anticipation of the bread. Trudi let Louisa run down to the water's edge, where she was immediately surrounded by at least a dozen ducks, all conversing loudly and padding impatiently around at her feet. Laughing, Louisa lifted the bag up high out of their reach and threw down a few crusts, which sent them scattering.

Trudi kept a close eye on Rosy, who dashed after her sister, calling, 'Me feed ducks, me feed ducks!'

'Give Rosy a few,' said Trudi. Louisa broke a few crusts apart, passing Rosy a handful to throw down herself.

One by one the ducks jumped into the water, but they hovered close to the bank, quacking expectantly. Trudi stood close to Rosy so they could toss a crust or two between them. The little girl shrieked with laughter when two ducks squabbled over their spoils. Louisa was dancing up and down, flinging the bread morsels into the air and whooping in delight whenever a duck caught one in its beak.

All at once the ducks took off in flight, with much flapping of wings and loud squawks. Rosy turned to Trudi in fright and clung on to the hem of her coat. As Trudi scooped her into her arms to comfort her, she glanced around for the cause of the disturbance, her heart pounding at the idea that there were Nazis lurking nearby. 'It's all right,' she soothed. Then as she turned she saw a figure she hadn't noticed before disappearing along the canal path, hidden under an umbrella even though it wasn't raining. She could see it was a man from the trousers and brown lace-up shoes visible below the wide black umbrella. Her heart gave a jolt. She was sure there'd been no one on the path a moment ago. Alarmed, she looked around to see where he might have come from. Was he following them? But the glimpse she'd had of him was so fleeting that the next moment she thought she must have imagined it.

Rosy was upset and crying. Louisa whined at Trudi to be allowed to go home. But Trudi refused to let this little drama upset their outing. She calmed them down as best she could. 'Let's go to the park, shall we?'

Her tears forgotten, Rosy was soon laughing and trotting after Louisa, who skipped down the path leading away from the houses and towards the nearby park. Here, they could briefly let off steam before it was time to return for another day confined to the attic and safety. It seemed so unfair that the lives of these young children and their parents had been devastated by the Nazis, who seemed determined to wipe out the Jewish population of the Netherlands. All over Amsterdam and Haarlem families were fleeing their comfortable homes, being hounded from the very businesses they had built and prospered from to seek refuge with friends, acquaintances and anyone determined to thwart the Nazis' evil intentions. If only it didn't have to be this way, thought Trudi, silently cursing this war that was making everyone fearful of encountering German soldiers whenever they stepped outside their front door.

As the girls whirled around on the grass, up and down, back and forth, pretending to be aeroplanes, Trudi kept a sharp lookout for the man with the umbrella. But there was no sign of him. All it was was someone out for a walk, she told herself, as she started to regain control of her nerves.

'Come on, girls, it's time to go home,' she called, clapping her hands.

Louisa was now playing 'it' and was running in circles, but not too fast, so that Rosy could catch her.

'My turn!' cried Rosy, bursting into giggles, and dashed away before Louisa could tap her on the shoulder.

Trudi was reluctant to spoil their fun so soon, but it was past seven now. Their mother would be waiting anxiously for their return and Trudi couldn't allow that. She pretended to join in the sisters' game, before quickly catching Rosy round the waist and lifting her up high. 'That's enough now. Time to go.' She joined in the little girl's effervescent laughter before setting her back down. Still making a game of it, with a girl on either side, she broke into a run, back the way they had come and up to the main road.

At the point where the path joined the pavement, Louisa let go of Trudi's hand and ran on ahead. As Trudi called to her to wait at the crossing, she caught sight of the man with the umbrella out of the corner of her eye. He had his back turned away from them and was waiting to cross the road while taking down his umbrella. He was wearing a long dark-grey gaberdine coat and black trilby hat. Trudi's heart began to beat faster as she stared at the tall familiar shape of him, but she was unable to place him.

Louisa had arrived at the crossing just as two German army vehicles came roaring by.

'Louisa, come back here now,' called Trudi, her voice coming out louder than she intended.

The man slowly turned his head to see what all the fuss was about. His face was broad, with small dark eyes peering out below thick brows. When the road was clear he hastily crossed, and disappeared down a side street.

Trudi felt relieved. She hadn't known the man after all, despite his unnerving stare. But her relief was short-lived. For everything was about to change in ways she never could have imagined.

TWO

It was normal for the families to tell each other if they saw anything suspicious, but Trudi decided against sharing her fears with Maria and Hans, Rosy and Louisa's parents. They had more than enough to be worried about, and there was nothing she could do about the stranger she'd seen. She was certain he'd gone before they'd made it home; even if he had been watching her and the girls and been suspicious of them, she was sure he'd be unable to find them again.

Hans and Maria Friedman were devastated when they were forced to flee their imposing town house in the centre of Haarlem. It had belonged to Maria's parents and her grandfather before them, so it was full of childhood memories: writing hidden on the walls from when Maria was a child and hiding places in nooks and crannies only she'd ever discovered. The Friedmans were long-time friends of Trudi's family and Trudi remembered visits to the house with great fondness. Before the war, the couple had been great entertainers and used to throw lavish parties to which they invited their extended family and friends. Music, song and laughter regularly filled the grand drawing room filled with treasured family possessions: the walls

were lined with paintings by well-known artists and the floor
was covered in richly coloured Persian carpets that had been
passed down the generations. The centrepiece was a majestic
Steinway grand piano. The excitement among the guests had
been palpable whenever Hans had raised his hands for quiet
and settled into his repertoire of numbers from the popular
musicals of the time. Maria, dressed in one of her elegant silk
evening dresses, always stood beside him and her beautiful
voice soared and swooped, delighting the assembled guests.

But when the Nazis occupied the Netherlands and their
intentions towards Jews became apparent, the Friedmans
realised they could no longer carry on their lives as normal.
Such lavish soirées only drew attention to themselves, so they
had to stop. The family withdrew from society and led a much
quieter life, but even that wasn't enough when Jewish acquaintances began disappearing from their homes. The raids invariably came in the dead of night, when people least expected
them: and if they didn't open up immediately at the pounding
on the door the soldiers would force entry and drag unsus-
pecting inhabitants from their beds and take them away. Maria
and Hans were terrified that it was only a matter of time before
the Germans came for them, so they made the heartbreaking
decision to leave their family home in a hurry, taking their two
young children and a couple of suitcases between them, leaving
everything else behind. It had been Trudi's idea that they
should come and hide in her family's attic. It wasn't the first
time her family had offered the attic rooms to a family in need.
Her mother felt strongly about protecting those less fortunate
than themselves, and, although her husband had needed a little
persuading, he had come round to the idea of lending their attic
room to a young Jewish couple for a time, until they left to go to
another house in the countryside where they would be safe.

The Friedmans' move was only meant to be for a couple of
weeks, but any hope of a swift return home for the family had

now been dashed. The raids across the city intensified and whole streets of Jewish families were emptied out. And then there were the rumours that Jewish people were not returning to Holland. Maria and Hans had no choice but to stay put until a more satisfactory arrangement could be found. Friends had talked of helping the family to move to Switzerland, but the recent escalation of hostilities meant they had no choice but to sit it out. It would be too dangerous to try to leave the country.

The attic wasn't such a bad living space for the family of four. It spanned the whole of the top of the house and was divided into two rooms; one was simply furnished with a divan that could be pulled out into a double bed, and two camp beds were put up each night for the girls; the other room was where they spent their days. It was sparsely furnished to avoid giving the impression that anyone might live there; there was a squashy, faded sofa that had seen better days and a wooden table with chairs that could be folded away when not in use. Behind a curtain in one corner were the WC and sink, with a small cooker in the space next to it, which could be hidden away behind a screen. One of the walls had a floor-to-ceiling book-case. But it was much more than that: in the centre, realistic books had been painted on, but in fact it concealed a panel that, when pressed, swung open to reveal a long low cupboard big enough for them all to hide should the need arise. Thankfully, that time had not yet come.

Even though the space was large, Trudi knew how hard living there was for Maria. Losing her freedom, her job and the community around her must have taken its toll, and Trudi wanted to do everything she could to help. Since leaving school at eighteen, the year war broke out, Trudi had been unsure of her future and had taken temporary positions as a domestic help for families in town. When she came in from work she helped her mother prepare meals for the Friedman family, which she took up to them. Often she would eat with them, or help out by spending time with the children, or simply stay and chat. Louisa could no longer attend school, but her old teacher provided her with schoolbooks so she didn't fall behind the rest of the class. Trudi found Louisa to be a naturally studious child and helped her with her schoolwork to keep her occupied, while Maria entertained Rosy, which was no mean feat – Rosy was a ball of energy and was unable to sit still for more than a few minutes at a time.

Maria did her best to remain cheerful, but Hans wasn't much help. Since their arrival, this formerly gregarious man had sunk into a deep gloom and mostly sat hunched over his small table, scribbling away in a notebook. It was obvious he was feeling lost after being ousted from the university, where he'd been a classics professor; he spent long hours writing letters to the authorities about the injustice of being forced out of his post because of his religion. But the letters just piled up, because it was too dangerous to send them by post. When Trudi offered to deliver them by hand herself, he refused. She suspected he was scared; he just wanted to get his anger out, but knew he couldn't change authorities' minds. He must have been aware that the power the Nazis had over them was already too strong.

The only time Hans came out of himself was on Friday nights, when the couple invited Trudi to join them to celebrate Shabbat. Hans would light the candles and lead the family in prayers, singing quietly in his gentle tenor voice. Despite not being Jewish herself, Trudi was invariably moved by the beauty of this weekly ritual and its reassuring rhythms, the flickering candlelight, prayers, song and quiet talk. After prayers had been said, the family tucked into matzo ball soup and baked chicken, provided by a local Jewish charitable organisation for families in need. Sometimes there would be cake too, which Maria always tried to give to Trudi and her family as a thank you for all they'd done for them. At the end of these evenings, Trudi went to bed with mixed feelings: happiness at sharing such special occasions with her dear friends, but dread that sooner or later the Nazis would find a way to put an end to it all.

'Girls, come and see what Tante Trudi has brought you.' Maria clapped her hands together as Trudi undid the flimsy metal clasp of her box of treasures she'd brought to show them and tipped it out on the floor.

She had been tidying her chest of drawers when she came across the old wooden cigar box of card games she and Frida used to play when they were children. As she'd examined the tattered, worn packs of cards, she had been reminded of those times, with a mixture of fondness and annoyance. The cards would come out every evening and the whole family joined in. Frida was the competitive one and would burst out crying if she lost a game – on more than one occasion she tore cards or scribbled on them in her frustration.

Rosy let out a squeal when she saw the picture of a donkey on the front of one of the packs, and immediately tipped the cards out into a messy pile. 'Horse. Dog. Pig,' she said, identifying each picture correctly.

Louisa waited for Trudi to explain each of the games, before asking to play Snap with her. Rosy, who had quickly lost interest in her cards, had gone to sit on Maria's lap, where she sucked her thumb while intently watching Louisa and Trudi at play.

'Rosy, would you like to join in?' said Trudi, catching her eye as she dealt the cards.

Rosy shook her head, but couldn't resist jumping off her mother's lap and snatching at a card she liked the look of.

'No, Rosy. I'm playing with Tante Trudi. You're too little,' said Louisa petulantly, and tried to snatch back the card. Rosy held on tight and let out a piercing shriek.

'Not so loud, girls. Louisa, let Rosy have the card,' said their mother quietly but firmly.

'Why should I? She always gets her own way.' Louisa pushed her bottom lip out petulantly.

'Mama!' Rosy cried, her eyes swimming with tears, but she'd managed to get hold of the card, which now lay folded in two in her little fist. She gave her sister a triumphant look.

With a sense of foreboding, Trudi could see the situation escalating out of control; and that had to be avoided at all costs. It was early evening and the next-door neighbours would probably be in. It was a big risk having a whole family in hiding in the attic. All it would take to alert the neighbours to the presence of children across the dividing wall was a single child's cry. Although Louisa was old enough to understand the need to be quiet, Trudi appreciated that she couldn't help but be riled by her little sister. She knew the feeling only too well.

'Louisa, you can still play your game without that card,' said Maria.

'Go on. We don't need it,' said Trudi as calmly as she could.

Louisa looked daggers at Trudi, but she did as she was told. Within minutes, she had forgotten all about the outburst and was happily playing snap with Trudi, though under strict instruction not to shout out when she had a matching pair. Rosy, meanwhile, had also forgotten all about the card and was down on her hands and knees pretending to be a dog.

'I'll make us a cup of tea,' said Maria, getting up and going to fill the kettle at the sink. 'Hans, can you keep an eye on Rosy?'

Hans, sitting at the table engrossed in a book, looked up at his wife distractedly. Rosy was crawling towards him. 'Daddy. Me doggy. Woof, woof!' she called out excitedly.

'Snap!' went Louisa at the same time.

'Shh...' Trudi said, and put a finger to her lips, suddenly alert to the sound of loud banging down below. The children fell instantly quiet. Trudi could hear it more clearly now, the repeated pounding of something hard against the front door.

With a gasp, she rose to her feet in alarm. 'They've come. Quick, you must all hide.'

Louisa and Rosy both fled to their mother in fright and clung on to her. Trudi, seeing Rosy's face begin to crumple, quickly went over and gave her a tight hug. 'Shh... shh,' she soothed, as she tried to still Rosy's rigid body before she could emit an ear-splitting cry. 'It's all right, Rosy. There's nothing to worry about,' she whispered against Rosy's hot cheek. Gradually she felt the little girl relax and her short staccato sobs subsided.

But Trudi remained tense as the sound of German voices, loud and demanding, carried up the two flights of stairs. Trudi could also detect her own mother's raised voice trying to deflect them, and knew she was buying time for the family in hiding in the attic.

Trudi's eyes darted from Maria to Hans. They were whispering urgently to one another as they tidied away the cards and the other toys the children had been playing with. *Are they oblivious to the imminent danger to their own lives?* Trudi thought in alarm. She bent down and prised Rosy's little fingers away from her legs.

'Let me help you all hide. There really isn't much time.' She thought of the dark, long, low bookcase cupboard: although it was where they'd always planned to hide them if something like this happened, she didn't really know if they'd all fit in.

Maria and Hans straightened up and exchanged a terrified look with one another. It was Maria who spoke, in a low voice as if she didn't want the children to hear. 'Hans and I have been expecting this for some time. We've come to the conclusion that they'll find all of us if we try to hide.' She drew in a shuddering breath as she went on in a whisper. 'But if it's just the girls... I trust you. I know you'll keep them safe.'

Trudi listened in shock. Could her friend be asking her to save her children, while sacrificing herself and their father? 'No...' she began and vigorously shook her head. But Maria was already on her knees, clasping Rosy to her and telling her to go with Tante Trudi, like a good girl. Hans had tears in his eyes as he went over to Louisa and lifted her up in his arms and hugged her tightly. Trudi watched him gently stroke the back of her head. Louisa was quietly sobbing against his shoulder.

Trudi could see that the couple had made up their minds and there was no point trying to dissuade them.

They were just moments away from the Germans storming the attic. Already, she could hear heavy footsteps climbing the stairs. There was no time to lose – she had to act fast. She ran to the bookcase and fumbled for the panel to release the catch, panicking when at first she couldn't locate it. Then Maria was at her side and found it for her, and Trudi realised she must have practised this many times before.

The panel slid back. Trudi crawled in first. Maria and Hans handed first Louisa, then Rosy into her arms.

'Be good,' stuttered Hans, his eyes glistening in the half-light.

'Goodbye, my darlings.' Maria was weeping as she spoke. She turned to Trudi. 'I know you will take good care of our babies. Please make sure they don't come to any harm.'

Trudi was too choked up to reply and could only nod. Of course she would look out for them... how could she refuse?

With an arm clasped tightly round each little girl, she watched as the door slid back in its groove. She was left with her friends' beloved children in complete darkness.

THREE

'Trudi! Are you up there?'

The man's deep voice seemed to come from far away. Trudi stiffened and held a finger first to Rosy's, then Louisa's lips. 'Don't make a sound,' she whispered as quietly as she could. Even though she knew who was calling her, she had to be sure this wasn't a trap laid by the Germans before she revealed herself. She tried not to think how long they had been stuck in this cupboard – could it have been an hour, even two?

After her initial terror listening to German boots stomp over the floorboards, inches from where the three of them were cowering – the scuffles and shouts, which receded as the parents were taken from the attic, with neither Maria nor Hans protesting, probably to save their children from further anguish – it had gone completely quiet. Louisa had queried why they weren't allowed out, but Trudi had sensed it was too early for that. She had quietly sung a lullaby, which seemed to soothe the girls, who were pressed against her. Gradually, she'd felt Rosy grow heavy as she'd fallen into a fitful sleep.

'What's going on up there?' called another voice, her sister's, followed by her light, quick tread on the staircase.

'Nothing. There's nobody here. Do you know anything about this, Frida?'

'Of course not, Papa. But I think I can guess.'

Trudi heard Frida's soft footsteps approach their hiding place, then her fast breathing close to as she slid back the panel.

Frida's worried face peered in. She let out a sigh. 'I thought I'd find you here. Thank goodness you're safe. Are you all right?'

Trudi nodded, but, after the pitch darkness, needed a moment to come to. She blinked several times. She was grateful to see her sister and knew she could rely on her. It was a relief to know that for now the danger was past.

Rosy gazed out at Frida with large distrustful eyes. Louisa was squeezed into the far end of their confined space, where she had tried to make herself as small as possible.

Trudi crawled out and felt her knees buckle as she made to stand up. She was turning back to help the children when her father spoke, his voice irritable and gruff.

'Where's your mother? I didn't expect to come home and find an empty house.'

Trudi felt anger surge up at his lack of concern for her welfare. Now, of all times, she wanted him to say that she'd done the right thing by saving these two small children as well as herself. 'Is that all you can say? If you'd been at home like any normal father, you could have stood up to those *moffen*. But no, it was just me, alone in the house with Mama. She was downstairs and I was with the Friedmans up here. And now they've gone too.' She realised she'd gone too far when she heard Louisa emit a loud sob. 'Sweetheart. Don't cry. Everything's going to be all right. I'll make sure of it,' she said, gripped with remorse that she'd made her cry.

'Where have Mama and Papa gone?' Louisa asked in a choked voice, her dark eyes swimming with tears.

Trudi pressed her lips together as she tried to think of something that would appease her without resorting to a lie. Fortunately, Frida came to the rescue. She crouched down and lifted Rosy towards her.

'Shall we go and find happy bunny?' Frida asked, lifting the little girl's chin so she could look into her eyes. Rosy gave her a faint nod. 'And Louisa, come and help find him, will you?' She spoke coaxingly and straightened up, taking each girl by the hand. She threw Trudi a look of sympathy before taking the girls off next door, leaving Trudi alone with her father.

Suddenly Trudi began to shake with the emotion of it all; her legs felt weak as she stumbled over to the sofa and flopped down. 'What do you think has happened to Mother?'

'I don't know,' said her father in a resigned voice. 'We can only hope the *moffen* don't interrogate her about the children left behind. She's a strong woman and has nerves of steel. With any luck she'll have the sense to keep quiet. And hopefully they'll let her come home soon.'

Trudi covered her face with her hands. She felt terrible knowing it had been her idea to persuade her parents to bring the Friedmans into their house, despite her father's reluctance. And why had she been so stubborn in ignoring her mother's warnings about taking the children outdoors? What if that was what drew the Nazis here? It was too late now, but how stupid she'd been to ignore the danger. And her father knew it. She looked up into his face, hoping for sympathy but finding none. 'What are we going to do?' she whispered, feeling helpless.

He gave an exasperated sigh. 'You tell me. I've warned you on more than one occasion not to get mixed up in things you know nothing about.'

Trudi's shoulders sagged. She knew he was right, but how could she stand by and do nothing, especially when young innocent Jewish children's lives were at risk? She thought of Rosy and Louisa next door and resolved to do everything in her power to help them.

Trudi stared at her father and realised he was probably as scared as she was, but she needed to appeal to his better nature. 'Father, I may not have been able to save Maria and Hans, but I carried out their wishes. Maria begged me to save their children. I need your support if I'm to give them the protection they need. Will you do that for me?'

He was silent for a long moment and Trudi grew worried about what he would say. So often he'd lost his temper at her. He was clearly upset now, and she wouldn't put it past him to do so again. But whatever response he gave, she knew she had to win him over.

'Listen to me, Trudi,' he began, as he so often did when he was about to launch into an argument he expected to win.

Trudi folded her arms and waited for him to continue.

'I know I haven't been the best father to you and sometimes we get off on the wrong foot.'

Trudi bit her lip, forcing herself not to interrupt. She was relieved to hear Rosy and Louisa's soft laughter from the next room.

Her father followed her gaze towards the muffled giggles; his voice caught as he went on. 'But it doesn't mean I don't care for you.' He smiled, surprising her, and she caught a glimpse of the father she used to know before he lost his job at the engineering works the year the Germans invaded Holland. The father who came home at the same time each evening and sat with his family round the supper table. What had happened to change him so, she wondered.

Then almost as quickly his face hardened again. 'I'm afraid those girls can't stay here, not now we've been raided. The *moffen* could so easily come back. No, it's far too risky. You'll have to find somewhere else for the children to go.'

Trudi began to tremble, but she knew he was right. It took her a moment to gather her thoughts to decide on the best course of action. Then she remembered talking to an acquaintance about a man who worked for the resistance, who might be willing to help and was trustworthy. Trudi had made a note of the man's name, thinking he might be a useful contact. She hadn't known how useful this contact would prove to be.

FOUR

Trudi turned her bike into the narrow street that would take her along the canal to the outskirts of town. Barely five minutes had passed since she'd left home, but it seemed longer as she bounced over the uneven cobblestones with a force that reverberated through her entire body. *Hurry, you must get away before the* moffen *come back...* Her father's words as he'd almost pushed her out of the door were still ringing in her ears, urging her to pedal even faster. Her heart hammered in her chest as she tried not to think about the two little girls, safe for now and tucked up in bed, but for how much longer? She was petrified that the Germans would come back and show them no mercy. It was imperative that she move them to safety.

At the bridge, she could make out the dark shape of the trees above the houses, denoting the edge of the expansive Haarlemmerhout and the more expensive part of town. A right and a left and then she arrived at the property in a quiet and leafy street. His was a tall red-brick building, three storeys high with dark-green shutters. Trudi slowed her bike to a stop and looked up at the imposing house. She couldn't see any lights on, but that didn't mean there was no one in. A gravel path led to the house and there was a metal bike stand out front. A single bike was parked there. She put hers next to it and locked up. Quickly glancing around to make sure she wasn't being followed, she hurried to the front door and rapped softly. A minute or two passed and she was about to knock again when the door opened an inch.

'Who is it?' The woman's voice was abrupt, sounding suspicious – as well she might, for it was long past the time for any visitors.

'My name's Trudi Oversteegen. Is Frans home?' Trudi said, her breath still shaky from her ride.

The door opened a little wider, revealing a woman of about sixty with wavy, short, greying hair. Trudi guessed she was probably Frans's mother. 'He's not in and I don't know when he'll be back,' the woman said in a cold voice.

'I've cycled all the way from the other side of town. Would you mind if I wait inside?' Trudi suddenly felt panicky and wished she'd telephoned ahead. It was stupid of her to assume he'd be in. 'I need his help,' she said, hating herself for having to plead.

The woman looked her up and down as if assessing her. 'I suppose you'd better come in,' she said finally, huffing out a sigh and standing aside to let her in.

Trudi looked around at the big hallway with its central staircase and pieces of antique furniture lining the walls. Frans must be well off, she thought, feeling rather small and insignificant as she stood in her second-hand coat that was frayed at the cuffs and her scuffed outdoor shoes.

'I'm the housekeeper. Live-in housekeeper,' the woman said in a smug tone of voice. She tilted her chin and glanced towards the staircase, which Trudi could see winding up several flights.

Trudi was taken into a small room off the hallway that had a bureau in one corner and two chairs either side of an unlit fireplace. The housekeeper checked to see the curtains were drawn tightly shut before she turned on a lamp on a small side table. 'Please take a seat.'

Outside the room, the hall clock struck the hour.

'Do you think he'll be long?' said Trudi, ignoring her request to sit, her anxiety mounting again. The longer she was forced to wait, the greater the chances the Friedman children would be discovered. She simply couldn't allow that to happen.

The woman shrugged, but appeared to soften a little as she became more talkative. 'He never tells me where he goes and probably doesn't know himself half the time. All manner of things crop up in his line of work and we often get people knocking at all times of the day or night. Mostly, they've been forced out of their homes and come here seeking shelter. Frans never turns anyone away and it does get crowded at times. You're not one of *them*, are you?' Her expression took on a faintly disgusted look, as she screwed up her eyes the better to scrutinise Trudi's face.

Trudi felt unnerved and shuddered inwardly. She was wary of revealing too much about the reason she had come, but at the same time was relieved to hear that Frans gave people shelter. Maybe he'd let the Friedman children stay here till an alternative could be found. 'No, I haven't come asking for shelter,' she said firmly. 'But I do need to speak to Frans tonight, so if it's all right with you, I'll wait here for him.'

The woman said nothing further and left the room. Trudi could hear her footsteps recede as she crossed the tiled floor and climbed the staircase.

Left alone with only the loud ticking of the hall clock for company, Trudi became anxious again. Had she been too impetuous and made a mistake by rushing here and expecting Frans to help? She barely knew anything about him, other than that he worked for some sort of resistance organisation; she had no further details than that. She only had the word of her acquaintance, who was a teacher, that Frans could be trusted. But what if she was mistaken?

The clock kept ticking. Next to her chair was a pile of magazines, which she began flicking through to pass the time. Halfway down, she noticed a copy of *Vrij Nederland*, hidden in between two others. She knew it was an underground newspaper published illegally by people who opposed the Nazis. There were many in circulation, but she had never read this one before. It was so different from the stencilled eight-sheet student paper she'd seen Sem put together each week. He'd been the editor in charge of deciding which stories were included and had done a lot of the writing himself. She remembered her time with him with a stab of fondness. Can it really have been only six months ago?

The sound of a key scraping in the lock and the front door opening brought Trudi back to the present. Her heart began to pound as she left the room to investigate, and saw a tall lean man shake his arms from his long grey coat, remove his hat and hang both on the rack. She cleared her throat. 'Excuse me, I hope you don't mind the intrusion. Are you Frans?'

He spun round at her voice. 'Oh. I didn't realise there was anyone here. Can I help you?'

'Your housekeeper let me in. Can we talk in here?' She glanced over her shoulder at the room where she'd been waiting.

'Yes, of course,' he said, frowning slightly. He followed her in and closed the door behind him. 'What is the problem?'

'My name's Trudi Oversteegen. I came straight here because I understand you help Jewish people.' She waited to see if he would acknowledge this fact, but he didn't react. Her words came out in a rush. 'My family has been sheltering a Jewish family. This evening we were raided. It happened so fast. I was in the attic with the family and managed to squeeze into a cupboard with the two children, but the parents were taken away. I'm sure the Germans must have had a tip-off. I have my suspicions that someone must have known about those children, maybe even seen me with them. You see, I took them out for a walk early yesterday morning before anyone was up and about. I thought we'd be safe, but it looks like I was wrong. When we were down by the canal, I swear I saw someone I recognised. I thought he was following us, but he hurried off before I could see his face. He could have informed on us.'

Frans looked thoughtful. 'It's possible you're right, but I don't think you can read too much into that. When the Germans conduct raids, they tend to be of a broad area, usually a whole street at a time. Are the children still in your house?'

'Yes, up in the attic.' Trudi's voice dropped to a whisper as it occurred to her that the housekeeper might be listening at the door. 'But it's too dangerous to let them stay there.'

'Is there anyone you trust who can look after them till I can find somewhere else for them?'

Trudi felt the panic rising in her chest. She had to make him understand the urgency of the situation. 'I don't trust the neighbours and you're the only person I know of who can help. I'm worried that the *moffen* will be back soon – they may even be returning as we speak. Would it be possible to bring the children here?' Her voice had grown shaky and she realised how much she was trembling.

'I'm afraid I don't have the space. If there are raids we may be next. Let me think for a moment.' Frans pursed his lips into a thin line as he paced the room, from the door to the window and back again, while Trudi stood by sniffing, suddenly overcome by emotion.

'I have it.' Frans's face relaxed into a brief smile. 'I have the keys to a garage that belongs to a friend who's away. He lets me use it for storage and there's not much in it right now. It won't be particularly comfortable but it will be fine for a night or two.'

'Where is it?'

He gave her the address.

'That's close to where I live. Will we be safe there?'

'Safer than staying put. How old are these children?'

'Seven and three.'

'Hmm. Too young to be left alone. Can you stay with them?'

'Yes, of course. They trust me.'

'Good. Give me a moment while I fetch the keys and I'll take you there.'

'Thank you, Frans. You've no idea—'

'No need to thank me,' he interrupted with a dismissive wave of the hand. 'As I say, it's a temporary solution before something better can be found.'

FIVE

The night had turned cold as they set out on bikes along the deserted narrow streets, over the bridge and along the canal. They pedalled quickly as they concentrated on covering as much distance as fast as possible. Trudi felt reassured to have Frans beside her, but dreaded the prospect of finding that the children had already been taken. To take her mind off her meandering thoughts she asked Frans about the housekeeper.

'Mevrouw de Wit has worked for me for years and has been in the family a long time. She's quite reliable.'

'She told me that you take in people who come knocking for help. And then she asked if I was one of *them*. The way she said it... it was rather strange.'

Frans made a scoffing sound. 'I wouldn't worry about her. In the past few weeks, we've had more people turn up at the door. I try not to turn anyone away, but we're going to have to come up with a better solution than using the cellar and attic. I suspect that Mevrouw de Wit is probably a bit fed up having to open the door to the homeless. As I said, she's been with us for years. She's perfectly trustworthy.' He spoke brusquely, almost defensively, as if he wouldn't have a word said against her.

But Trudi couldn't let it go. 'I'm probably just jumpy after everything that's happened today. It was the way she said it. As if she disapproved.'

Frans gave her a sharp look. 'You're wrong. She has a heart of gold. She once gave up her bed to a young woman who was fleeing with her child when her family home was raided. I don't see that as the action of a woman who holds anti-Jewish sentiments.'

Chastened, Trudi decided against saying any more about the matter, but she wasn't entirely won over by Frans's explanation. Perhaps she'd heard one too many stories about people who had started out by helping people who were being persecuted only to end up as Nazi sympathisers. Mevrouw de Wit's unsettling comment made Trudi suspicious of the woman's real motivation.

They were nearing her home now, but Trudi didn't recognise these backstreets by the canal. Many of the houses were boarded up and had a desolate air about them. 'Where exactly is this garage?' she asked, unease rippling through her.

'Patience. We're nearly there,' said Frans – and suddenly stood on his brakes.

A black and white cat had darted across their path, causing Trudi to swerve and almost overbalance. She braked hard, stopping inches from the canal's edge. Her heart thumped as she found herself staring into its inky depths.

'No need to get back on. We've arrived,' said Frans, dismounting. He wheeled his bike towards a dark alleyway between two houses. Still shaken, Trudi righted her bike and quickly set off after him.

At the back of the houses stood a row of four dilapidated lock-up garages. Frans walked up to the one at the end, fiddled his key into the stiff lock till it turned, and swung open the wooden doors. He took a small torch from his pocket and shone it around inside. The beam bounced off a stack of objects piled up in one corner, half covered with a tarpaulin, and an old wooden chair without a seat. Several taped-up boxes stood in the middle of the concrete floor.

'Where will we sleep?' asked Trudi, surveying the place in dismay, but Frans didn't answer. Instead, he went over and began moving things around. He propped the lit torch up on a pile of junk and began heaving out a large mattress that had seen better days. In one corner, Trudi spied a large moth-eaten woollen blanket. *So we're not the first ones to stay here,* she pondered to herself.

'Help me, will you?' Frans gestured for her to take one end of the mattress and together they manoeuvred it forward. He pushed the cartons aside to make space in the centre of the room. 'There. Maybe you could bring a couple of cushions from home and it'll be fine.' He surveyed the makeshift bedroom with satisfaction, before catching the expression on Trudi's face. 'Look, I'll make sure it won't be for long. A couple of days at most. I need to sort out a few things my end first. Then I'll tell you what I have in mind. Trust me.'

Trudi looked up at him. He laid a hand on her shoulder and she felt herself relax.

But the feeling was short-lived as she mounted her bike and rode away through the dark streets back home. These days most people didn't venture out much after dark and those who did were usually in a great hurry to get home in case they ran into trouble. The streets were so empty, no people out walking or on bikes – it was unnerving. Trudi tried to put her fears out of her mind, for she knew she would be retracing her steps very shortly with Rosy and Louisa. How would they cope with being shaken from sleep and asked to leave home that instant, not knowing where their parents were or what fate awaited them?

· · ·

It was close to midnight when Trudi crept through the back door and switched on the kitchen light. Everything was the same as when she'd left, which meant her mother couldn't have returned. She took the stairs two at a time and pushed open her parents' bedroom door to find her father, who was snoring lightly with one arm sprawled over the empty space where her mother should be. Inhaling a sharp breath at the sight, Trudi realised there was nothing she could do about it. She tiptoed past Frida's door, which stood ajar, up the steep stairs to the attic, and pushed open the door to see the two children lying curled up together, deep in sleep. After a moment's hesitation at the prospect of disturbing them, she went over and gently shook Louisa awake.

'I need you to be really quiet,' she whispered, stroking Louisa's dark curls that lay in a tangle against her forehead. Louisa's eyelids fluttered open, then closed again. 'Louisa, wake up now.' Trudi kept stroking her hair till her eyes blinked open. Louisa gave a little gasp, but Trudi held a finger to her lips. 'We're going on a little adventure, just the three of us, but I need you to be quiet and calm for Rosy's sake. Do you understand?' She lifted Louisa's chin and looked into her eyes, willing her to agree, even though she knew she was probably asking too much of a seven-year-old child.

'Where's Mama and Papa?' said Louisa, tears filling her eyes.

'They've had to go away, also on a little adventure.' Trudi hated herself for lying but couldn't think what else to say. 'Now get dressed quickly and put on a warm jumper.'

Rosy stirred at the sound of their voices and let out a cry, followed by a plaintive 'Mama'.

'Shh, it's all right,' whispered Trudi, and clasped her to her. Rosy put her thumb in her mouth and stared up at Trudi with big sorrowful eyes. Trudi forced a smile. 'Let's get you dressed.'

Rosy didn't resist as long as she was allowed to suck her thumb and cuddle her toy rabbit.

The two little girls obediently followed Trudi down the stairs; she told them to take care to be quiet, 'so that you don't wake Oma and Opa.' Grandma and Grandpa... the familiar names she used to describe her own parents to the children brought a lump to her throat. How could things change so suddenly in the space of a few hours? The parents of these two innocent children snatched from their children in an instant, and her mother also gone.

Each careful step that Trudi and the children took down the steep staircase seemed so final, so irrevocable; it felt like they would never return.

SIX

As Trudi led the children through the dark deserted streets, she was struck by the enormity of their situation. They had been lucky that the Germans hadn't come back. An image of the figure under the umbrella down by the canal flashed through her mind. She glanced at the girls on either side of her, each holding tightly to one of her hands, and knew she must do all she could to protect them. 'Can you try and walk a little faster?' she said to Rosy, who was beginning to drag her feet. She didn't answer, but they couldn't afford to dawdle. 'Would you like me to carry you?'

Rosy nodded. Trudi adjusted the heavy bag she was carrying on one shoulder and lifted the little girl onto the other. But instead of going faster, she was forced to walk more slowly as Rosy's head lolled against her and the child fell into sleep. At least Louisa sensed the urgency of getting to their destination as quickly as possible and kept walking a few steps ahead, turning and waiting for Trudi to catch up. They carried on like that until they reached Canal Street, when Trudi caught sight of a car idling by the side of the road. The fact that it wasn't a German vehicle did little to assuage her suspicion that someone was lying in wait for them. *You're imagining things*, she told herself, glancing in through the back window. She could just make out the shape of two people. It made her heart lurch. She hurried past the car without a further glance and took a sharp left.

'We're nearly there. Just a bit further,' she said to Louisa, who had moved closer to her side. 'See that opening on the left? That's where we're heading.'

From behind, Trudi heard the throb of an engine. She knew it had to be the car they'd just passed, and it was right behind them. She was too scared to look.

'Along here.' Her voice came out in a desperate whisper. She hoisted Rosy a little higher and grasped Louisa's hand, and together they ran towards the narrow opening between the houses. Their footsteps clattered over the cobblestones. They had just reached the end of the alley when Trudi heard footsteps sprinting in their direction.

'Stop! Right now!' yelled a man's voice. Dutch, not German, but that was small consolation against the terror Trudi was experiencing.

With a huge effort, Trudi dashed forward to the garages and set Rosy down. 'Mama,' Rosy whimpered, clinging to Trudi's skirt.

'Not now,' Trudi whispered, as she fumbled desperately in her bag for the keys. Louisa gave Rosy a clumsy hug and said, 'I'm here, Rosy.' Trudi threw Louisa a brief smile as she located the key and jabbed it in the lock. It engaged and she turned it and leant her weight against the door.

'Quick... In!' Not daring to turn on the torch, she blindly pulled the children inside and hastily locked the door behind them.

Moments later, a fist pummelled against the door. 'Don't think you can hide. I know you're in there.' The man was shouting in Dutch, his voice hoarse with rage.

Trudi crouched down and clasped the children to her. 'Don't make a sound.' Her voice was scarcely a whisper. She closed her eyes, willing the man to leave. But he kept on shouting and thumping. Then she heard more footsteps, which came to a halt outside the door, and another man's voice.

'How do you know they are in there? Did you see them go in?'

The pounding stopped. 'No, but where else would they be?'

'Hasn't it occurred to you they might be in any one of these garages?' the second man yelled, clearly irritated. He swore and kicked the door with such force that the wood splintered inwards, but it held firm. Terrified, Trudi waited until the voices grew fainter and she could be sure they were moving away. In the silence, her mind raced with the possibility that these men were scouring the streets for Jews so that they could turn them in to the German authorities in exchange for a monetary reward. Opportunists. What else could they be? Some moments passed before she dared switch on the torch. She saw the children's faces looking pinched, almost ghostly.

'We're safe. They've gone,' she murmured, though her heart still hammered in her chest. She didn't want to think about the possibility that the men would come back, perhaps bringing something heavy to knock down the door. She had to stay calm. 'Louisa, take the cushions and lay them side by side on the mattress.'

Louisa nodded weakly and did as she was told; then she immediately flopped down with exhaustion. Rosy, thinking it was a game, lay down beside her with a giggle. Trudi's mood lifted briefly as she regarded them, marvelling in their childish ability to put aside their fear in an instant.

From far off she could just make out a church clock chiming the hour with a single stroke.

'Time to go to sleep,' Trudi said, suppressing a yawn. She moved her bag off the mattress and settled Rosy between herself and Louisa, before spreading the blanket so that it covered them all. She lay on her back, her heart still racing, and waited until the girls' breathing became slow and steady, while she stared up into the pitch-black darkness.

Much later, Rosy's cries woke Trudi from a troubled sleep and she wondered if she'd even managed to drop off at all. Louisa stirred, rolled over onto her side and settled with a sigh. Rosy, though, was wide awake and sobbing pitifully. Trudi reached for the torch, which had rolled off the mattress. She switched it on and its eerie light cast unsettling wavering shadows into the corners of the room.

'What is it, Rosy?' she soothed, though she wasn't expecting an answer. She guessed what was troubling the little girl as she felt around till she found her toy rabbit, which Rosy grabbed gratefully and pressed to her chest. When her sobs had subsided, she allowed Trudi to lay her back down.

But Trudi was unable to settle and spent a long time fretting about what she should do once it got light. Frans had promised to come early, but could she afford to wait for him to turn up, knowing that their hiding place had been compromised?

SEVEN

The knocking was soft at first, but gradually became more insistent. Trudi came to with a start and sat bolt upright. 'Who is it?' she called out without thinking, before scrambling to her feet. Her heart began pounding in her chest as she realised her mistake. She shouldn't have replied; she didn't know who it was. And she was surprised she had even managed to drift off.

'It's gone eight o'clock,' Frans said from outside.

The girls were curled up beside her, still fast asleep, and she carefully shuffled away from them so as not to disturb them and stood up to let him in.

He pushed the door shut and removed his hat. In his other hand he held a brown paper bag. 'Mevrouw de Wit made up jam sandwiches for you all. And there's a bottle of milk.'

Under his gaze Trudi felt a mess. She straightened out her clothes as best she could and scraped her fingers through her hair. 'That's very kind of her. So you told her about the children?'

Frans tilted his head slightly, not quite a nod nor a shake. Trudi took it as the former and let out a sigh. Perhaps she had misjudged the housekeeper after all, she thought, as she accepted the bag of provisions.

'How was your night?' asked Frans, ignoring her sigh. 'You look tired.'

'Now there's a surprise. I had a terrible night.' Trudi turned her back on the slumbering children so she could tell him more. 'We were followed by two men in a car who then chased us on foot. As you can see, we managed to get inside safely, but I've been up most of the night worrying they'll come back.' She whispered, not wanting to wake the girls.

Frans sucked in a deep breath. 'Did you manage to take a look at them?'

'No. It was too dark and I was in too much of a hurry to get the children out of harm's way. But there were two men and they were in a car with a Dutch licence plate – that much I know. Frans, it's far too dangerous for us to stay here. I'd rather be at home. I've decided that when the children are awake, we're going back.'

Frans shook his head and gave her a pained look. 'I'm afraid that's not a good idea. It's not safe for you to be anywhere near your home, especially with two fugitive Jewish children. You're going to have to go into hiding too.'

'What do you mean?' Trudi could hardly believe what she was hearing.

'I went to check on your house just now and saw a group of Germans smoking and talking next to their van at the top of the street. I walked away before they could see me, but it looked to me as if they were embarking on more raids.'

Trudi thought of her father and Frida left behind in the house and was suddenly scared for their safety. Frida would stand up for herself – she always did – and would be fine, Trudi reassured herself, but her father was capable of sudden fits of rage, especially if wronged. 'I can't leave my family to the mercy of the Germans after what they've done to Rosy and Louisa's parents. It's a risk I have to take. I have to help them.'

'And you want to take these children with you? Trudi, you need to make up your mind – either it's your family you save or the lives of these two children.'

Trudi heard Louisa stir. The girl opened her eyes and stared straight at Trudi and she quickly looked away. Had the child heard their conversation and was waiting to hear what Trudi would decide? Trudi despaired that Frans was putting her in such an impossible position. How could she be expected to choose?

'That's not fair,' she said quietly, quickly glancing over at Louisa, whose face was very still and expectant. Would she, could she choose her family over these defenceless children?

She couldn't meet the child's gaze as she came to her decision. Of course she wasn't about to abandon Louisa and Rosy. She'd made that promise to their parents. Her father and Frida could fend for themselves. They weren't Jewish.

'I'll stay away from the house,' she told Frans in a low voice, 'but you must see it's not safe to stay here another night. I have a great-aunt who lives alone in a village not far from Haarlem. She's helped the family out once before. But I need help getting there, and it can't be for long as she's quite elderly and it would be unfair on her. I'll stay there with the children but, as soon as it's safe to do so, I must return home.' What she really wanted to discuss with Frans was what to do with the children if their parents weren't coming back. It was an appalling notion, but one they must face up to. Not now, though, she thought, aware that Louisa was still listening intently to their conversation. It was important that she kept Louisa and Rosy as calm as was possible under such trying circumstances. She hoped Frans understood this.

'Very good. That sounds like a good solution. Now, you eat

your breakfast and we can all get going.' He gave Trudi a reassuring smile. 'I knew I could rely on you.'

Trudi managed to return his smile, but suddenly felt intensely alone. Unable to return to the support of her family, however difficult things had become, she now bore the responsibility of ensuring her friends' daughters remained safe and far from the prying eyes of the Nazis. She thought of Sem and wondered what he would have said if he'd been here at her side. Strong, handsome Sem, who she'd believed was the one for her. But the war had intervened and put a stop to any dreams that she – they might have had. Trudi let out a quiet sigh as she remembered the way he'd made her feel that time she first set eyes on him.

EIGHT

SIX MONTHS AGO

Sem was tall, even for a Dutch boy, with white-blond hair, startling blue eyes and a deep tan from spending his days selling fresh fish at his father's stall on the quayside. He also had a mischievous smile, which he turned on for all his female customers that was guaranteed to get them to spend more than they'd been intending to.

The first time Trudi saw Sem was when her mother had sent her on an errand to the coast to buy fresh fish for their supper. It was blowing a strong wind that day, and she arrived on her bike, rosy-cheeked from her exertions, with her fair curls dancing around her face. She parked her bike at the stand opposite the fish stall and heard his deep clear voice calling out the special offers of the day. Normally so full of confidence, she hesitated and watched him serving customers before walking over, suddenly forgetting what she had come for. But Sem had spotted her locking up her bike and greeted her with an enormous grin, as if she were a long-lost friend.

'I have a special offer just for you, five herring for the price of four. Show me your lovely smile and I'll let you have them for half price. What do you say?' He held two silver-scaled herrings up by their tails. 'I gutted and filleted them myself.'

Trudi laughed at his expression, so earnest and yet so beguiling; she didn't have the heart to refuse. 'Go on then. I'll take five,' she said, before she remembered her mother's request. She got out her purse to count out the coins, suddenly realising she couldn't also afford the piece of haddock her mother had so expressly asked her to get. But he had already wrapped up the herrings in white greaseproof paper and slapped them down on the counter.

'I'm afraid I can't take them after all. I came for haddock and my mother won't be too pleased if I turn up with those. I'm sorry.' She felt her cheeks burn up.

'No need to be. Listen' – he glanced over his shoulder at the older man with his back turned who was preparing the catch at the back of the van – 'I shouldn't have made you. You can have these ones on me. How much haddock do you want?' He leant forward over the counter and gazed intently into her eyes.

Trudi was lost for words. Why was this stranger being so nice to her? In her limited experience of boys, she was the tall gawky girl that boys never chatted up. But this one not only had the conversational skills but seemed genuinely interested in her. Her stomach gave an unfamiliar flip. 'Thank you, but you really don't have to...'

'But I want to. Now, how much?' He straightened up and looked over her head at the gathering queue of customers.

'A pound please,' she said quickly before she lost his attention altogether.

He gave her a lopsided smile as he turned to cut and weigh her order. She noticed that the fish was heavier than the brass weight he'd put for balance on the scales, but he simply wrapped it up and handed it across. 'I'm helping my dad out when it's busy. I'll be here again on Friday morning,' he said, taking her money. 'Will I see you then?'

Trudi fought back a smile. 'I can't say. I'll have to see.'

As she walked away, she was sure she could feel his eyes on her, but she didn't dare look back. For some reason, and she had no idea why, she felt self-conscious, as if she might trip over or something; but inside her heart was soaring.

Her mother was surprised when she turned up with the extra fish. Trudi couldn't bring herself to tell her the truth, so lied that the fisherman was trying to get rid of his surplus stock. Her mother didn't question her, but on the Thursday evening, when Trudi offered to go and buy fish the next day, her mother narrowed her eyes and said, 'Is it a young man you're going to meet?'

There was no point pretending otherwise – but then again, Trudi told herself, she wasn't really going to meet him as such. 'The fisherman's son is helping out at the stall. He was just being friendly and asked if I was coming again on Friday. I thought I would.'

'Well, that's nice for you. But be careful, won't you?'

'Yes, Mother. You know I will.' Trudi sighed. It was something her mother always said whenever one of her daughters left the house by themselves – and she had reason to be concerned. They were, after all, under German occupation since the Dutch had capitulated following the terrible bombing of Rotterdam. Life for many Dutch people more or less carried on as normal, though, and schools, theatres, cinemas and public transport all functioned as before. True, the Germans were an increasing presence on the street, though Trudi chose to ignore them as she went about her daily life. It was inconceivable that things could get any worse.

Friday morning dawned bright and sunny with the promise of a warm day ahead. The wind had dropped and Trudi enjoyed the sun on her face as she pedalled along the coast towards the fish stall and the boy she'd been thinking of non-stop all week.

He was between customers, and waved to her as she went to park her bike in the rack opposite.

'You came,' he exclaimed, after she'd locked her bike and walked over. 'I was afraid you wouldn't.'

'My mother needs fish,' she said unconvincingly, her smile telling him otherwise. She was secretly delighted that she hadn't read him wrong and that he actually was hoping she would come.

'Forget that for a moment. Listen, I finish work at midday. I can prepare us a couple of sandwiches and we can go and sit on the sand. Would you like to do that with me?'

'I'd love to,' Trudi said with a laugh, and wondered if he'd been planning it all along. 'But I don't even know your name.'

'Sem.' He wiped his hand on a cloth and held it out to her. His hand was warm with a firm grip, and Trudi felt a stab of pleasure shoot through her.

'I'm Trudi.' She was unable to take her eyes off him.

'That's settled, then.' And his eyes seemed to dance with delight. 'I'll meet you over by the blue fishing boat you can see at the end of the beach. It's my dad's.'

Trudi walked away as if she were floating on air. Her head was full of him, and she kept repeating his name to herself and hearing his voice, not quite believing that he wanted to be with her.

It was still quite a while until midday. The tide was out, so she decided to go down to the shoreline and walk along the extensive beach and back again. She carried her sandals in one hand and luxuriated in the feel of damp sand between her toes and the rush of cold seawater frothing over her feet. By the time she arrived back to where they'd arranged to meet, Sem was already on his hands and knees spreading out two tea towels for the picnic he'd brought for them both.

'Hello. Do you want a hand?' she called, sweeping away her curls, which were blowing round her face.

As Sem got to his feet, his face lit up. Trudi found herself looking up at him, something that rarely happened with the boys she knew, who invariably were her height or a few inches smaller than her.

'No need. It's all ready. I hope you like fried fish,' he said, taking her hand and pulling her down to sitting. 'I put some in bread rolls with gherkin and mayonnaise.'

Trudi discovered she was ravenous and her stomach made a gurgling sound, which made him laugh. 'I'll take that as a yes, then.' And he handed her a soft white bread roll, oozing mayonnaise at the sides and smelling divine.

'I've never tasted anything this good,' she said, after she'd bitten down on the still-hot succulent fish and finished by licking the mayonnaise off her fingers.

'It's what we're famous for,' Sem said with a laugh, and held her gaze for a long moment. 'People come from all over to taste our *kibbeling*. It's my father's secret recipe.'

'Will you take the stall over when he retires?' She followed his gaze and saw he was watching a figure walking along the pristine yellow beach that stretched for miles.

When he turned his head back, his expression seemed sad. 'My dad would love me to, but I've told him my studies must come first. This is just a holiday job till I start back at Amsterdam University in September. I'm halfway through my science degree, you see. He thinks I'm wasting my time, but I don't expect him to understand – I'm the first in my family to go to university.'

'That is surely something for him to be proud of. Do you have any siblings?'

'No, it's just me. I never took an interest in going out on the fishing boat with Dad. It was always books for me.' He gave an apologetic laugh.

'University was never an option for me and my sister. I was only ever good at art, but you can't earn a living from that.'

'You're an artist. But that's wonderful,' said Sem, gazing into her eyes with interest. 'What do you paint?'

Trudi felt her cheeks grow hot. No one had ever shown an interest in her work before. 'I sketch mainly, and did some pottery at school. I'd love to be a sculptor.' It was the first time she'd said the words out loud, and it felt good.

'Then you must,' he said encouragingly.

'Maybe I will one day after the war.' This idea, which had only just come to her, seemed thrilling.

A cool breeze had blown up, and Sem moved closer till their thighs touched, then tentatively put an arm round her shoulders. 'Are you cold? Do you want to go back?'

'No, I'm not cold.' Trudi smiled into his handsome face and thought she'd never been as happy as she felt right then. 'But shouldn't you get back to the stall?'

'No, I've finished for the day,' he murmured, and moved even closer. He hesitated, before leaning in to kiss her softly on the lips. Closing her eyes, she became aware of the sighing of waves breaking gently against the shore and the warm sun on her face. Time seemed to stand still. All that mattered was that Sem was kissing her – and she was kissing him back.

NINE

Twice a week, Trudi cycled over to the coast to meet Sem for long walks along the sandy beach. More often than not, he brought a picnic of warm fish sandwiches and they would sit side by side in a favourite spot in the dunes, engrossed in conversation while staring out towards the blue horizon. One long lazy afternoon, when they were lying together, soaking up the last of the late-August sunshine, Sem mentioned that he would soon be going back to university to start the new term. Trudi listened as he spoke with enthusiasm about student life and the student group he had joined the previous year that met weekly in a backroom of an Amsterdam bar to debate politics. Lately, the discussion had taken on a more serious tone, as they mulled over the implications of living under occupation by the Germans, leaving Sem uncharacteristically gloomy about the future.

Sem hoisted himself onto his elbows. 'I have a bad feeling about it all. You can't go anywhere in Amsterdam these days without seeing German soldiers on the street stopping people and demanding to know what their business is. I've heard rumours that they'll introduce ID cards next. But it won't end there. They'll be closing theatres and cinemas soon, and then the universities. Bit by bit Hitler will take over until all our freedoms have been taken away from us. I'm afraid it's all part of his bigger master plan to make Germany the greatest nation on Earth.' He turned his head to look at her, but had to squint against the bright sunshine, making it impossible for her to read his expression.

'I haven't noticed anything myself. Do you really think it'll be as bad as all that?' she said, a feeling of cold dread snaking up her spine. If what Sem was saying were true, she feared for their relationship, which had been so perfect up to now.

'That's the point. They want us to believe that they're here for our own good. You only have to look at what's happening in other countries to realise they'll stop at nothing until they've taken us over completely.'

'I just hope you're wrong,' Trudi said, wondering what it would be like to lose Sem. They'd grown so close so quickly that it was unthinkable; and yet, she was aware of something shifting in their relationship that meant their idyllic existence was about to end. 'Would you fight if you were called up?' she asked uncertainly, hoping he'd say no.

Sem sighed and turned his face away to gaze into the far distance. He picked a long strand of marram grass from beside him and began pulling it into little pieces. 'No. I definitely won't join the army to go and fight. My grandfather was a fisherman in Scheveningen and lost his life when his boat was torpedoed by the Germans in the last war. It was so senseless and brutal and he paid the price with his life. But I may have no choice but to sign up. If that's the case, I'll find a way to get an exemption.' He rolled over onto his side and began twisting one of her curls round and round his finger. 'I'm sorry I brought all this up, but it's been on my mind for a while. Let's not talk about all that anymore. You're right – it may never happen.' He then pulled her into his arms for a long kiss. When he pulled back, he stared into her eyes with an intensity that startled her. 'I can't bear the idea of anything terrible happening to you. Trudi, I want you to know I love you and that I always will.'

'I love you too, Sem Schipper,' Trudi replied, breathless at his sudden announcement. She kissed him hard on the lips, but her joy was tinged with a shiver of fear that their happiness couldn't possibly last.

Grey skies and blustery weather ushered in the end of summer and the end to their languid afternoons spent whiling away time in each other's company. And after that intense conversation, they stopped talking about what might happen in the future and simply enjoyed being together. They still took long walks together, and whenever the rain came pulsing across in sheets from the sea they were forced to dash for shelter.

Finally, the day arrived when Sem finished his summer work on the fish stall. Trudi saw less of him, as he was back home getting ready to resume his studies in Amsterdam. Meanwhile, Trudi carried on with her job working as a domestic help for families in Haarlem.

It was her day off when Sem came round to her house unannounced. 'Can you come right away? Everyone's talking about the news screening at the theatre in town in half an hour.' He was breathless from his bike ride, and ran a hand carelessly through his hair, which no longer looked white-blond but dark from a sudden rain shower. He looked so handsome, Trudi thought, distracted. She had never seen him this enthusiastic about anything before.

'Give me a minute while I grab my coat,' she said, feeling excited that Sem wanted her to accompany him.

'Hurry, I don't want to miss it,' he called out impatiently as he wheeled his bike down the path through a patchwork of puddles.

The clouds parted and the sun came out as they cycled side by side into the centre of town, where a large noisy crowd was gathering in the main square. Sem found them a place to leave their bikes and, holding on to Trudi's hand, pushed through to the front of the queue. Several men protested, but Sem turned on his charm and said they were working at the theatre. He managed to get them in, and found them seats right at the front of the stalls. All around them, people were filing in and talking at the tops of their voices, but as soon as the loud music came booming over the loudspeakers announcing the beginning of the newsreel a hush descended on the whole theatre. A fuzzy black and white image flickered and danced until it came into focus, showing crowds of people standing with their arms held in a stiff salute and shouting 'Heil Hitler!' Their noise was deafening. This cut to an equally chilling image of dozens of Wehrmacht tanks trundling across a bleak, devastated landscape. It was followed by footage of German soldiers wearing metal helmets and crouching in ditches as they operated heavy artillery. All at once, Trudi's attention was drawn to a soldier in officer's uniform who had removed his helmet and was rubbing his hand over his short spiky blond hair. Unnerved, she glanced at Sem, then back to the screen, but the footage had already switched to crowds of people swarming round the entrance to a theatre. The camera focused on a poster pasted on the door bearing two words: 'Jews Forbidden'. The newsreader confirmed her worst suspicions: that the Germans were singling out Jews everywhere for persecution. Where would it all end, she thought despairingly, unable to keep watching, as she realised that Sem's predictions about Hitler and his ambitions were starting to come true.

There was more of the same and then, when the newsreel came to an end, Sem squeezed her hand and whispered for them to leave. Outside, the town centre had almost returned to normal, with just a few cyclists criss-crossing the square and other people going about their daily business. The church clock rang out the hour. This was their reality, she tried to tell herself; but how could she forget what they'd seen only moments before? And how could all these people around her not know what was happening all around them? She realised that she was trembling. 'I need to sit down,' she said.

'Let's go and get a cup of coffee.' She was reassured by Sem's deep voice and let him steer her across the square to a side street and into a small café where one or two people were sitting at tables. The coffee he ordered for them both was warm and comforting and he insisted on stirring an extra spoonful of sugar in hers to help calm her down.

'Sem,' she began, a question in her voice.

'What is it? You've gone quite pale beneath those pretty freckles of yours.' He smiled and stroked her cheek.

She gave a weak smile. 'I've never asked you, but do you have German parentage?'

Sem frowned, glancing around to make sure they weren't being overhead. He spoke in a low voice. 'My mother was born in Frankfurt but the family moved to Haarlem when her father got work at the shipyards. She was just a baby. We must still have family in Germany, but my mother considers herself to be as Dutch as the next person and never talks about coming from Germany. Especially these days with all the anti-German senti-ment around. Now does that answer your question?'

'Yes, of course. It's just... well, with your blond hair and blue eyes you might be mistaken for German.'

'Along with half the population of the Netherlands, in case you haven't noticed. I'd rather be mistaken for a German than a Jew.' He laughed, but Trudi didn't laugh with him. She was shocked by his throwaway remark. Sem noticed the look on her face and straight away apologised, but Trudi said nothing. Her mind had returned to the newsreel they'd just seen.

'Did you see the look of elation on those people's faces who were saluting Hitler? I don't understand how they can salute a man who is hell-bent on destroying people's lives. Jews in particular. Sem, I'm scared that people are blindly accepting whatever he tells them, putting all our lives in danger.' She took an inadvertently large gulp of the hot coffee, which made her cough.

Sem put an arm round her and whispered quietly, 'It doesn't have to be that way. Not if enough people stand up to him.'

'What are you saying? What sort of people?'

'People like us. The student group I meet with have been talking about it for some time. Listen, here's not the place to discuss it, but why don't you come along with me tonight and hear what they have to say?'

TEN

It was Trudi's first experience of a political student gathering and she was spellbound. Finding herself to be the only woman in attendance, she decided to sit at the back where she could watch and listen. The room was cramped and hot and the discussion became overheated as students held forth on ways to resist Nazi rule and discourage further support of Hitler in Holland. Trudi was fascinated to discover about the small resistance groups that were emerging all over the country with ambitious proposals to intercept German plans. She was horrified to hear that the Germans were making all 200,000 civil servants register by filling in an 'ancestry form' detailing their religion and that of their parents and grandparents. It was a blatant attempt to monitor and keep track of Jewish citizens. As she listened in appalled silence, the thought occurred to her that maybe she should not stand back when there was still so much to be done.

The more she heard about the injustice meted out to innocent people, the more she wanted to help others, but, looking around at the fervent faces of those around her, she was struck by how many men were here and how few women. It occurred to her that if she were to become involved she would have to do so on her own terms.

Glancing over at Sem, she couldn't fail to see how comfortable he was in this environment and how calm he remained while others around him lost their tempers. She noticed how when he spoke others listened, and it was no surprise to her when he was voted in as editor of the organisation's underground news-sheet. He spoke so fervently about its aims to challenge German propaganda and urged more people to resist.

At the end of the evening, they left together and Sem talked excitedly and almost non-stop about the meeting.

'This is what I meant when I said that people like us can make a difference. With this newspaper we'll finally be able to get the truth out about what the Germans are really up to. I'll probably have to write most of it myself to start with, but once I've got a group of people on the ground, observing what the Germans get up to first-hand and feeding me the truth, it'll go much more smoothly.' He stopped suddenly and placed his hands on Trudi's shoulders. 'You could help me too,' he said, as if the idea had only just come to him. 'You can write, can't you?'

'Of course I can write,' she said indignantly, 'but I'm sure there are people you know who can write better than me. Your student friends, for example.' It came out more harshly than she intended, but she was unable to disguise how she felt. Sem was different to her and he was also better educated – this evening had opened her eyes to the fact.

'I'm sorry, I didn't think for a moment you couldn't write,' Sem went on. 'It's the first thing that came into my head. But you're right, I should ask my friends at the university. We're all used to writing essays and giving speeches, that kind of thing.' He interlaced his fingers with hers and they set off again, each lost in their own thoughts.

'But I do want to help,' said Trudi eventually. She looked up at him, anxious that he had disappeared into his own head and forgotten about her. 'I may not be as good with words as you, but I am practical and can get things organised.'

Sem blinked back to the present and smiled at her. 'Then you can help with stencilling and getting the news-sheet ready for distribution. I'd love nothing more than to have you work alongside me.'

ELEVEN

Trudi took a house-cleaning job with a wealthy German Jewish family who had moved to Holland several years ago. Herr Goldberg had been an outspoken critic of the Nazi regime and was forced to flee with his wife and ten-year-old son when he learnt that he was about to be arrested. They managed to get out at a time when it was still possible to bring their furniture and valuables with them, establishing a quiet comfortable life for themselves far from danger. At least that was how things had seemed, until the Germans invaded the Netherlands and started to make life difficult for the Jews. Although the couple were always cheerful in her presence, Trudi guessed that they always carried this heavy burden with them, knowing that they too could be singled out.

Trudi was heavily involved in Sem's operation, which he ran from his digs in a large scruffy town house on one of the outer canals in Amsterdam. He shared it with three other students, who also helped out putting the paper together. Sem typed most of the articles himself, bashing them out on an ancient typewriter one of his student friends had lent him.

Trudi became a dab hand at running off copies on the clunky stencilling machine. She sorted and folded the printed paper into news-sheets ready to be distributed. She learnt not to interrupt Sem when he was deep in concentration. Once, when she needed his help for something or other he shouted at her in irritation. He immediately apologised and made it up to her with a kiss. She was willing to forgive him, but soon discovered that he was prone to losing his temper when things didn't always go his way.

It was easy to forget his sudden outbursts when the two of them were alone together. At least once a week he took Trudi to the cinema, where they sat at the back cuddling up to one another. More often than not, Trudi had no idea what the film had been about, but she didn't care. All that mattered was being with him and hearing him whisper how much he loved her.

One morning, Trudi was in the Goldbergs' dining room polishing the large mahogany table when the doorbell rang. She heard Mevrouw Goldberg open the door to greet her visitor.

'Ursula, what a surprise to see you! Is everything all right?' she heard Mevrouw Goldberg say.

'Hilde, can I come in a moment?' said the visitor in a quiet but pleading voice.

Trudi moved closer to the dining room door, which stood ajar.

'Of course, you're always welcome. Would you like to join me in a coffee?'

Trudi took several steps back from the door in case they discovered her eavesdropping. Normally she would never listen in on other people's private conversations, but there was something in the visitor's tone that made her anxious and want to hear more.

Mevrouw Goldberg's friend declined the offer of coffee and wasted no time in explaining why she had come round. 'The

Meissners at number thirty-four are leaving tomorrow for America. It's all arranged. As soon as I heard, I came straight over, because I think you should take your family away from here as soon as possible. The Netherlands is no longer safe.'

Trudi heard Mevrouw Goldberg begin to protest, but her friend interrupted her.

'Hilde, there's no point pretending it won't happen. Hitler hates the Jews and will stop at nothing to get rid of them. The signs are everywhere and things are only going to get worse. I know the man who arranged the Meissners' passage and I'm sure he can do the same for you, Aron and little David. Please tell me you'll consider it.'

Trudi was unable to make out Mevrouw Goldberg's reply, spoken in urgent tones, but shortly after she heard the front door close with a click. Shaken by what she had heard, her first thought was to talk to Sem, telling herself that this was the kind of news he was always looking for. With his skill, she was sure he would turn it into an important story which would serve as a warning to others that the threat posed by Hitler was very real.

But first she needed to speak to Mevrouw Goldberg. She found her sitting in the kitchen with her head in her hands.

'Mevrouw Goldberg... is everything all right?' Trudi asked from the doorway.

She couldn't have heard Trudi come in. As she looked up, Trudi could see the tears welling in her eyes. 'You heard?' Mevrouw Goldberg said.

Trudi nodded. There was no point in pretending she hadn't. 'I'm so sorry you are faced with this awful dilemma. What will you do?'

'I don't know, but it's not fair. What have Aron and I ever done to hurt anyone?' She gazed pleadingly at Trudi, as if she could provide the answer, but Trudi could find no words to console her.

. . .

After work, Trudi went straight by bus to Amsterdam. The short journey was one she usually enjoyed, staring out at the beautiful old buildings in Haarlem centre, before the bus trundled out into the green countryside towards the suburbs of Amsterdam. But today her thoughts were troubled as she wondered if the Goldberg family would heed Ursula's advice and abandon their comfortable life in Holland for the uncertainty of an unknown destination thousands of miles away. She was brought back to the present by the dinging of the bell as the bus rounded a corner and drew to a halt. Trudi climbed off and hurried along Sem's street edging the murky-looking canal. She had to avoid the bikes parked two and three abreast, some leaning precariously near to the water's edge. It was only when she arrived outside his house that it occurred to her that she hadn't seen Sem for over a week. She wasn't even sure if she would find him at home, as it was the middle of the day, when he was usually in lectures at the university.

The bell sounded shrilly somewhere deep in the house. After a couple of minutes, the door was opened by one of Sem's housemates.

'Hello, Wouter. Is Sem in?' She seemed to have woken his friend judging by his hair, which stood on end, and his enormous yawn.

'Come on in,' he said, still yawning, before calling to Sem over his shoulder.

Sem was sitting at the kitchen table, nursing a cup of tea. He was dressed in a shabby dressing gown and looked decidedly the worse for wear, but his face cracked into a smile the moment he saw Trudi. 'To what do I owe this surprise?' He stood up and came over to kiss her.

Next to him, Trudi felt self-conscious in her fawn tweed coat and dark-blue felt hat, which she quickly removed. 'Aren't you going to the university today?' she said, laying the hat on the table.

Sem blinked several times, as if he needed to process her question, then shook his head. 'There's a strike on. All lectures are off. So a few of us decided to share a few drinks together. It got rather late.' He gave her a rueful grin before rubbing his hands over his face.

'A strike? What about?'

'Nothing much. At least not yet. It started with a left-wing group who are protesting about Hitler's persecution of Jews. But not much is happening yet in this country, so I don't see what all the fuss is about.'

'Don't you?' she said, surprised by his comment. He was normally so enthusiastic about the work he did for the resistance, but now he seemed utterly deflated. She sat on a chair at the opposite side of the table. 'I've come from work where I overheard a conversation between my Jewish employer and her friend. The friend is desperately worried about her family's safety and is urging her to leave Holland for America. She knows of other Jewish people who are planning on fleeing the country. I thought you should know this is happening and that you could write about it.'

Sem frowned as he sat back down in his chair. 'I would, but I'm afraid it's out of my hands.'

'What do you mean? You're the editor, aren't you?'

'Unfortunately, not,' he said with a scoff. 'I had a falling-out with editorial over the protest, which I didn't think was a big enough story for the front page. A new editor was appointed yesterday, so I'm now redundant. But, no matter. I resigned before they could get rid of me. It suits me quite well, actually; all this writing and editing has become a burden. It's been taking up too much of my time.'

'So you'll be able to concentrate on your studies,' she said, trying to second-guess what lay behind his words. It occurred to her that he might have lost his passion for the resistance.

'Yes, I suppose you're right,' Sem said, but sounded doubtful.

'Well,' she said. 'There won't be any need for me to help out with the stencilling anymore.' She stared at him, waiting for an answer.

'The truth is, I'm a bit disillusioned with it all,' Sem said with a sigh. He didn't appear to have heard her last comment. 'I felt so passionate about the paper when I could see a reason to work at it. But things aren't quite turning out the way I expected.' He got up and went to pick up a packet of cigarettes lying on the sideboard. 'Want one?' he said casually, after he'd taken one for himself and lit it.

'I don't smoke. You know that,' said Trudi, annoyed that he should ask and surprised to see him smoke. What else didn't she know about him? Can it have been so long since they'd sat down together and talked about things that mattered? She regarded him with a pang of nostalgia for what they so clearly no longer had. He was still as handsome as ever, but he seemed to have lost the vivacious charm that had first attracted her to him. Maybe it was because they were all more anxious these days, she told herself. Since those early heady days of summer when the only thing that mattered was being together, their lives had moved in different directions. She wondered if they even had that much in common.

'Sem,' she said, plucking up courage for what she was about to say.

'Hmm?' Sem blew out a lungful of smoke.

She then spoke the words still forming in her mind. 'I think we should stop seeing each other for a while.' Suddenly, she wanted this conversation to be over and done with.

'What are you saying?' Sem quickly stubbed out his cigarette in a saucer overflowing with butts. He moved towards her.

She stepped back. 'No, Sem. Don't hold me. I've made up my mind.' She was surprised by the force of her words. She hadn't intended this when she'd walked through the door, but perhaps she'd seen it coming for some time. She looked around the messy student kitchen with its pile of unwashed dishes in the sink and open textbooks strewn about the place. 'It was different when it was just the two of us. It didn't matter when we were working together on a common cause that we both believed in, but I've seen the change in you each time I come here. When I'm here with you, I can see I don't fit in. Your life is here among like-minded people who share your interests.'

'Trudi, please don't say that. You're seeing what you want to see, not the reality. Just because I'm living the life of a student with other students doesn't mean that I've changed. I'm still the boy who worked at his father's fish stall, the one who fell in love with the beautiful, wonderful person that you are.' His voice was soft as he moved a little closer so he could touch a curl that had fallen across her face – the way he used to. Trudi couldn't help but stare up into those intense blue eyes of his, remembering the first time she'd looked into them and felt captivated. She could feel herself weaken.

'Don't make this harder than it already is,' she said quietly, and removed his hand, which was cupping her face. 'There really isn't anything more to say... except that I hope we can remain friends.'

'Trudi, wait...'

The despair in his voice almost made her falter.

'I'm sorry, Sem,' she said. And before she could change her mind, she retrieved her hat from the kitchen table and walked away quickly, stepping over the clutter in the hallway, before opening the front door onto the street. She took a deep breath in. It was busier than when she'd arrived. She was able to slip away down the steps and into the crowd, and ran all the way back to the bus, which was about to depart. She managed to jump aboard as it began to move off, and found a seat at the back. Only then did the tears stream down her cheeks. Had she done the right thing by ending it? She really couldn't tell. But it was done now, and it wouldn't be until later that she'd truly understand the reason why.

TWELVE

NOW

Trudi carefully carried a tray with two cups of coffee and two glasses of lemonade out onto the terrace and placed it on the round wrought-iron table. She took a seat on one of the matching chairs and waited for her Great-Aunt Lieke to join her, keeping an eye on the children, who were happily playing ball on the lawn. Smiling, she marvelled at how quickly the girls had adapted to their new home after their ordeal in the lock-up garage. It must be the innocence of childhood, she mused, wishing that she could move on from the traumatic events of the past months as easily.

In those early weeks after she'd split from Sem, she'd often thought about him and wondered whether he had given up on his studies, but he'd made it clear he wouldn't return home to work on his father's fish stall. She wondered if he'd had a change of heart and regained his enthusiasm for the resistance. Several times she'd been on the verge of contacting him – she genuinely wanted to find out – but then events had overtaken her. First, there was the shock of the sudden and unexpected raid and disappearance of the Friedman parents, and after that her priority had been to ensure their girls' safety. And all this time she was considering how she might contribute in some way to opposing the Nazis.

She smiled at Great-Aunt Lieke, who had come out of the back door and was walking slowly towards her. The elderly woman suffered from arthritis and was unable to get around without a stick, but said she was pleased to help out as long as Trudi stayed around to look after the children. Despite having problems with her mobility, she revelled in having the company and enjoyed sitting out here watching the children playing in her walled garden, which wasn't overlooked by inquisitive neighbours. She'd lived in the same beautiful cottage in a quiet village outside Haarlem all her life. Trudi had wonderful child-hood memories of playing in this garden, scrambling up the old apple tree with Frida and afternoons baking cinnamon biscuits and apple cake with her great-aunt.

'Come and drink your coffee before it gets cold,' Trudi said, standing up to pull out the other chair.

'It's so lovely to have you here. But I can't get around as quickly as I used to.' Her great-aunt lowered herself onto her chair with a contented sigh and gazed fondly at Trudi, before taking a sip of coffee. 'I'm so grateful that you asked to come and stay with these dear children. I love having you all here. In fact, I've been thinking for some time that I'd like to do something to help others, but it's not easy to know how at my age.'

Trudi nodded sympathetically. 'The Germans are every-where now, but I don't think I'll ever get used to them, which is probably a good thing. It makes you wary whenever you go out, that feeling you're being watched. You can't imagine what a relief it is being here.'

Just at that moment, the children's ball came bouncing towards Trudi and landed at her feet. 'Whose is this?' she said, scooping it up and holding it aloft.

'It's mine!' exclaimed Louisa, running over and trying to snatch it before Rosy caught her up. Rosy began to cry plaintively, which stopped Louisa in her tracks. 'It's OK. You can have a turn,' Louisa said, a tiny look of worry crossing her face. It was a small thing, but it pleased Trudi to see the motherly concern Louisa was showing her little sister so soon after being separated from their parents.

'That's a nice thing to do,' she called to Louisa, but the two girls had already run off to resume their game. As she watched them Trudi realised that, despite everything, this was the happiest she'd felt in ages.

A week later, Frans turned up with news that he'd found a place for Louisa and Rosy to stay with a family who lived in a small village on the edge of the Kennemer dunes. They wouldn't be alone as they would be close to several other families sheltering Jewish children from Haarlem. Frans had supplied them with new identity cards without the incriminating letter J, which meant Louisa could attend the local primary school without raising suspicions.

Under the circumstances, it was all Trudi could hope for – the girls would stay together and be well cared for. Until they could be reunited with their parents, it had to be the best possible solution. But it was still a wrench for her and Great-Aunt Lieke to say goodbye to them, and she forced herself to hold back her tears as they waved them off with the promise that she would see them very soon. The Kennemer dunes were within easy cycling distance and she suggested to Frans that she deliver ration coupons and food weekly to the whole Jewish contingent. Great-Aunt Lieke insisted on sending them home-made biscuits too, whenever she could get hold of the ingredients.

The day after the children left with Frans for their new home, Trudi was clearing away the breakfast things when her great-aunt came into the kitchen holding a letter addressed to her. Trudi immediately recognised her sister's handwriting. 'It's from Frida,' she said, taking the letter and sitting down to steady herself in case of bad news. She tore open the envelope, relieved to see that it hadn't been tampered with. The letter was short, written on a single sheet, but enough for Trudi to read between the lines. She longed to know more, but knew she'd have to wait to hear the full story till she saw Frida in person.

Dear Trudi

The house has been unbearably quiet since you left. Just me and Papa. That is until Mama returned home, a little shaken but otherwise well.

I think of you every day and hope nothing has happened to you. I miss you so much and can't wait to see you.

Your loving sister

Frida

She folded the letter in half and inserted if back in its envelope. 'Everyone back home is well,' she said, looking up at her great-aunt, who was watching her expectantly. 'And Mother is back – isn't that wonderful news?' She leant over and hugged her great-aunt, who had tears in her eyes. It must have been such a relief to her that Cornelia, Trudi's mother and her favourite niece, was safe and sound. 'Dearest Cornelia, I'm so glad,' she said, taking out a handkerchief and dabbing her eyes.

Trudi bit her lip as she felt tears prick behind her eyelids. 'I really should go back,' she said with a tremor in her voice.

'Of course you must, though I want you to know you're welcome to stay longer.'

'You've been so kind to me already, Tante Lieke. I wish I

could, but it's not practical. I need to find work and Haarlem is the best place for it.'

'Will you stay here until you do?' her great-aunt asked hopefully.

'I will.' Trudi leant over and kissed her great-aunt on the cheek. She hadn't realised how lonely Great-Aunt Lieke must have felt living on her own since her husband had passed away.

THIRTEEN

The letter continued to play on Trudi's mind and she realised how much she missed her sister. So she was surprised and thrilled when, out in the garden one morning planting potatoes and carrots, she saw Frida appear at the kitchen door.

'Frida, is it really you?' Trudi dropped her trowel in the earth and ran over to her. Heedless of her filthy hands, she threw her arms round Frida and gave her an enormous hug. 'Why didn't you say you were coming?' she said, holding on tight.

'I didn't know I was until this morning,' said Frida breathlessly. 'Until this man turned up at the door and introduced himself as Frans. I didn't know who he was at first, then he told me he was the one who helped you hide Rosy and Louisa. It was such a surprise. He said he was coming to see you and would I like to come too. Of course I said yes. But let's not go inside just yet. I've so much to tell you.' She hooked her arm through Trudi's and they went over to the wooden seat nestled beneath a lilac tree in full bloom. Frida breathed in the delicate scent, so redolent of spring. 'Gorgeous. It's so peaceful here. You can almost believe there isn't a war on.'

'If only,' said Trudi with a sad smile. 'Tell me, have there been any more raids?'

'Not since that dreadful night, thank goodness. I think the *moffen* got who they were looking for and that's why they haven't bothered us again.'

'And Mama? How is she after her ordeal?'

'She won't talk about it, apart from to say that they interrogated her about the Friedmans. It must have been awful for her, but she managed to keep silent about the Friedman children, thank goodness. Frans tells me they've moved to a village over at the Kennemer dunes. They should be safe there.'

'I'll make sure of it and will visit them whenever I can. I only wish the girls could stay there indefinitely, but Frans says it must only be temporary until he can move them to a foster home. He hasn't had any news yet about Maria and Hans and says we should remain hopeful, but it's hard with all the rumours circulating about Jews disappearing on transports to Germany. I can't bear to think those two little girls might never see their parents again.'

'Do you really think that's a possibility?' asked Frida, screwing up her forehead.

Trudi nodded. 'Yes. The longer we have no news...' she began, but didn't finish. Her mind filled with the appalling images she'd seen in the illegal newspapers of crowds of people being herded into cattle trucks. Then, changing the subject, she said, 'You haven't mentioned Papa. How is he?'

Frida pursed her lips into a smile. 'I think the raid shook him up more than he's willing to admit. He's at home a lot more now and doesn't go out in the evenings. It's weird, but Mama and Papa seem to be a lot closer now.'

'I don't think it's weird. It's good,' said Trudi, relieved to hear some positive news. 'Let's hope it lasts.'

Frida nodded. 'What will you do now, Trudi?'

'I've been thinking about things a lot since I split from Sem.

Although it didn't work out between us, I learnt a lot from him about what people can do to stand up to the Germans. So I've started delivering anti-propaganda magazines and newspapers for a couple of organisations. *De Koevoet* is aimed at young people but it's very small. Then there's *De Waarheid*, which is the banned newspaper of the Communist Party. I feel quite strongly about helping people to understand the truth about what is really happening under the Germans. It's just a start, Frida. Helping Rosy and Louisa escape from the Germans was terrifying, but was probably the most meaningful thing I've ever done in my whole life. There are so many children like them whose only hope is to disappear to safety before they are taken by the Nazis. I want to be the one who can make that happen.' She took a steadying breath, before she went on. 'What about you... how's your work?'

'As always, being a nurse it's constantly busy on the wards, but I've recently asked if I could move to the emergency department to help with all the victims of bombing. It's tough work, but every life we save is worth saving, whichever side that person is on. Many of the patients we see have suffered serious gunshot wounds and of course some don't recover. Some of the staff joke that it's like the Wild West out there, not that it's in the least funny. I suppose they say it to lighten what is a truly awful situation.' She slowly shook her head.

'Oh, look, here comes Frans,' exclaimed Trudi.

'Your Great-Aunt Lieke has been making a fuss of me,' quipped Frans as he crossed the lawn carrying a tray holding tall glasses. 'She insisted I drink a glass of her home-made lemonade with her while we had a very nice chat. I had to tear myself away to come and talk to you. I hope I'm not interrupting.' He deposited the tray on a rickety metal garden table and fetched a fold-up chair that was leaning against the garden fence for himself. 'Have I missed anything?' He handed Trudi and Frida glasses of lemonade.

'I'm just hearing from Frida how things are back home. I'm glad to hear the *moffen* haven't returned,' said Trudi with a smile.

'And Trudi's been telling me she's a bit too comfortable here and is ready for a new challenge,' Frida quipped.

'That's not what I said.' Trudi gave her a playful slap on the arm. 'I'm very grateful to Great-Tante Lieke for all she's done for the children and me. But it's time I moved back to Haarlem. This whole experience with the Friedmans and their children has opened my eyes to the plight of so many Jewish families who are unable to fend for themselves. I've been thinking of joining the resistance ever since I used to help my ex print and distribute student material. Then after we stopped seeing one another, I got involved in delivering copies of *De Waarheid* in town. I wait at bus stops where it's busy and slip copies into people's bags when they're distracted boarding or leaving the bus. I like to think that by reading these papers people get to understand what is really happening, not what the Nazis tell us. It's a small thing, I know, but I want to do more. Would you be able to help?'

'That's interesting to hear. I am setting up a group in Haarlem and I have plenty of young men eager to throw themselves into all kinds of dangerous assignments, but no women. It's not really the kind of thing women want to get involved in. But there's always a call for people to distribute anti-Nazi pamphlets and news-sheets and, as you've already been doing that, I'm sure I can arrange it.'

Trudi shook her head so vigorously her curls bounced. 'No, that's not what I had in mind. It's not safe for Jewish people as long as the Germans are in charge. I want to help others like I helped Rosy and Louisa. I'm not afraid of what it entails, if that's what you're thinking.'

'No, I don't think that at all. I've seen you in action when you took the Friedman children into hiding. You were brave and determined and these are qualities that are necessary. But you must be aware that this is dangerous work and that if you get caught the Germans will show you no mercy, nor will they spare the lives of any Jewish person they discover you're protecting.'

Trudi was growing impatient. It was as if he didn't believe she was up to it. But what if he were right and working for the resistance was too dangerous when she had her responsibility towards Louisa and Rosy to consider? 'What are you saying?' she asked.

'If I'm to take you on, you will need to convince me you can defend yourself. Is that something you could see yourself doing?'

'Potentially,' she said warily. 'What would it involve?' She was loath to commit herself to something she knew so little about. Frans may have said he'd seen her in action, but she hadn't considered that hiding children from the Germans would mean she would have to be armed. The very thought of it made her extremely uncomfortable.

'Good. Then we'll get you started on courier work. Don't worry – not newspapers, but delivering vital messages to resistance cells on the coast who are aiding the Allies. You will need to deal with German soldiers at the various checkpoints and be prepared to be searched. Naturally, it's dangerous work, so you'll need to be trained in how to use pistols and hand grenades. And from there, how to detonate a bomb. Once you've got the hang of that, you'd need strong nerves. How do you feel about firing a gun?'

'I don't know how to use one, but I could learn if it would keep people safe,' said Trudi with a conviction she wasn't altogether sure she had. How could she possibly know if she could use one unless confronted with the situation?

'Do you think you could shoot?' Frans stared at her but she was unable to hold his gaze. 'It's not something you can learn,' he went on. 'It comes from within.' He thumped his chest with his fist. 'There's a big difference between knowing how to shoot and actually pulling the trigger. Let me ask you again – do you think you could shoot someone?'

Trudi knew he was testing her nerve, but needed a moment to think over his request before answering. If she were being followed and thought her life was in danger, would she have the nerve to pull the trigger? She was sure her instinct would be to run away. But what if she knew it was a Nazi or a collaborator who was responsible for the deaths of innocent people, people she knew and loved? In that case she knew she would be prepared to risk her life. 'If he's a Nazi, then yes, I would.'

Frans frowned. 'It may not always be obvious in the heat of the moment. In that split second, you may not be able to work out their identity. Let me put it another way – if it were a Dutch person – and don't forget it could be a woman – someone who has been betraying a fellow countryman to the Nazis... would you shoot them if you believed it would save a life?'

Trudi hated that he put her on the spot, but had to admit that the way he put it made her reconsider her answer. Last autumn, her mother had given shelter to a young couple for several weeks, before the resistance had found them a safe haven in a small Jewish settlement in the Veluwe woods some thirty miles away. While they were in hiding in the attic, Trudi's mother had warned her daughters about making any casual remarks to the neighbours in case there was a traitor among them. Trudi remembered the quiet teacher, who lived only two doors away. He was always so polite when they exchanged a greeting in the street – but what would she do if she discovered he'd been passing information about the inno-cent couple hiding under her roof? Would she dare to pull a gun on him? It was a question she hardly needed to ask herself, though the thought of it made her tremble. Then she remem-bered the look of sheer terror on Marie and Hans's faces moments before they were dragged away. 'If I had intelligence that the person was a danger to innocent people, then yes.' This time her voice was firm.

'Good,' Frans said, leaning back in his chair, and Trudi wondered if she'd passed his test. 'We would never send our people after someone we suspect is passing information to the Germans unless we are certain to have proof. I want to assure you of that.'

Frida had remained quiet during this exchange, but now spoke up. 'I work at the hospital and every day I see patients who have suffered terribly at the hands of the Germans. Many die from gunshot wounds or are left with life-changing disabilities. Like Trudi, I think women are as capable of working for the resistance as men. I would also like to be one of those women.' She reached for Trudi's hand and clasped it in hers. 'I'm sure Trudi and I would make an excellent team.' She squeezed her sister's hand. 'What do you think?' she said, addressing Frans.

Trudi was both elated and comforted by Frida's suggestion. She wouldn't have to face the dangers alone and they would be working for a common cause – thwarting the Germans. And Frans would surely be glad to recruit them to his group. But instead of agreeing, he appeared to have second thoughts, and said they should give the matter serious consideration before taking such a big step.

'Think it over for a few days,' he said,' and if you're still keen then come along to a meeting I'm holding for new recruits, so you can get a flavour of what the work entails.'

Trudi wondered if he'd been expecting her to be more enthusiastic about the idea of killing Nazis, but she couldn't pretend to be something she wasn't. More than anything, she wanted to assist Jewish families in need and protect their children, but she realised she still needed to convince Frans that she was the best person to do that.

FOURTEEN

The sun was setting as Trudi and Frida walked round the outside of the park towards the meeting place. They had discussed long and hard whether to go through with it. Trudi still had misgivings about getting involved in an organisation that expected its members to take up arms against the enemy. Frida didn't see it that way. She was excited to be doing some 'real resistance work', as she liked to call it. 'All we're doing is going along to hear what he has to say. And if we don't like it, we'll walk away. But just imagine being part of a group that takes a stand against the Germans by saving innocent lives.' Frida's eyes sparkled as she spoke, and Trudi found herself agreeing with her assessment. Perhaps she was right – wasn't helping ordinary people unable to defend themselves what this was all about?

They turned in to the park through the tall black iron gates and headed over to the pond. Beneath a tall lime tree stood a huddle of men smoking and talking quietly among themselves.

'No other women,' whispered Trudi.

'I'm glad there are two of us,' said Frida, clutching at her arm, as one of the men stopped talking to give them an appraising look.

'Me too. But look who's come.' Trudi nodded in the direction of a fair-haired, stocky man, about her age, whose face lit up when he saw them. 'Hello Wim. So you also got the message?' She smiled, relieved to see someone familiar. She'd known Wim at school, not so much as a friend but someone to stop and chat to occasionally.

'That's right. Nice to see you and your sister. Though I wonder if we've all been stood up,' he said with a chuckle.

'No such luck,' said another man out of the side of his mouth as Frans came hurrying towards them, his long coat flapping round his ankles. He took up a position with his back to the pond and facing the park gate.

'Sorry I'm late, but I was held up at a meeting that overran. I'm glad you all made it.' Frans swept his gaze over each of the participants till it fell on Trudi and Frida and he gave each of them a smile.

Trudi looked away, then stared uncomfortably at her feet. The last thing she wanted was anything that could be seen as favouritism in front of all these men. She realised that she and Frida had more to prove if they were to be accepted into the group; they would need to be shrewd and quick-thinking, not just handy with a gun.

'I'll keep it short as I don't want to draw attention to us,' said Frans. 'But if anyone accosts you...' he paused to check if anyone was coming through the gate, 'the story is that we are gathered here for exercise, and that I am your coach. You all know I've been working to create a subgroup of the main Haarlem resistance organisation. My aim is for it to become the sabotage arm involved in more active forms of resistance. That's not to say that minor acts of resistance, such as spreading anti-German information and acting as couriers, aren't also vitally important. We still need people on the ground to counter the appalling propaganda fed to us by the Germans daily from all quarters.

'I will be in charge of this group's activities, including training on how to use firearms correctly. I am confident that together we will work to remove the problem at its very root. We will hunt down and flush out any person – German or Dutch – who is on the side of the Nazis and betraying ordinary citizens in exchange for money or other favours. And especially anyone with a hatred of Jews. Make no mistake – if there is no other choice, we must be prepared to use force.' His voice rose as he delivered this last line with vehemence and punched the air.

Trudi caught Wim's eye and he widened his eyes at her. She wondered if, like her, he was uneasy with Frans's rhetoric. She wished he would get the speech over with and tell them exactly what they were expected to do.

'So here's my plan for this evening,' Frans went on. 'I'd like you to get into twos or threes. Your first task is to go looking for Germans in uniform. Follow at a discreet distance. Be subtle. They like to go drinking after hours, so stake out the bars they frequent down by the canal and eavesdrop on their conversations. Find out anything that could help us sabotage their plans. And when they leave, trail them and look for opportunities to attack.'

'What are we supposed to do? Cosh 'em on the head?' said a good-looking man with dark curly hair.

'Quite so,' said the young man next to him, as laughter erupted from the rest of the group.

'Or strangle them with our bare hands,' quipped another, raising his voice above the din.

'He makes a serious point,' said Trudi quietly to Frida. The talk made her feel uncomfortable. 'What chances would we have against a *mof* if we're not armed?' Since Frans had seeded the idea of her handling a live gun, she'd been mulling over the possibilities of ambush and whether shooting was the right thing to do, or if she'd even have the nerve to shoot. Holding a gun in her hand would undoubtedly give her a feeling of control and without one she knew she would be as good as dead. She turned to look at Frans and noticed the high colour in his cheeks. Was it anger, or nervousness, she wondered? Perhaps he wasn't as sure of himself as he made out.

Frans raised his hand for quiet. 'This is no laughing matter. Until we can arm ourselves, we won't be able to make progress. Do any of you possess a firearm?'

Wim scoffed into the silence. It was a stupid question that no one was prepared to answer in the affirmative, even if they did have a gun on them.

Trudi was getting impatient as she addressed Frans. 'But you must have a gun. Would you let one of us use it?'

'Or maybe it's you who should be the one going after the *moffen*,' said Wim, who seemed emboldened by her comments.

There were murmurings of agreement and Trudi wondered if Frans was losing control of the meeting. But he merely laughed, saying, 'I could – and I will if needs be. But the issue here is that we need to get hold of more weapons. They're not easy to come by and we don't have the funds to buy any. The alternative is to steal from the Germans. If you're clever and work together, it should be possible. There will be plenty of opportunities to target bars where Germans are off duty and drinking. Where they're off guard. One of you gets talking.' His eyes landed briefly on Trudi, before he went on, 'Maybe distracting him by pretending to spill your drink, while your partner steals the gun.' Frans obviously noted the dubious expressions on their faces; he went on, 'Well. We can work up to that and I don't expect you to do any of this yet. So for this evening, I want you to get a sense of how this might work by watching and observing, and, if there's a chance for a conversation, don't underestimate what you might learn about their movements and intentions. Wim, I see you already know the girls, so you can go with them. The rest of you, find someone to team up with. Before you set off, discuss tactics together and make sure you all spread out. We'll meet back here tomorrow evening at the same time so we can discuss next steps.'

FIFTEEN

'I suppose he thinks we're incapable of doing this without a man in charge,' Trudi whispered fiercely to Frida as they exited the park and started walking towards the main city canal and the bars that many Germans were known to frequent.

'Hmm,' said Frida, nodding in grim-faced agreement.

'Wait for me,' Wim called, half-running to catch them up. 'Listen, let's keep away from the others. I know of a bar just off Raamsingel that's a favourite with the *moffen*. Let's try there first.'

But Frida had already spotted a couple of men in German uniform walking ahead of them. They were engrossed in conversation as they turned down a side street and strode towards a bar.

'No, we'll follow these two. Wim, you stay here and keep a lookout for trouble while we go in,' Frida said.

'But...' began Wim. Frida wasn't listening; she linked her arm in Trudi's, propelling her across the road.

'What are you doing?' said Trudi, worried that her sister was about to do something foolhardy.

'Wait and see,' said Frida with a knowing look.

It was only when they were through the door that Frida admitted she'd come out without her purse. 'Do you have enough on you to buy us both a drink?'

'Maybe enough for one drink. One of us will have to ask for a glass of tap water,' said Trudi with a puzzled look.

'That'll have to do,' said Frida, nudging her arm.

The bar was quiet, with only a few people sitting at tables, keeping to themselves. Trudi and Frida walked up to the bar and stood behind the two uniformed Germans, who were deep in conversation. The bartender was quick to serve the men with large glasses of frothy beer and a glass of jenever each, which he slid across the counter. 'On the house,' he said in a low voice with an ingratiating smile.

Without a word of thanks and with the barest of nods, the men accepted the drinks, each tipping the jenever back with a loud *Prost!* Then the taller of the men caught sight of Frida. Trudi touched her sleeve as a warning, but Frida was already flashing the German a smile, and stroked her fingers through her hair in a suggestive gesture.

'*Guten Abend*, or should I say good evening,' the German said, switching easily to Dutch. He was young, no more than nineteen, thought Trudi. She could tell he was taken with Frida by the way he also ran a hand over his short-cropped hair, but somewhat more self-consciously.

'I'm Fritz and this is Manfred,' he said, nodding to the other man, who looked a little older and had more insignia on his jacket lapels.

'I'm Greta,' lied Frida, before turning to Trudi. 'And this is my friend Corrie.'

Trudi nodded, momentarily lost for words. They hadn't prepared for this. It always surprised her how easily Frida was able to lie while switching on the charm. Trudi's instincts were to be wary; first she wanted to get the measure of these two Germans.

'Ladies, let me buy you both a drink. What will you have?' said Fritz, addressing Frida.

'A soft drink please.'

'I'll have one too, please,' echoed Trudi.

'Really? Not even a small glass of wine?' said Fritz. Briefly, his face twisted into a look of disdain. Manfred watched impassively. Trudi felt her stomach clench. She'd heard how little it took to rile the Germans and wondered if they'd made a mistake in turning down their offer of alcohol. Then she remembered that they had the perfect excuse. At least part of what she was about to say was true.

'We're working a night shift at the hospital later. We only popped in because Fr— Greta said she was thirsty.' Instantly, Trudi felt her cheeks flood with colour at her near blunder over Frida's name, but the two Germans didn't appear to have noticed. Fritz clicked his fingers at the barman and ordered two lemonades and two more beers. They took their drinks over to a table by the window and soon the men were chatting to them about their move to Haarlem from Germany.

'This bar seems rather quiet. Where do you girls normally go for a night out?' said Fritz, taking a large mouthful of beer. He had a mischievous glint in his eye.

'We mainly see friends at home. We don't go out much, do we?' said Trudi, refusing to be drawn. She glanced meaningfully at Frida, who shook her head and seemed to get her message.

'You could always go to Amsterdam. It's not too far by train or bus,' said Frida.

Manfred frowned. 'That's no good to us now we're stationed out here. They've put us in accommodation out of town, where there's nothing going on. We pulled the short straw coming to Haarlem instead of Amsterdam. Our army colleagues tell us the nightlife there is incredibly lively. From what we've seen so far, this place is a dump.' He gave a derisive sniff.

'We like it well enough,' said Trudi a little defensively, thinking that if they didn't like it they could shove off back to where they came from. But of course she didn't say anything of the sort, and instead steered the conversation back to safer ground, asking where they came from in Germany and what they did before the war. She was surprised to hear that the war had interrupted their schooling, which must have made both of them no more than seventeen or eighteen years old.

'I suppose we'll have to take our final exams after the war,' said Fritz with a derisive laugh.

'That seems pretty pointless now we're doing a proper job. If it hadn't been for the war, we wouldn't have learnt how to use one of these beauties.' Manfred took a small gun out of his inside jacket pocket and twirled it admiringly through his fingers before showing it off in the palm of his large hand.

Frida gave a small gasp and quickly covered her mouth with her hand. 'Have you used it?'

Manfred let out a loud laugh. 'Of course. That's what we're trained to do, *nicht wahr*, Fritz?' Fritz laughed too. Manfred leant forward and spoke in a low voice. 'Last week, we received information about a man who was hiding a Jew in his garden shed. How foolish to hide him there. He was easy to find and then he tried to make a run for it. I hit him first time.' He made a shooting sound, but thankfully did not lift the gun to demonstrate.

'No!' said Trudi with a sharp exhale, horrified by his callous remarks. 'Did you kill him with that?'

Manfred sat back in his chair and looked thoughtful. 'No, unfortunately. Just grazed him on the leg. But there is always next time.' He looked over at Fritz and they both laughed heartily, before Manfred slipped the gun back into his pocket.

Trudi had heard enough of their bragging. 'Greta, have you seen the time?' She held up her wrist in an exaggerated move-ment. 'We should go.' She was in shock and couldn't wait to get away. If this was what trailing the enemy involved, she wanted none of it. She quickly drained her glass.

'We're in town for the next few weeks. Perhaps we'll see you here another time?' said Fritz, looking hopefully at Frida.

'Perhaps. Thank you for buying us a drink,' Frida replied for them both and they quickly stood up to go.

Outside, a cold wind had whipped up. Wim was waiting in a bus shelter across the street.

'What took you so long? I thought I'd die of boredom and the cold out here.' He rubbed his hands together in an exaggerated movement.

'Sorry, but we couldn't very well walk out after they'd just bought us a drink,' said Frida, glancing back over her shoulder towards the bar.

'Did they tell you anything interesting?' Wim said, lighting himself a cigarette.

'Not really. They've only just moved to Haarlem and don't think much of it here.' Frida shrugged. 'But one of them showed us his gun. He used it to shoot a Jewish man they found hiding in someone's shed.'

Wim's eyes widened in alarm. 'You know you should have let me come in with you.'

Trudi thought for a moment. 'I don't think they'd have spoken to us if you were there,' she said disdainfully. 'And besides, it wasn't as if we were there to enjoy ourselves.'

Wim looked disappointed. So they didn't tell you anything useful. Did they?'

'Look, these things take time,' said Frida. 'You heard what Frans said. We need to get the measure of them before doing anything rash.'

'I don't know what you were expecting, Wim, but it's not that simple extracting information without it appearing obvious,' added Trudi defensively. 'The point is, they trusted us. They were disarmed and friendly.' She was starting to see exactly how a woman could make a difference in the resistance. How they'd never be suspected of anything by the Germans. The reality struck her that men always underestimated women. Addressing Wim, she said, 'Tell us what you've been up to.'

Wim shrugged and narrowed his eyes as he pulled deeply on his cigarette.

Waiting for a reply, Trudi stared at him, until she lost patience and said, 'I've had enough of this. Come on, Frida. Let's go home.'

'You're right. We're finished here,' said Frida, and started to walk away.

'No, wait,' said Wim. 'I'm sorry if I gave the impression I could have done better. Er... it's only the first time any of us have done this, so we all need a bit of practice. And once we work out a way of arming ourselves...'

Trudi shook her head. 'I think we'll be working on our own from now on. Let's go, Frida,' she said urgently, not giving Wim a chance to reply. She was in a hurry to get away before the two Germans emerged from the café and saw them still standing there with Wim. But more than anything, she was annoyed with Wim for failing to make any contribution to their plan.

Then a niggling thought came to her, something she knew she'd be unable to shake off. 'Frida?' she said, once they had put some distance between themselves and Wim.

'What's going on? You seem angry.'

Trudi stopped to look at her sister. To her annoyance, tears came to her eyes and she tried to swipe them away. 'No, I'm not angry. I just don't think I'm tough enough to go through with this.' She set off quickly before her tears could overwhelm her, as Frida ran to catch up and tried to stop her with a hand to her arm.

'You mustn't think like that. You underestimate yourself. I

couldn't do the things you do, the lengths you went to, protecting Louisa and Rosy. Can we at least talk about it?' Frida tugged at Trudi's sleeve, then slipped her arm into her sister's. 'Please,' she said.

Trudi softened, but wasn't ready to talk. She suggested they walked until they arrived back at the park, where they found an empty bench in a quiet spot.

'I just can't forget the look on Manfred's face when he was talking about shooting that poor man. He seemed so smug about it. Barely more than a boy and already a trained killer. I don't want to end up like him.' Trudi studied her hands in her lap. 'Hearing Frans talk about guns unnerved me too. It seems we have no choice but to learn to use them if we've any chance of protecting ourselves. But I just can't come to terms with shooting another human being.'

'Hmm. I'm struggling with the idea too,' said Frida, and Trudi looked at her, surprised.

'But you came across so confident. The way you spoke to those two.'

Frida shrugged. 'I was more nervous than I've ever been, but I wasn't going to show it in front of a couple of *moffen*.'

'Really?'

'Yes, really. This is new to us both and we're going to have to feel our way. And maybe learning how to fire a gun isn't such a bad idea. It doesn't mean we have to use one, does it?'

'No, I suppose not. But there must be ways of resisting the Germans without brandishing a gun.' Her thoughts returned to Rosy and Louisa, two innocent children caught up in this terrible war, and she vowed to do all she could to protect others who found themselves in an equally precarious position.

SIXTEEN

After a shaky start, Trudi heard Frans's resistance group was soon inundated with requests from young men who opposed the order to work in German factories for the war effort. They were prepared to do anything they could to help from the inside, even if it meant in the evenings when they weren't working. However, she'd expressed her concerns to Frans about the violence involved in his plans; she had already seen an opportunity to offer help of a different kind.

Increasingly, Trudi was hearing how Jewish families were terrified by what the new restrictions would mean to their freedom. She hadn't realised just how grave the situation had become until it became apparent that Jews in their hundreds were disappearing from the streets of Amsterdam. She'd heard that families who had been forced to leave their homes by the Nazis were being taken to cramped housing in specially formed ghettos called *Jodenbuurten*, or 'Jewish neighbourhoods'. It was almost impossible to get information on these and she hadn't yet figured out if this was where Rosy and Louisa's parents had ended up, but she never gave up looking for them. As new regulations and restrictions to Jews' freedom were introduced, they were pushed further into social isolation. People were led to believe that the ghettos were just temporary – until it became obvious that trucks and trains were being prepared to transport the Jews to unknown destinations.

Many people were handing their children over to total strangers, and it left Trudi with an uneasy feeling. Could these strangers be trusted? She remembered the shouts of the men who had been so intent on catching her and the children when they were racing to get to the lock-up garage. The reason was clear: the Germans were offering money to people who turned Jews over to the authorities, especially children. She simply couldn't allow that to happen, so she arranged to meet Frans in the park to discuss her proposal.

'The Jews are under threat and it's only going to get worse,' she told Frans as they walked beneath the tall beech trees. 'I've helped the Friedman family, but I know of at least three other Jewish families, all friends of theirs, who want to get their children to safety but don't know how to. It relies on the cooperation of bewildered young children who don't understand why they are being taken from their families. I believe that with my experience and your help I can offer support to Jewish families to bring their children to trusted safe houses far from the city centre. I'd accompany them, of course.'

Frans listened attentively and she was relieved he agreed with her idea; but he wanted to be sure she knew what she was taking on. 'You must prepare yourself for the possibility of being stopped and questioned. Any confrontation with German soldiers could turn nasty. Those Germans will stop at nothing and, if they suspect you're aiding a Jew, will show you no mercy. I'm aware that this work is no less dangerous than taking direct action against Nazi targets. But I have faith in you, Trudi. I'll give you whatever help you need by putting you in touch with families on the run and getting hold of false identification papers and tickets for travel.'

Trudi's heart felt lighter than it had done in ages as she walked away contemplating this latest plan. She was pleased that Frans had agreed so willingly.

It was only a couple of days till he came back to her with her first assignment. Trudi was to pick up Lottie, an eight-year-old Jewish girl whose father had been arrested at the university where he was a lecturer. He'd never returned home and his wife feared she and her daughter would be targeted next. She didn't dare leave the family home in case he turned up, but she knew she had to save her child by sending her away.

Trudi arrived to find Lottie waiting in the hallway, dressed in a coat and hat with a small duffel bag by her side. Her mother was doing her best to comfort her daughter, but the girl clung to her in floods of tears. She cut a pitiful figure and it was all Trudi could do not to offer to take the child and look after her herself, but she knew she must be strong for them both.

'Lottie, would you like to come with me on an exciting adventure?'

Lottie stopped crying for a moment and seemed to notice Trudi standing before her for the first time. She looked to her mother for her agreement; her mother smiled and wiped away her daughter's tears with her thumbs. 'It won't be for long and when you come back we'll take a trip to the beach together,' she said with forced brightness.

'With Papa?' Lottie said through her tears.

'With Papa,' echoed her mother, and straightened Lottie's collar before hugging her close. 'Look after her,' she said to Trudi, her voice breaking, and stood up to hand her the girl's small bag of possessions.

'I will.' Trudi gave her a sympathetic smile, before taking Lottie's hand and leading her from the house. She lifted the girl onto the back of her bike, instructing her to hold on to her bag tightly between them, before setting off on the long ride to a small village in the countryside. She reassured Lottie, comforting her with kind words, and then decided distraction would probably be a better technique.

It was late, but still light, and Trudi was grateful that the roads were quiet and there were no Germans about. At first, all she could hear was Lottie's choked sobs from behind her as she sang songs she remembered from her own childhood. It took a few attempts to console her until she hit on 'Alle Eendjes Zwemmen in het Water' – all the little ducks are swimming in the water.

'You must know this one, Lottie. Please join in.' And after singing it through twice, she heard Lottie's soft tremulous voice join in from behind. It would have been enjoyable, Trudi thought, had the circumstances not been so sad.

They were a few miles from their destination when they came across a group of German soldiers standing by the side of the road. They looked as if they were interrogating two men. Her heart beat fast as she approached, but the Germans didn't even turn to look. She pedalled faster once she'd passed them, just in case they decided to call out, but there was nothing. She was just a woman out for a bike ride with her friend's daughter: invisible and unlikely to be up to anything that might attract their attention.

By the time they arrived at her new carers' home, Lottie was in slightly better spirits, though she clutched tightly to her bag and Trudi knew she must be feeling apprehensive. The husband and wife welcomed them into the living room, where a drink of squash and a biscuit were laid out ready for Lottie, which she accepted politely, and nibbled and sipped while staring at them.

Trudi decided to stay a while, and asked to see where Lottie would be sleeping. Her room belonged to their son, who was away, and was opposite the couple's bedroom. Lottie's lips lifted into a smile when she saw the pile of children's books on the bed. Trudi took the opportunity to give her a hug and tell her that her mama would write soon.

Cycling home along the dark lanes, Trudi wanted nothing more than to crawl into bed and sleep. But she knew she couldn't rest till she had returned to Lottie's mother to reassure her that she had delivered her daughter into safe hands.

Her next assignment was more problematic. She was to escort a fourteen-year-old Jewish boy from the centre of Amsterdam to the country, because he was proving to be too much of a handful for the elderly couple who were caring for him. They lived in cramped conditions in a town house on one of the canals in the centre of Amsterdam; there was no outdoor space. Needless to say, the boy was growing restless at being cooped up and spent hours gazing out of the ground-floor window in full view of the street, despite being repeatedly scolded for doing so. And when they found him listening to music on an illegal wireless set loud enough for the neighbours to hear through the walls, the couple despaired and turned to Frans. He found the boy a place to stay on a farm, where he would have the freedom to roam outside in exchange for helping the farmer feed and milk the cows.

Trudi walked with the boy a little way to the tram stop, where a small crowd had gathered.

'Now remember that you are my younger brother and that we are visiting our uncle who's a dairy farmer outside Haarlem. That's all you need to say if anyone accosts you. I'll take care of our papers.' Frans often arranged for the children to have false IDs under Trudi's surname. 'Do you understand?' She was worried when he didn't immediately answer.

'I don't want to do this,' Aaron muttered, shooting her a sullen glance.

'So you'd rather remain here, would you?' Trudi knew she

had to be firm with him. After all, he was old enough to understand what was expected of him.

'No, but I don't want to be stuck out on some smelly farm.'

Trudi could feel herself losing patience, but caught herself just in time. 'I'm sure you don't, but if you come with me you won't be stuck indoors any more. And you'll have more freedom out in the country.'

They both looked up at the dinging of the bell as their tram drew up to the stop with a high-pitched squeal of brakes. It was busy and they were the last to board, taking their place on the platform at the back. Then, just as the tram began to pull away, the driver jammed on his brakes, causing Trudi to stumble and almost lose her footing. She had just managed to steady herself by grabbing on to the metal pole when the doors flew open and four helmeted men in Gestapo uniform climbed aboard, brandishing machine guns. Trudi instinctively dropped her gaze to her feet, willing them not to look in her direction. She held her breath, waiting for the men to pass through the tram as it set off again. But they'd spotted her.

'*Guten Morgen, Fräulein.*'

Trudi kept her eyes lowered to the German's knee-high black boots. She didn't want to engage him in conversation, so glanced up at him quickly with a cursory nod. He smiled and offered her a cigarette.

'*Danke,*' she said and took it, while keeping her gaze averted. *Now please leave me alone,* she begged silently, certain this was a prelude to him questioning her. He flicked his lighter open – just as the tram came to another shuddering halt.

'*Verdammt!*' He swore.

Trudi was forgotten in an instant as he turned to see what was causing the incident. She took the opportunity to let the cigarette drop to the floor and covered it with her shoe. She held on tight to the pole, as people all around her cried out in panic;

they had realised what was happening on the tram tracks, right in front of their eyes.

'Keep calm,' Trudi whispered to Aaron, trying to keep the fear out of her voice. Aaron stared out of the window with a terrified expression. Out there a terrible scene was unfolding: dozens of men, women and children were walking quickly, some running, blindly, right in front of the tram. All were hampered by heavy suitcases and bags that banged against their legs. From a little way off, a dozen or more German soldiers came running, this time firing their heavy, grey machine guns indiscriminately into the moving crowd. Trudi's heart lurched when she noticed a little boy of about four trip over a tramrail and land flat on his face. He screamed in shock. Just behind him, a soldier showed him no mercy and kicked him aside with the metal tip of his shiny black knee-length boot. A weeping woman – she assumed it was his mother – rushed to the boy's aid but a rifle butt caught her behind the knees, causing her to crumple beside the little boy, who was wailing loudly.

Everyone on the tram was now either crying or screaming. Aaron had gone quite white, and she rested a hand on his arm to reassure him. It was a tragedy that one so young should be brought face to face with such violence.

Meanwhile, the German soldiers on board the tram were attempting to restore order by barking out commands and shoving aside people who had become too hysterical for their liking.

Trudi was trembling so violently that she didn't realise the German who had offered her the cigarette was still standing right beside her. He was bragging loudly to his comrade in German.

'That's two less to worry about,' he said with an unpleasant snigger.

'And the others won't stand a chance either,' retorted the

other, looking pleased, and they both burst out laughing while slapping their thighs.

Trudi stiffened, and inadvertently caught the eye of the one standing nearest to her. He winked. Disgusted, she turned away, but not before she discerned the glint of metal in his hand. But instead of fear, she felt anger rise up in her. If only she had the nerve to grab this soldier's pistol, she knew she wouldn't hesitate to shoot him at point-blank range. And then she would turn the pistol on the soldier who had so brutally attacked the defenceless mother and her innocent child.

Fear mixed with shock raced through her as she grappled with these thoughts. Was this what it would take to shoot someone? It dawned on her that Frans had been right and that the only thing holding her back was her inexperience in handling a gun. As much as she despised the idea of killing a person, she realised that once she had trained to use a gun, then she would be able to defend herself and others.

The moment passed. The tram started up and the German soldiers separated, each taking up a position guarding one of the exits.

'What's the matter?'

Trudi swung her head round to see Aaron staring at her. She felt the blood rush to her face. Was it so obvious what she'd been thinking?

'This is our stop,' she said, as the tram slowed. It wasn't, but she couldn't trust herself to spend another minute on this tram with all these people. Most of the other passengers clearly had the same idea and began surging towards the doors. She grabbed Aaron's hand tightly and pulled him roughly to her side, not letting go.

'Not so fast.' The German soldier she'd been trying to avoid stood in her way, holding his machine gun away from his body and barring her exit. 'No one is to get off until we have checked all your papers. *Fräulein*, I wish to start with you. And this boy. Is he travelling with you?'

'Yes, we're together. He's my brother.' Trudi reached into her bag and brought out the documents, wishing her hands wouldn't tremble so. She gave Aaron a warning look, but the boy looked too scared to do anything other than comply.

The German took his time examining the papers. Aaron began to fidget beside her and she started to feel her own patience grow thin.

'We're on our way to help out on our uncle's farm in the country.' Trudi could have kicked herself for volunteering such unnecessary information, but it was too late.

The soldier looked at her, now interested.

'Kijkduin,' Aaron said, answering for her. 'It's quite a long way from here and we're running late. My Uncle Joop isn't at all well and runs the farm all by himself. He asked us to come as soon as we could. We need to take two more trams before we get there.' He gave the soldier a pleading look.

'Hmm.' The German gave him a hard stare, before handing Trudi back the papers. 'You may go,' he said gruffly and stood aside to let them off.

Trudi felt proud of Aaron's quick thinking, but had no time to tell him so as she hurriedly exited the tram, half-dragging the boy with her. The two of them sprinted away down the street. She didn't care where she was or where they were heading; she just needed to get away from the tram and the Germans as fast as possible.

Later that day, Trudi cycled out to the Kennemer dunes to visit Rosy and Louisa. Still on edge from her earlier encounter with the Germans, she made sure that the ration coupons she was carrying were hidden in a secret compartment in her saddlebag. Even though they were indistinguishable from the real thing, and Trudi was rarely searched, she knew there was always a chance that she could be and that the Germans would show her no leniency if anything incriminating was discovered on her. She knew where each of the checkpoints were along the coastal road as well as the detours, and managed to pass through without incident.

The house where Louisa and Rosy were staying was on the edge of a village with sweeping views across the dunes. Trudi loved these visits, seeing the delight on the girls' faces whenever she came to visit, and the walks they took out on the windswept dunes.

It was a chance to chat things over with Mevrouw Berg, who had two children of her own besides looking after the girls.

'Did you know that the Germans are putting in new check-points towards Katwijk?' Mevrouw Berg said, as they walked side by side onto the dunes. 'There are rumours they're building new fortifications to stop the Allies landing on the beaches.'

Trudi squinted in the direction she indicated, but it was all sand dunes and marram grass waving in the stiff breeze as far as the eye could see. Louisa and Rosy were running hand in hand ahead of them and trying to keep up with the two faster, older boys, aged eight and nine. It gladdened her to see how happy and carefree the girls were in this place. Any threat seemed a long way away.

'I'd heard something of that kind, but didn't realise it was so close to home. Do you worry about it?'

'Not at the moment. But we should take any increased German presence seriously.'

'Yes, of course. You must tell me if it becomes a concern. I don't want to put your family or the girls in any unnecessary danger.'

'No, but I thought you should know. Just in case we need to make alternative arrangements.'

Mevrouw didn't need to spell it out, but with even the

inkling of a discovery the girls would have to be moved quickly. 'Don't get me wrong. I'm more than happy to do my bit by looking after the girls.'

'And I'm so grateful to you for all you're doing. It's a big favour I'm asking of you, and it's only right that you tell me your concerns.'

SEVENTEEN

It was Frans's idea that Trudi should move away from home. She gave up her work as a domestic helper; her time was now taken up with his resistance group on various assignments, both ferrying children to safety and as a courier. These missions were increasing in number as the moves to oppose the Germans intensified. While she was undertaking risky work for the resistance, he said, it was better for her to lie low – for her own safety, but also for her family, who might still be a target for raids. And to be on the safe side, Frida moved into nurses' accommodation at the hospital where she worked.

Trudi moved to a room in a four-storey town house in a pleasant part of town with a view of the Haarlemmerhout park. It was her second address in as many weeks and she hoped its quiet position would provide her with the privacy she so craved. Her previous accommodation had been close to the centre of town, and at night she would wake in fright to the clatter of hobnailed boots on the pavement outside her window. Until she moved to her new more peaceful home, she hadn't realised just how tense she'd been feeling. A feeling exacerbated by the quantity of her assignments, which always took more out of her than she realised. Even the most straightforward of tasks, involving a walk through the streets of Haarlem holding the hand of a small child, filled her with apprehension and sadness. One episode in particular stuck in her mind: of the little boy, still in nappies, obediently trotting by her side, oblivious to where she was taking him, and his trusting smile as she handed him over to his new carer. That scene was somehow more heart-breaking to witness than the pale, frightened children who cried pitifully at being taken from their mothers.

Trudi wearily climbed the stairs to her third-floor room wanting nothing more than to kick off her shoes and lie down for a rest. She had cycled back along the coast from Zandvoort, a small seaside town, where she'd taken the daughter of a Jewish couple who had taken refuge in an attic that was only big enough for two people. Unusually, Trudi had been stopped on the way there by two German soldiers, and she'd needed all her powers of persuasion to convince them she was the girl's aunt and was taking her back home. She'd been so lucky up to that point when out visiting Louisa and Rosy, and it troubled her how shaken up she'd been by the incident, despite having prac-tised scenarios such as this one time and again with Frans, who was meticulous in providing her with the details of every assignment.

'Oh, hello. Have you just moved in?'

Trudi raised her head to see a girl at the top of the stairs, waiting for her to pass. She had striking red shoulder-length hair, pale freckled skin and an open smile. 'My name's Hannie. My room's that one.' She lifted her chin in the direction of the room next door to Trudi's.

'I'm Trudi,' said Trudi as she drew level. 'My room's next door to yours.'

And the two of them exchanged a smile.

'Well, it's nice to have someone my own age to talk to. People are forever coming and going in this house – they're mainly middle-aged or older. Not that I mind. You wouldn't like to join me in a cup of tea, or do you have something else that needs doing?'

Trudi found herself warming to her and realised it was company she needed, not a lie-down. 'Tea would be very nice. Give me a moment to take off my outdoor things and I'll join you.'

Trudi was careful not to say too much about her work. She'd been trained not to talk to strangers about being a part of the resistance, but she was taken with this friendly girl who, like her, had recently moved away from home. Hannie told her she was a law student at the university in Amsterdam.

'Why don't you live in Amsterdam?' asked Trudi as they sat on Hannie's bed sipping tea.

Hannie pulled a face before replying. 'I'd love to, but my parents don't think it's safe living in the big city with German soldiers roaming the streets. They wanted me to stay at home, but I managed to persuade them to let me move into digs in Haarlem. I thought I'd be moving into a student house, but it hasn't worked out that way.' She sighed theatrically, then laughed. 'Tell me – what do you do, Trudi?' She pulled her feet up underneath her.

'I work for a family in the town centre. Housekeeping duties, that kind of thing.' She didn't want to lie, nor did she want to tell the truth. She gave an apologetic shrug, hoping that Hannie wouldn't guess.

'And you're earning your own money. If this war carries on as long as people say it will, it'll be years before I do,' Hannie said wistfully. 'I sometimes wonder if I should be helping with the war effort rather than locking myself away in my room studying.'

Trudi nodded, trying to look sympathetic. She was sorely tempted to talk to Hannie about her resistance work, but managed to stay cautious.

. . .

Then, two days later, while she was walking by the side of a canal in the centre of Amsterdam, she heard her name being called. She glanced quickly across the water and saw Hannie waving at her. She was walking along arm in arm with another girl, also a student, Trudi guessed. Trudi felt herself redden, as if she'd been caught red-handed. She nodded a quick greeting at Hannie, before glancing down at the young girl whose hand she was holding and urging her to keep moving.

'Who was that little girl I saw you with the other day?' asked Hannie the next time they crossed on the stairs.

Trudi had been expecting this question and was ready with an answer. 'A friend of mine isn't well and asked if I could take her daughter to her cousin's. She'd offered to look after her.'

'And the cousin couldn't come and fetch her herself?'

Their eyes locked for a moment and Trudi realised that Hannie must have guessed what she'd been up to.

'Come inside,' Trudi said, opening the door to her room.

She shut the door behind them and turned to face Hannie. 'You mustn't tell anyone what I'm about to tell you. Do you promise?'

Hannie held her gaze as she gave her word.

'The little girl you saw me with is Jewish and I was taking her to an address outside Amsterdam where she won't be found by the Germans.'

Hannie widened her eyes. 'Something tells me this isn't the first time you've done that.'

'You're right. I've escorted more than twenty Jewish children to safety so far. As long as the Germans are in power, I suspect there'll be many more.'

'Oh Trudi, that's such a brave thing to do. Do you ever worry about being caught?'

'All the time. I make sure I'm on my guard.' Trudi frowned and wondered if she'd revealed too much.

But Hannie was looking pensive. 'My best friend at the university is Jewish. Sonja always thought that she'd be safe there, but with everything I've been hearing recently I've been having my doubts.'

'Is that who I saw you with the other day?'

'Yes. Sonja and I had finished lectures and we were off to have a bowl of soup at the student café. I wonder for how much longer, though.' Hannie's expression was sad as she went on. 'It must be a terrible thing having your freedom taken from you.'

'Which is why I want to help those who can't help themselves,' said Trudi. 'I just wish it wasn't so hard.'

'Yes. I can understand that.' And Hannie gave Trudi a sympathetic smile.

Their conversations over cups of tea in one or the other's rooms became a regular occurrence. In Hannie Trudi found a soulmate, someone with whom she could exchange views freely. From Hannie, she learnt about life as a student, the people she mixed with, and the student society she'd recently joined with links to the resistance, who she hoped might help her friend Sonja. In return, Trudi explained about the struggles endured by the Jewish families she met and the dangers she faced whenever she set foot outside with a Jewish child at her side.

It was late one afternoon when Trudi went to knock on Hannie's door. She received no answer and glanced at her watch, thinking it strange – Hannie was usually home by now. A click from across the corridor caused her to look up and she saw it was her neighbour, an elderly woman called Mevrouw van Houten, opening her door.

'Hello Mevrouw van Houten. Have you seen Hannie?'

The old lady slowly shook her head, as if she knew something she couldn't quite believe. 'Hannie has moved out.'

Trudi frowned, not quite comprehending what she was hearing. 'I'm sorry, but I only saw Hannie this morning.'

'It's true. I was watering the plants on my balcony and heard noises. Doors opening and closing, people running up and down the stairs. I went out on the landing to investigate. Hannie was shutting her door and asked me if I could take her key for her. I asked where she was going, but she wouldn't say. Someone was calling from the bottom of the stairs. She apologised, saying she had to leave right then – and then she was gone.'

'Did you see who was with her?' Trudi was struggling to make sense of Hannie's sudden disappearance. Why hadn't she mentioned anything earlier?

'No, I'm afraid not. But I could hear it was a man's voice and he was urging her to hurry up.'

Trudi must have looked dismayed, for the old woman went on, 'I wouldn't read too much into it, dear. It's not the first time I've seen it happen in this house. War causes people to move for all kinds of reasons, often unexpected ones. There may be a perfectly reasonable explanation. Now, would you care to join me for a cup of tea? I don't have much company these days and it would cheer me up enormously.'

EIGHTEEN

'Call me Oma. Everybody else does,' the old lady said with a tinkling laugh as Trudi stepped inside.

'I'd like that... Oma.' It didn't feel at all strange to call her that. She had never known her two grandmothers, who had died before she was born.

It was the first time Trudi had been inside the old lady's room and she was surprised to see how large it was. It extended across the width of the house, with a large window opening on to a balcony covered in plants. The room was full of dark mahogany antique furniture, trailing plants on ornately carved wooden stands and a bookcase that covered one wall from floor to ceiling. Along another wall stood a divan bed spread with a Javanese blanket and an array of batik cushions in hues of blue and orange. Mevrouw van Houten emerged from behind a dark-blue velvet curtain with a tray of tea things, which she put down on a low coffee table in the centre of the room.

'Come and sit next to me and tell me all about yourself,' she said, lowering herself onto a small plush sofa. She poured two cups of tea and handed one to Trudi. 'I'm curious to know why a young girl like you wants to live in a big house with strangers.

Have you fallen out with your parents? Or is it for some other reason?' She gazed at Trudi, her dark-brown eyes alive with interest.

Trudi hesitated and took a sip of tea, a little taken aback by the direct questioning. Remembering Frans's words of advice to be innately suspicious of strangers, she knew she shouldn't let on too much. And telling the truth might only lead to more questions about her work, which she was reluctant to talk about until she felt she could get to know her neighbour a little better. Best to be cautious, she thought. 'I haven't fallen out with my parents. I simply wanted to spread my wings a bit and see what it would be like to live on my own. I work during the day and do housework for one or two families nearby, so living here seems like a good solution. And my parents understand.'

The old lady replaced her cup in the saucer and watched Trudi with an appraising look. Trudi shifted awkwardly in her seat and wondered if it was so obvious she wasn't telling the truth. She smiled brightly and changed the subject. 'I couldn't help noticing all the Indonesian furnishings you have. Did you spend time in the country?'

'Once, a long time ago. I have one daughter. Corrie married an Indonesian man called Ismaya. They moved some years ago to Malang, where he runs a business exporting spices. They have one daughter, Amanda. She'll be the same age as you.' She paused and gave Trudi a wistful smile, before carrying on, 'I've only met my granddaughter twice: once as a baby when my husband and I travelled out by ship to stay with them for three months. And then in 1940, mere weeks before the occupation began, the family came back for my husband's funeral. It's a great sadness that I've missed seeing my granddaughter growing up. I often sit here and wonder if I'll ever see my family again.' She looked away and fished in her skirt pocket for an embroidered hanky, which she dabbed at her eyes.

'I'm sorry. That must be so hard for you,' said Trudi, and to her surprise her own eyes began filling up with tears as Rosy and Louisa came to mind. 'It's not the same, but I had two little girls in my care, who—' Trudi shook her head and took a deep breath.

'My dear girl. What is it? You can tell me what happened.' The old lady reached out a bony hand to comfort her.

Trudi blinked away her tears. The memory of their escape from the Germans still haunted her, even though they were so much happier since moving to the Kennemer dunes. But gradually she opened up and told her story of how she'd run through the streets with the two children at the dead of night, and only just managed to escape her pursuers by hiding in a lock-up garage.

Oma was sympathetic and handed her a clean handkerchief from the handiwork bag at her feet. 'What you've done must have taken a lot of courage.'

Trudi felt a little comforted as she smiled through her tears. 'I didn't feel courageous at the time. I'm sure anyone would have done the same in my position. I just hope that the children are safe.'

'Our country could do with more young women like you. Have you ever thought about helping others caught up in the war?'

'Oh yes,' Trudi said enthusiastically, before she could stop herself. 'I love working with children and I've helped a few other Jewish families find safe places for their children.'

'Jewish, did you say?' Oma's attention seemed to sharpen at the word.

'Of course. They're the ones who need help. You must know how terrible things are for the Jews, especially in Amsterdam where so many are being harassed by the Germans.'

Oma sat back in her chair and took her time answering. 'Jewish families. Yes, there are so many of them. Well, that sounds like an admirable thing for a young woman like you to be doing,' she said finally with a smile.

Back in her room, as Trudi sat darning the elbows of her one and only cardigan that had become threadbare through incessant wear, she reflected on all that had happened that day. The shock of Hannie's departure had been softened by Oma's overtures of friendship. She'd felt relaxed in the old woman's company, but she did wonder about her strange reaction to the mention of Jewish families. She hadn't wanted to probe, in case Oma was harbouring painful memories of someone close to her who was Jewish. Or maybe it wasn't that at all, and Oma actually disapproved of the Jews. Perhaps she was a Nazi sympathiser. Trudi found that idea hard to reconcile with the kindly old lady who seemed to approve of her efforts to help children in need, but she told herself to be more careful in future.

She set aside her darning, stretched and yawned. Perhaps the war was getting to her and she was reading too much into it all. She walked over to the window and was drawing the curtain against the gathering dusk when she thought she recognised the woman in a headscarf standing with her back to her. It was clear she was in conversation with a man in what looked like German uniform. Trudi couldn't be sure, and leant forward to get a closer look. The man lit himself a cigarette, and the two exchanged a few more words before he walked away. The woman turned to go back into the house, and as she did so she adjusted her scarf. Trudi was now able to see her face more clearly: it was definitely Oma.

NINETEEN

It was a hot cloudless afternoon and the sea sparkled in the brilliant sunlight. Trudi and Frida were cycling side by side, engrossed in conversation and enjoying the wind at their backs. They hadn't seen much of each other as Frida had been working all hours at the hospital. Despite her tiredness, she was eager to keep up her work with the resistance.

If they had been men, they would run the risk of being interrogated and arrested by the Germans, but they knew that no one would ever suspect them of any wrongdoing. Of course, they were used to stopping at the roadblocks and being questioned – everyone was – but they never let on where they were heading, sometimes more than fifty kilometres along the coast and all the way to The Hague. The important thing was to avoid saying anything that could arouse suspicion and result in a thorough search. Usually, all it took to be waved on was a ready answer and a friendly smile.

On this occasion, they were delivering two packages they'd been told contained, hidden among clothes, documents with vital information concerning German activities and movements in the area. In the hands of the Allies this would be like gold dust. If the parcels were to attract the attention of German soldiers at checkpoints, it wouldn't be immediately obvious that they contained anything more than the clothing, which they would say they were delivering to a relative in need. On closer inspection, though, the clothes would be found to be interleaved with coded messages. Of the two packages, wrapped in brown paper and tied with string, one was much heavier, and Frida was convinced it contained ammunition. They had been told to handle certain cargo carefully as it came with the risk of an explosion; but they never allowed themselves to think of that possibility. All that mattered was that the package was compact enough to fit easily into a saddlebag, the one with the secret flap that concealed a compartment at its base. It was a dangerous assignment, but the prospect excited Trudi.

The road shimmered in the heat, making it hard to see more than a few yards ahead. Suddenly, Trudi became aware of two uniformed Germans stepping into their path.

'Leave them to me,' whispered Frida. 'I'll see if I can distract them.'

'*Halt! Ausweis!*' both Germans shouted in unison, and held out their arms in a stiff salute.

Brazenly, Frida stopped her bike inches from where they stood, while Trudi kept her distance, stopping a little way behind.

'Good afternoon, officers.' Frida spoke in good German. 'I certainly need a breather after all that cycling. Isn't it warm today?' She ran her fingers through her hair and angled her face to catch the sun's rays.

The Germans seemed to have forgotten they had asked for her ID. While they kept their eyes glued to Frida, Trudi wheeled her bike to the side of the road.

'Please don't say you're going to stop us from passing through,' Frida said playfully, this time in Dutch. She tipped her head coyly and threw the soldiers a flirtatious look.

'Well, *Fräulein*,' said the one standing closest to her. 'Strictly speaking, I should, but maybe I will make an exception on this occasion.' He just couldn't take his eyes off her; but the other one became distracted by Trudi's movements.

'Are you the boyfriend?' he said rudely in a loud voice.

Trudi wasn't in the least perturbed, for she sometimes wore her father's cast-off trousers, held up with braces. The notion that she could be taken for a young man on occasion amused her. Defiantly, she kept her eyes on him as she removed her cap and let her blond curls tumble around her face. 'No. As you can see.'

'Did you see that, Dieter?' he spluttered, turning to his partner in astonishment. 'It's a girl!' They were so surprised by this revelation that they let the sisters pass without further questioning.

Moments later, the two were pedalling away to their destination over by the dunes, where their resistance contact was waiting for them. Their saddlebags were intact and they were barely able to contain their mirth. They hadn't planned these tactics in advance, but quickly realised that it was the perfect way to distract the Germans from interrogating and searching them.

The following evening, Trudi and Oma were sitting together in companionable silence. Oma was reading a book and Trudi had her head bent over her sewing. Since noticing Oma talking with that man on the street she'd had no further reason to suspect the woman, and Oma had made no more disquieting comments about Jews. But that day still worried Trudi and she wanted to know whether she could really trust Oma. Without looking up she said, 'The other evening I saw you outside the house talking to a man. It was you, wasn't it?' She glanced quickly at Oma, who closed her book and put it down on the small table beside her.

'You must be mistaken. I never go out after four o'clock in the afternoon. What did he look like?'

'He was in uniform, so I assumed he was German. And he was deep in conversation with... well, I thought it was you.'

Oma shook her head vigorously and chuckled. 'Now why would I do that? I avoid the *moffen* at all costs. And if I was going to have a secret conversation with a German, I certainly wouldn't do anything like that in full view of everyone.' Still chuckling to herself, she picked up her book again and Trudi went back to her sewing, not entirely convinced by the old lady's seemingly innocent explanation.

Examining her efforts, she didn't appear to be making any progress with her sewing. It was obvious she was having problems pulling the needle neatly through the fabric.

'Do you need a hand with that?' said Oma, laying down her book again and leaning forward for a closer look. Trudi had her coat turned inside out on her lap and was attempting to sew long strips of material into the lining. Her cheeks were flushed with the effort.

'Yes, would you mind?' she said, letting out a deep sigh. 'I can't seem to keep the two sides of the material together and they keep sliding apart. I never was any good at sewing.' She showed Oma her ragged attempt, which made them both laugh.

'Let me see what I can do with it.' Oma took the coat from her and examined Trudi's work. 'I assume you're trying to sew in pockets that can't be detected.'

Trudi gave her a despairing look and nodded.

'Let me show you how,' said Oma.

Trudi watched as her nimble old fingers deftly attached the fabric to the lining in no time at all. 'You've obviously done this before,' she said in admiration.

Oma smiled, but didn't answer. 'Now, are you going to tell

me what you intend to carry in your pockets?' she asked, when she'd secured the last stitch and had cut the thread with a tiny pair of scissors from her needlework box.

Guns. But how could she admit to it? Her heart beat faster at the very idea of carrying a gun in self-defence. Everything she had done up to this point had relied on her ability to outwit the Germans, whether it be running through the streets protecting Jewish children or working as a courier, transferring confidential intelligence and essential items from one resistance cell to another. Despite her misgivings, Frans insisted it was time she carried a gun with her and was prepared to use it for her own protection. It had been his idea to get her to sew deep pockets into the lining of her coat so that she could conceal a pistol and draw it while riding her bike. Although he promised to show her how it was done, the thought scared her. Could she actually ride one-handed while shooting with the other hand? And what if she dropped the gun while trying to get it out of her pocket?

'There must be a reason you want such big pockets,' Oma said, a smile curling at her lips. 'Whatever it might be, I'd better add another row of reinforcing stitches to prevent whatever it is from falling through the lining for all to see. I'd never forgive myself if that happened.' She kept smiling as she carried on her work in silence while Trudi marvelled at the speed at which she ran her needle in and out of the material and up and down the seams.

When Oma had finished her handiwork, she handed back the coat. 'Will it be the first time you've used a gun on someone?' She asked the question so casually that Trudi had wondered if she had heard correctly.

Trudi briefly closed her eyes. 'How did you guess?'

'I trained as a seamstress and worked for many years at a dress salon in Amsterdam. We used to have people come in with all kinds of requests for alterations. I particularly remember the gentleman who brought in his greatcoat and asked me to reinforce the pockets so he could carry his guns. We were told never to ask questions, so I didn't know what he was up to, but I always wondered if he put my handiwork to good use. Or bad, should I say.' Still smiling, she held Trudi's gaze for so long that Trudi felt she could trust her a little more.

'I'm not sure I'm comfortable with carrying a gun. It's not something I'd do lightly.' She hoped she hadn't revealed too much.

'Nor should you. I should know.' Oma kept her gaze locked on Trudi's as she went on. 'A long time ago, during the last war, I lost a brother to gunfire. He wasn't even on the front line, but was caught in crossfire when he was helping move a fellow soldier to a field hospital. I often think about Robbie and the life he missed out on, all because of that stray bullet.'

As Trudi listened, she realised how little she'd known about this woman's life and how quickly she had jumped to conclusions that she was colluding with the enemy. Oma's revelations left her feeling chastened.

'Remember, a gun is always a weapon and should only ever be used as a last resort. When the time comes, you will know what to do.' Oma nodded her head as if she had first-hand knowledge of using guns. 'And I have every confidence that the decision you make will be the right one.'

TWENTY

On market day, Trudi liked to cycle into the centre of Haarlem to shop for provisions. Food was more scarce these days, but the stallholders kept coming, even though it meant selling their wares under the watchful eyes of German soldiers. For many it was their only means of eking out a living. As it was high summer, fruit and vegetables were more plentiful, and there was always a bargain to be had at the bakery stall, such as yesterday's left-over loaves sold for half price or four currant buns for the price of three.

Trudi was sauntering among the market stalls before deciding what to buy when she was stopped in her tracks by a familiar voice that rang out above the din of other stallholders shouting out their wares.

'See this lovely herring, freshly caught this morning. Buy two and I'll slip you an extra one for free. You won't get fresher than this.'

Trudi couldn't help herself smiling at the way he held the wet silvery fish up by their tails and slapped them down on the counter while charming the customers with his sales patter. She watched him chat cheerfully to a middle-aged woman who was haggling for a lower price. It was Sem, and he was just as she remembered him that first time they'd met.

Sem was finishing wrapping the woman's purchase and taking her money when he caught sight of Trudi. He waved and called out a greeting above the heads of the waiting customers. Several people turned to see who he was addressing.

Trudi came forward to the front of the queue, ignoring the grumblings of a woman who was convinced she was being pushed aside.

'Do you mind?' said the woman, sticking her elbows out in an exaggerated fashion.

'I'm not here to buy fish,' Trudi said with an apologetic smile, and shrugged at Sem, who was grinning at her. He wiped his hands on a cloth, which he then handed to his assistant, a rosy-cheeked boy who looked no more than fifteen. 'Jaap will serve you. I'll be back in a few minutes.' He flashed a smile at the small group gathering in front of his stall, and left through the canvas flap at the back.

'What a nice surprise. I never expected to see you here.' Sem came striding over and kissed her warmly on both cheeks, and she was reminded of the old Sem, the one who had so beguiled her all those months ago.

'Will you come and have a coffee with me?' he asked.

She nodded and thought, *why not?* She was curious to hear what he was doing these days.

As they set off across the bustling *Grote Markt*, she stole a glance at him. Apart from his hair, which he now wore longer and brushed away from his handsome face, he seemed very much the same as she remembered. But she knew he wasn't the same, and nor was she – she had to remind herself that she really had moved on. And yet she was pleased to see him and looked forward to spending a little time in his company.

'I never knew you had a stall here. Has your father given up his one at Bloemendaal?' she asked.

'Not at all. He'd never give that up. Besides, it's right next to where he brings the catch in every day. But he's always done the weekly market here. Don't you remember? I'm sure I would have told you. Sometimes I help out. What luck I ran into you.' He gave her a playful smile, and she felt his hand cup her elbow as he steered her across the road, narrowly avoiding a German army lorry containing several armed soldiers that came speeding towards them.

They arrived at the café that she recognised from the time she'd been so upset after watching the newsreel showing the grim realities of war. 'I remember this,' she murmured, as Sem opened the door for her.

The café was crowded and the air heavy with cigarette smoke. Sem found them the last empty table, against the back wall. 'You mind if I sit with you?' he asked, and before she could object he slid in beside her. For a brief moment, it felt like they were still girlfriend and boyfriend, till she remembered that she'd been the one to break up with him and no longer felt that way about him.

He took a pack of cigarettes from his shirt pocket and offered her one. She shook her head. He shrugged and lit one for himself, catching the eye of the waitress, who came over and took their order.

'I want to hear all about what you've been up to,' he said, drawing on his cigarette. 'Are you still living at home?'

'No, I moved out some months ago.'

'Ah. Where do you live now?'

She named the neighbourhood, not the street, not wanting to divulge too much, and went on to ask if he was still living in the same student house in Amsterdam.

'Yes, the same old student house in Amsterdam,' he said

with a mock sigh, and relaxed back in his seat. 'I don't know for how much longer though. There's been a lot of disruption at the university. My tutor left suddenly halfway through last term and it doesn't look like he'll be replaced.'

'Why is that?'

Sem gave her a puzzled look, as if he thought she should know the answer. 'Because he's Jewish and he doesn't want the Germans to know where he's working. He's not the first to go, nor will he be the last.'

He stubbed out his cigarette as the waitress arrived with their coffees.

As Trudi watched him pay, she noticed his face looked quite drawn and wondered what could be bothering him.

'I suppose you won't stay on if there aren't enough tutors at the university,' she said, after the waitress had moved away.

'I doubt I will. Some of the third-year students are forming study groups. I tried it, but it's not the same as having someone teach you who really knows the subject.'

'What will you do?'

'Oh, I don't know. This and that.' He let out an exasperated sigh, before giving her a sideways look. 'Actually, I've been attending some student meetings with a friend of mine, and I've been really impressed with the speakers. They talk a lot of sense and have this wonderful vision for the future of our country – bigger and stronger than before the war.'

'You mean once we've defeated the Germans?'

'No, it's not going to be like that. Together with the Germans we'll be part of a new Europe. A *nieuw Nederland.* Sounds good, doesn't it?'

More like a slogan, she thought, dreamt up for impressionable people. She took a sip of her coffee and made a face. It tasted awful. Ersatz coffee would never taste like the real thing.

'You don't look convinced,' said Sem with a concerned look.

'Look, I know it seems like I've changed my tune, but I haven't. Well, not really. I just got bored churning out local news for the resistance. I realise now it was never about the bigger picture with them, about getting our freedom back. And, if I'm honest, I don't believe that fighting the Germans is the way to go about things.'

Trudi could hardly believe what she was hearing. 'That's not what you used to think. Don't you remember how you used to tell me that people like us could make a difference if we supported the resistance?'

Sem narrowed his eyes at her, then made a scoffing sound. 'I can't believe I was actually taken in by that. All I see is the resistance encouraging people to break the law – sending people into hiding and approving of Radio Oranje, which is illegal and spouts lies.'

Shocked, Trudi said, 'I don't see how you can say that. Can't you see that the resistance are the only ones standing up to the Germans, who are hell-bent on making life difficult for us all?' She was on the verge of saying more when a terrible thought occurred to her. 'This group you're part of, these speakers... it's the NSB, isn't it?'

'No,' he said quickly, his eyes sliding evasively down to the table between them. 'Not exactly, if that's what you're worried about. The NSB attracts a nasty type of person, often with a criminal background. I'm just keeping an open mind about it all. Hey, why don't you come along to our next meeting? I think you'd find it interesting.'

'No. Thanks, Sem. It's not for me,' she said, appalled he could even consider asking. She glanced at her watch. 'I'm sorry, but I really must go. And you must get back to the stall. It's been good to see you, Sem.'

'You too, Trudi.' He held her gaze for a moment, then picked up her hand and turned it over so he could kiss it. She gave an embarrassed laugh as she remembered the first time he'd kissed her, on the beach in Bloemendaal.

'Come by the stall soon, and we'll have coffee again,' he said with a lingering look.

'I will,' she said, though she doubted she ever would.

TWENTY-ONE

Frans arranged regular target practice every Sunday in the private grounds of wealthy benefactor and well-known Dutch sculptor, Mari Andriessen, who was generous in his support for the resistance. The targets were set up on his lawn at the back of the sprawling property and it was here that Trudi and Frida went along for their first lesson in how to handle and shoot guns. Frans had amassed an array of pistols for the purpose, most of which his members had stolen from the Germans and which he kept under lock and key when not in use.

Trudi was riddled with nerves at the prospect of handling a gun, and would probably have backed out if it hadn't been for Frida by her side. They were still the only women in Frans's group, which was now over forty and counting. It seemed that everyone was keen to have a turn with the guns, apart from the two sisters, who stood back to watch until Frans called them forward.

'Who wants to go next?' he said, after complimenting the first group on their accurate firing skills.

'Best get it over and done with,' Frida whispered to Trudi. She put her hand up and went to take up her position. She took the pistol from Frans, who murmured a few words of encouragement to her before saying, 'Now remember to take your time. When you line up the rear sight, make sure it appears in the centre of the front one, and keep the gun level as you pull the trigger.'

Trudi could see Frida was trying hard to concentrate, but she was slow in finding the centre of the target. At last she fired, the pistol jerked upwards and she missed the target by several inches. Frans was on hand to help and her next few shots made the target, but were way off centre.

'I don't think I'm cut out for this,' she said with a dismissive laugh, and lowered the gun. 'I'd rather be out gathering intelligence than firing guns. Trudi, let's see if you can do any better.'

'You were fine. Don't worry about it,' Trudi whispered. She could tell Frida was upset with herself. Frida's eyes glistened as she handed Trudi the gun, but Trudi didn't rate her own chances of doing any better. She waited for Frans's instruction, but he had his back turned and was talking earnestly to a man she hadn't seen before. They carried on like that for several minutes, before Frans turned to Trudi and introduced them.

'My cousin Piet. I invited him along tonight to help out. You'll find he knows as much as I do about handling a gun. Would you like to assist Trudi?' he said, turning to address his cousin.

Trudi gave a nervous smile, unsure what to make of this stranger and not wanting to reveal how little she knew about guns.

'Have you done this before?' Piet asked in a kind voice that helped to put her at her ease.

'No. This is the first time.' Trudi gazed at the pistol, which lay large and heavy in her hand. It wasn't surprising that Frida had had difficulty using it.

'Here, try this one. You'll find it easier to handle.' And he exchanged it for a smaller, lighter pistol from a bag at his feet.

'How many do you have in there?' Trudi asked, surprised.

'Not that many. But it is important to start with one that's right for you.' He stood beside her and put his hand over hers, gently positioning her fingers. 'Keep your thumb firmly on the grip, index finger along the top, and middle, ring and little fingers curled towards you under the trigger guard.'

Conscious that all eyes were on her, she raised the gun. But, to her frustration, she found she was unable to keep her hand steady.

'Take a deep breath. And pretend you're about to shoot a Nazi,' said Piet, standing a little closer. His voice was soft, persuasive, as she felt his breath against her ear.

She thought of that terrible night of the raid and the terror in Marie and Hans's eyes moments before they were hauled away. It wasn't difficult to summon up an image of the Nazi soldiers, for she remembered all too clearly their shouts, the desperate scuffles and the scraping of furniture being shoved aside. With a determined effort, she took aim at the target and brought to mind the idea of a brutish man in uniform with the German swastika pinned to his sleeve, running to snatch Louisa and Rosy from her with hatred in his eyes. Her heart pounded as she pulled the trigger. At first it wasn't obvious if she'd hit the target, as smoke from the gun billowed up and obscured her view of it. And then, as the smoke cleared, she heard Piet cry out, 'Well done, you hit a bullseye!' Astonished, she looked round as everyone broke out into applause. Then Piet said quietly, so that only she could hear, 'Whoever it was you were thinking about, that's who you need to have in mind. Every time you shoot.'

At the end of the session, the group began to disperse in twos and threes. Piet was carefully packing the pistols away. Frans asked Trudi and Frida to hang back as he wanted to fill them in on their next courier assignment, the delivery of documents to an address out of town. 'I received these just before I came out. I was rather hoping you'd go this afternoon.'

'I'm sorry, you'll have to count me out as my shift starts soon. Can it wait till tomorrow?' said Frida.

'No, I'm afraid it's too urgent to wait. It's needed today else the plan will fall apart. I would come with you but I have to be somewhere later.'

'I can go by myself if it's just one package,' said Trudi. 'I'm sure I won't be bothered by the *moffen*. You know how they like to take it easy on a Sunday.'

'I can go with you,' offered Piet and caught her eye.

Trudi gave an involuntary smile. 'Well...'

'That's settled then,' said Frans, taking a slim brown envelope from his jacket pocket.

'Is that it?' said Trudi incredulously. 'I was expecting something more exciting.'

'It's what's inside that counts,' said Frans, with a note of irritation. 'Now you'd better get going, before I change my mind.'

It was a warm afternoon, fragrant with the smell of late spring blossom and filled with cheerful birdsong. Trudi and Piet cycled side by side along the deserted rural roads with water channels on either side. It had been Piet's idea to come this way, as he knew it would be quieter than taking the main roads.

'Is this where you're from?' asked Trudi, enjoying the feeling of the breeze as it lifted her curls away from her face. If it weren't for the important letter safely hidden in her jacket pocket, they could have been just two friends out for a pleasant Sunday afternoon cycle ride in the country, far from any prying German soldiers.

'No, I'm an Amsterdammer. Surely you guessed that from the way I speak?' Piet turned to her with an amused look. 'Frans is too, but he's lost his accent. Our families lived next door to each other and we spent a lot of time together. We were like two brothers when we were growing up. He's quite a bit older than me and I always looked up to him, though he tended to be quite bossy. We lost touch in our early twenties when I went off to study architecture. I was barely a year in when this wretched war came along and everything changed. First it was identity cards, then all the propaganda the Germans were spewing out on what a great future we'll have under them. I just couldn't believe what was happening. When the general strike took place, I decided to join in. I was so angry about the way the Germans were treating Jewish people, but of course we didn't achieve anything by striking. So when Frans said he was joining the resistance, I decided to join too, though I stayed in Amsterdam.'

'It sounds like Frans has always liked to boss people about. He makes such a big deal of everything, but he never says exactly what it is he does. I must admit I sometimes have my doubts about him. But you obviously know him well. Do you think he's trustworthy?'

'What, Frans? To be honest, I've never doubted him. What makes you say that?'

'I'm not entirely sure. Maybe it's the way he never gets involved in assignments and always has an excuse that he's needed elsewhere.'

'That's just his way of showing he's important and he likes to be in charge.'

They had been cycling between open fields for some time when Trudi spotted a sign pointing up a track to a farm. She stopped by a tree on the side of the road and said, 'This is the address. Let's leave the bikes here and walk.'

The drop was routine and Trudi followed the procedure she'd had drummed into her. Four sharp raps on the front door, followed by two long ones, and when it was opened she gave the innocuous greeting, 'How is your aunt feeling today?' This told her contact she was who he was expecting.

They were let in by a silent surly-faced man. Piet closed the door behind them, while Trudi pulled the envelope from her jacket and handed it over.

'Better late than never. I've been waiting since morning for this,' the man grumbled. He almost snatched it, without a word of thanks.

'I'm sorry, but we came as quickly as we could,' said Trudi. 'I hope it's not too late.'

'No. It's not too late. It's just this war... it's getting to me,' said the man, then, as if remembering his manners, he asked them if they would like a drink before they went on their way. Speaking for the two of them, Piet declined his offer, and they left. Trudi felt an unexpected rush of disappointment that their mission was over so quickly. She hadn't realised how much she'd enjoyed being in Piet's company.

'I hope you weren't intending to stay,' said Piet, as they walked back to their bikes. 'You see, I happen to have a couple of bottles of beer in my saddlebag and I thought we could still make something of the day.' He gave her a shy smile.

Trudi looked into his eyes and felt a shiver of something she hadn't felt in a long while. 'I'd like that very much. But how come you've brought beer with you?'

'I thought I'd be spending the afternoon with Frans. That was before I met you. I'd much rather spend it with you.'

'Me too,' she said, and laughed with happiness.

'We're not far from the Zandvoort dunes. Let's go there,' Piet said with a sparkle in his eye. 'Do you know it?'

'I've done a few courier drops along the coast near Zand-voort, but I've always been too busy avoiding being stopped by the Germans to spend any time there. I'd love to see it.'

'That's settled then. I used to come to Zandvoort for the

summer holidays when I was a child. The dunes are breathtaking.'

They approached the dunes, after cycling through the pretty seaside town of Zandvoort itself and picking up an un-made-up path that zigzagged to the sea. When it got too sandy to keep cycling they pushed their bikes to the top of a dune, where they could stop and sit and gaze out to the horizon. They were the only ones around for miles.

Piet brought out the beer bottles and, squinting against the bright sun, chinked his against Trudi's.

'This reminds me of picnics when I was a child. Sorry it's only beer. I'll make sure I think it through next time.' There was that shy smile again and Trudi felt her stomach flip at the prospect of there being a next time.

TWENTY-TWO

The following week, Frans sent Trudi a message to come to his house, saying he had something in mind for her, which he would explain face to face. Intrigued, she wondered what it could be, but hoped he wasn't about to send her on a violent mission that required her using a gun. He had no shortage of men in the group who were keen to get experience in what Frans described as 'active resistance'; she had no desire to be part of it. Although she'd made it clear that her preference was to keep working with children, she knew that Frans was keen for her to develop other skills and she knew she had to be prepared.

She arrived at the house and rang at the door, which was opened by Frans's housekeeper. Mevrouw de Wit clearly didn't recognise Trudi from the last time she'd come and regarded her with suspicion.

Trudi gave her a friendly smile. 'Hello, I'm Trudi. We met that time I came for Frans late one night, if you remember.'

The housekeeper lifted her chin, the only indication that she did remember her. 'Frans is with someone. Come inside and I'll tell him you're here.'

'Thank you,' said Trudi, relieved to have passed her test, though it could hardly be described as a warm welcome. She stepped into the hallway while the woman went to tell Frans he had a visitor. What a palaver, Trudi thought, as several minutes passed while she could hear the murmur of voices from the small sitting room, before Frans came out to greet her. Behind him, she glimpsed Piet, and felt her spirits soar. She hadn't seen him since their trip out to the coast, but he'd been in her thoughts almost constantly.

'Thanks for coming over at short notice. Piet and I were just talking tactics,' said Frans, ushering Trudi into the room. 'Come, and I'll explain it all to you.' He walked over to a desk under the window, where a map was spread out, and proceeded to roll it up. Trudi caught Piet's eye and raised her eyebrows. Clearly, the two of them had been discussing things that Frans didn't want to mention to her.

'No need to go into the details just yet, as there's a bit of reconnaissance work to be done first and I'd like you to be involved,' Frans went on. 'Piet will be joining our group for a while. He understands and speaks good German and has been doing quite a bit of this kind of work in Amsterdam. He's been following the movements of an SS officer we suspect of holding valuable information about the secret movement of stolen goods by rail to Germany. The officer has recently moved to Haarlem. I thought the two of you could work together to track him down and find a way to learn more about his plans.'

'It's not something I've done before. Are you expecting me to carry a gun?' said Trudi warily.

'No, that shouldn't be necessary, though Piet will be armed should things grow nasty.'

Trudi frowned at the idea that Piet might get hurt and that she'd be unable to help him. 'So what exactly is my role?'

Frans looked quickly at Piet before answering. 'It'll make

Piet's job easier if he has you with him. You can pretend to be a couple so that you won't draw attention to yourselves. You'll be going to the Café Wolkers down by the canal. It's a regular haunt of our German and where he goes to meet other officers. Piet will take things from there.'

'We need to get a move on if we're to go,' said Piet anxiously, glancing at his watch. 'The next part of the plan depends on it.'

'Was it your idea to have me tag along?' said Trudi as they walked quickly along the leafy streets towards the centre of town. As much as she was pleased to have something new to work on, she couldn't help feeling this little assignment was a waste of her time and abilities.

'Actually yes,' said Piet, shooting her a guilty look. 'And perhaps an excuse to see you again, though I wonder if I shouldn't have simply asked you out for a drink.'

Trudi felt her irritation melt away. 'Sorry, Piet. I didn't mean it to sound like that. It's just that I get the feeling that Frans doesn't value me the way he does the men in the group.'

He looked at her, surprised. 'No. You've got that wrong. Frans thinks highly of you. He tells me he's got you lined up for some weighty assignments. We've just got to get this one under our belts. I can't say too much for now, but everything will become clear.'

She had no time to consider what Piet had just told her; she had caught sight of a group of four or five Germans in uniform up ahead. They were banging on doors with their rifle butts and shouting at the tops of their voices to be let in.

'Stay back,' warned Piet, quickly pulling Trudi into an alley where they couldn't be seen. 'It's a raid. But from the looks of it something has really riled them.'

They watched as a middle-aged woman, still wearing her

apron and slippers, was dragged screaming from her house by two of the men and forced towards a car that stood with its engine idling by the side of the road. Her screams were ignored by the two brutes, who bundled her inside and slammed the door shut. The car moved off smoothly and the men crossed the street to join the others, who were continuing their rampage.

'We have to do something. That poor woman,' cried Trudi. She was about to break out of their hiding place, but Piet held her back.

'No, there's nothing we can do for her. Remember what we're here to do.'

The soldiers were now less than fifty yards from where Trudi and Piet were hiding.

'They could turn nasty if they find us. Is there another way we can reach the bar without running into them?' Piet spoke quietly but urgently.

'At the end of the alley there's a passageway that comes out by the canal. It's no distance at all.' Trudi clung to Piet's arm, trembling with the emotion of it all.

'Do you have ID on you?' he asked suddenly.

'Yes. It's fake though. It was Frans's idea.'

'Let me take a look at it. I'm good at spotting the bad ones and so will they.'

She handed over her card and he held it up to the dim light. Her unsmiling photo showed her with her head turned to show the left ear, a requirement of the German authorities. It bore a fake name and address, two fingerprints and the relevant stamps. 'OK, Gretel. Let's go,' he said, handing it back with the glimmer of a smile. He grabbed her hand and they ran off down the dark alley and away from the din of German soldiers wreaking havoc in their wake.

Café Wolkers stood on a street corner with large picture windows on two sides. It wasn't busy for a weekday early evening, and the pair positioned themselves at a table with a view of the door. They didn't have long to wait before the door flew open and four rowdy uniformed Germans came in and sat themselves at the next table. It was obvious to Trudi that they had been drinking heavily; she could smell the alcohol on them, as well as a whiff of stale sweat. She stiffened as fear mixed with revulsion crawled through her. Piet squeezed her hand and she guessed that he had spotted his man.

The waiter came over and the Germans ordered large beers and whiskies in loud voices amid much laughter.

'And make it quick, we haven't all day. We have important business to attend to,' said the one nearest Trudi with a self-satisfied smile. From the corner of her eye, she discerned him to be the most senior of the group, judging by his booming voice and the eagle insignia on his jacket.

The waiter looked nervous as he rushed to take Piet and Trudi's drinks order before scurrying back to the bar.

Piet leant towards Trudi and took her hand, interlacing her fingers in his. He spoke in a low voice. 'Keep telling me about yourself while I listen.' Trudi wondered what he was up to, but knew better than to say anything more about her work in earshot of the men mere inches away from her. Not that they were listening, for they were too engrossed in their own conversation. It wasn't hard to pick up how many houses they had raided that evening and that they were intending to return the following day for a more thorough search for Jews and young men in hiding.

As the men lowered their voices, she felt Piet squeeze her hand to continue. She forced herself to talk about herself, starting with how after she left school at eighteen the only work she could find was doing menial jobs that didn't stretch her. 'The only thing I was any good at in school was art. Drawing, painting, clay modelling. I would have loved to go to college and really learn my craft, but my parents were adamant I should get a job.' She carried on like this, wondering if Piet was taking in anything she was saying above the intense conversation from the next table.

The waiter returned with a full tray of drinks. Trudi stopped talking and noticed the Germans were now playing a card game. Her heart sank. She glanced at Piet, who frowned and gave a small shake of his head, as if he too was disappointed in the way things were going. 'You were saying,' he said, which she took as a sign she should carry on talking about anything, while he listened.

She didn't mean to catch the German's eye, but just happened to glance at him at the same time he looked at her. He immediately rose to his feet and came to stand beside her chair. 'I don't believe I have seen you in this bar before, *Fräulein*,' he said in an ingratiating voice. 'Perhaps you would care to show me your identification.' He swayed a little and grabbed a chair for support.

'Is this really necessary?' said Piet. Trudi noticed the flush in his cheeks, and hoped he wasn't about to lose his temper. 'The lady has every right to be here and have a quiet drink in peace.'

'It's fine,' said Trudi, her heart pounding, as she took the card from her purse and held it out for inspection. The German barely glanced at it before handing it back to her. Piet didn't wait to be asked but rose to his feet. 'Now, Gretel,' he said, using the name on Trudi's card. 'It's time we went.' He dug in his pocket to pay for the drinks and tossed a handful of loose change on the table, then grabbed Trudi's hand and made for the door.

'Walk quickly. We don't want them following us.' He made off along the canal, walking fast and dodging people on bikes. Trudi had to run to keep up. She was convinced the whole episode had been a disaster. Eventually they reached a crossroads with a signpost pointing towards the Haarlemmerhout.

'That didn't go too well,' began Trudi, wondering how

Frans would take it when he heard they'd come away with nothing. This wasn't at all how she'd expected things to turn out.

Piet looked puzzled as he turned to her and said, 'What do you mean? It all went perfectly to plan. Those stupid Germans had no idea I was listening to them. I now have all the information I need.'

TWENTY-THREE

Trudi was still somewhat confused by what exactly Piet had managed to glean until they had arrived back at Frans's house. She was astonished at how ignorant she'd been about what the Germans had been so freely discussing. But Frans was extremely pleased with what Piet had found out and congratulated him on a job well done.

'I can see that teaming you up was a good decision. We are now ready to move on to the next part of this assignment.' He unrolled the large map from earlier and carefully spread it out on the table. It showed the coastal area to the north of Haarlem, with certain points ringed in red ink. 'As you know, this is a key industrial area where the Germans have a specific interest. We weren't exactly sure what they were up to, but thanks to Piet he has confirmed they are planning to take over our factories and dismantle all the components to load onto freight trains.'

'Which they will transport by rail to Germany,' added Piet, poring over the map.

'I thought Germany had its own factories. Why does it need ours?' said Trudi, with a growing sense of unease.

'Their factories have already switched to manufacturing arms and ammunition, but it's not enough to support their war effort,' Piet said. He broke off to glance at her.

'So they think they can come here and steal what we have,' said Trudi, shaking her head in disbelief. 'What right do they have to do that?'

'None, but as they're the occupiers it's a small detail as far as they're concerned. Which is why we need to stop them. The next movement of goods will take place at eleven o'clock sharp on Saturday night. That's what the SS officer so carelessly spoke about when he was playing cards with his collaborators,' Piet explained with a wry smile. 'It's vital we stop them.'

'And sabotaging the train with explosives is the best way of doing it,' said Frans, turning back to the map. He pointed to a bridge marked with a cross. 'This is the bridge over the Spaarne River that links Haarlem to the industrial areas north of the city. When the German train leaves the factory depot here,' he said, moving his finger fractionally to the right, 'it will take three minutes to reach the bridge, which you will prime with enough explosives to derail the train.'

'So you're asking us to blow it up?' Trudi said, scarcely able to believe what she was hearing. Could she actually do this, when she'd never done such a thing before, she wondered.

'Precisely,' said Frans. 'But you'll be part of a team working together. In addition to the two of you, I'm sending along Jan, Wim, Andries and Elco, all experienced in resisting the Germans. It's a shame Frida is working at the hospital both nights, otherwise I'd have teamed you together. I thought you and Wim would work well as a pair. Wim's a steady chap, doesn't lose his head in a crisis, and you've always proved yourself to be courageous and willing to take on difficult assignments.' He paused, waiting for her reaction.

More than anything she would have wanted Frida at her

side. But why Wim and not Piet? She remembered how useless she'd found Wim the first time the three of them had gone out on an assignment. He must have proved himself in the meantime, for Frans to recommend him. 'All right,' she said, tentatively, but determined not to show her nerves. 'Tell us what we'll be doing.'

'First things first. On Friday evening, you'll need to go and check out the area. My colleague Gerrit trained with British commandos in the use of explosives. He lives on a secluded farm outside Velsen.' Frans showed the place on the map. 'He'll show you exactly how to prepare the explosives and attach them to the metal structure of the bridge. And then it's your job to go and check out the area and the bridge itself. Piet and Jan will lead the operation, helping to scope out the area, studying the movement of the guards on the bridge and working out the best place to attach the explosives. Then on Saturday evening, once you've planted the explosives, you'll need to give yourselves enough time to set the fuses and get away before they set the whole thing off.' He moved away from the map and added, 'I should ask you, Trudi – how do you feel about it?'

She was surprised to be asked. Extremely nervous, she thought, but she wasn't going to let that put her off. He'd always said this was what she'd been trained for, so she would carry out the plan to the best of her abilities. 'If we can put a halt to this despicable scheme, then I'm ready to do all it takes.'

He smiled. Then, turning to Piet, he asked 'You've done this before, haven't you?'

'In theory. From behind a desk – but I'm good at detail,' Piet said with a nervous laugh.

Frans made it sound so easy, though Trudi doubted he'd done anything like this either. She thought he hid it well as he brushed off Piet's remark with an airy, 'Well, there's a first time for everyone, and from what I know of you you're methodical and thorough, and I have every faith in you.'

'You can rely on me,' said Piet, though it was Trudi he was looking at as he said it. It was the reassurance she needed as she smiled back at him.

TWENTY-FOUR

On Friday evening the group assembled at a remote farmhouse belonging to Gerrit, the resistance member and expert in the use of explosives. Apart from Piet, Wim was the only one Trudi knew, and she hadn't seen him since their first recruitment meeting in the park.

'So we're to be teamed up together. Have you done much work for Frans?' asked Trudi.

Wim shrugged. 'Mainly office-based intelligence work passing information onto the Allies. Nothing like this, though.'

Trudi laughed nervously. 'I suspect none of us have done anything like this before.' Again, she wished that Frida could have been here for moral support, and because she thought she'd be good at this type of work.

Gerrit clapped his hands for attention. Their lesson in building and handling explosives was about to begin.

They followed him along a dirt track to a barn in a field, a short distance from the house. Apart from Trudi, the group comprised only men, who mostly seemed to know one other and walked along in pairs, chatting and making jokes while smoking.

They arrived at the barn, but before the farmer let them inside he gave a short lecture about the dangers of lit cigarettes.

'Under no circumstances are you allowed to smoke inside the barn. And that goes for whenever you're in the vicinity of explosives. We don't want any unfortunate accidents.'

The men all hurriedly extinguished their cigarettes underfoot.

The barn was empty except for a large, roughly hewn wooden table in its centre. The farmer bent down to retrieve a box, which he heaved onto the table with a thump. The group crowded round to watch as he lifted out what looked like a grey lump of clay with a fuse attached to one end. There were many more of the same inside the box. From another he brought out some glass tubes. 'These are the chemicals you need. This one needs especially careful handling.' He held up a tube containing a bright yellow liquid. 'It's highly effective but also highly explosive.'

The group watched while the farmer demonstrated how to assemble the explosives. He made it look so simple for something so deadly, thought Trudi, as she regarded the putty-like substance that reminded her of the clay she used to use in art class what seemed like a million years ago.

When he'd finished his lecture, everyone nodded approval, seeming impressed, though the atmosphere in the barn was markedly more subdued than when they'd first arrived.

Once they left the farm, everyone visibly relaxed and was chatting in their twos and threes. Jan, the man designated to lead them, turned up halfway through Gerrit's demonstration and was now deep in conversation with Piet as they led the march to scope out the area around the bridge.

It was pitch black and Trudi kept her eyes on the two men walking in front of them as they followed the path that snaked in between dense shrubbery towards the bridge. Was she the only one who was worried that someone might jump out and ambush them, she thought anxiously. But Jan had told them to stay quiet, so there was no opportunity to confide her fear to Wim. Instead, she concentrated hard on the path ahead and not putting a foot wrong.

Suddenly, there was an enormous bang up ahead. Trudi and Wim jumped to the side of the path and took shelter behind a bush. Several others ahead of them did the same.

'Is it Germans?' Trudi said, clutching Wim's arm.

'I don't think so. We'd know if it was. There'd be more noise.'

It was a tense wait. A few minutes later, Piet came striding back down the path and announced that it was nothing more than a car backfiring in a nearby street. The relief was immense; Trudi hadn't realised how jittery it had made her feel, but the incident was enough to make her grasp the seriousness of the situation. And that they had a job to do.

After they had resumed walking for a while longer, the bridge they were heading towards loomed large, spanning the wide canal. It had a single train track running across its length. Jan gathered the group together and told them to work in pairs. 'There's a footbridge over the canal lower down that will give us a good view of what's happening up on the bridge. Piet, you come with me. Wim and Trudi, you stay on this side as a second lookout.' He gave the others the instruction to spread out well and keep hidden from the German guards patrolling the area.

Trudi and Wim found a place where the bank dipped down, where they had a good view of the guards and any movement on the bridge. In the dark, they could pick out the guards' torchlights jerking up and down with every step they took as they crossed from one side of the bridge to the other and back again.

'We'll never be able to plant explosives while they're

around,' whispered Trudi, after another guard had passed by overhead.

'Patience,' said Wim, keeping his eyes trained on the bridge. 'I'm pretty sure they'll soon be knocking off and heading back to base. Remember this is just a scouting exercise for tomorrow.'

When they could no longer see the guards' lights bobbing up and down, Jan signalled with his torch, telling them it was safe to come out. They met at a designated point well out of sight of the bridge, where he instructed them to follow him to 'the bunker', a place used by the resistance cell during training exercises. 'It's a bit basic, but well equipped with food and drink. I thought we could discuss tactics for tomorrow and get to know one another better.'

The bunker was underground and hidden in nearby woodland. The entrance was so well concealed that it took them several attempts at shifting branches and ferns until Piet let out a shout that he had found it. He led the way down a ladder that took them into a small fusty-smelling room. Once he'd lit the oil lamps that hung down from the ceiling and checked that the ventilation shaft was working, the space immediately became more welcoming. There were comfortable cushions to sit on and a low table in the centre. It was a squeeze for them all to fit in, but this added to the feeling of camaraderie. Trudi found herself squashed up between Piet on one side and Jan on the other. Between them, they talked through the order of events for the following evening and what was expected of everyone. Trudi and Wim would be up on the bridge planting the explosives, and brothers Elco and Andries would be backup. Piet kept stressing that the operation was a team effort and that each member of the group had a responsibility to ensure that the rest of the group were safe. Once he'd finished his spiel, he said, 'Now, enough of the solemn faces. Who would like a beer?'

A cheer went up. After the earlier tension, the mood between them visibly relaxed, as if everyone just wanted to forget about everything for now. Trudi was just happy to be here, close to Piet, who had taken a seat next to her, and in convivial company. Hunks of bread, cheese and sausage were handed round along with bottles of beer. Once the beer was finished, someone produced a bottle of brandy and everyone cheered.

When the bottle reached Trudi, she took a mouthful. The brandy slipped down, instantly warming her insides. 'Want some?' she said, handing the bottle to Piet. She caught him gazing at her and gave him a smile.

He kept looking at her as he took the bottle from her. 'You're quiet. Is it about tomorrow?'

She made a sound like a low hum. 'It's a big thing that you're asking me to do. I can't help wondering what happens if it goes wrong.'

'Shh,' he said, putting a finger to her lips. 'You mustn't allow yourself to think that. Frans, Jan and I have meticulously been through every detail and we have every faith in you. You've more than proved yourself, and you won't be alone. You'll have Wim beside you and a backup team keeping close watch.' He helped himself to another mouthful of brandy and wiped his mouth on his sleeve. He held the bottle out to her. 'Here, have some more.'

As she tipped the brandy into her mouth, she relished the feeling of being pressed up against him. She noticed him shift his position and slide an arm round her shoulders. 'Do you mind?' he said quietly against her hair.

Trudi didn't answer. Instead, she closed her eyes and leant against his shoulder. As if from afar the voices and laughter washed over her, and she wished the moment would never end.

TWENTY-FIVE

The explosives weighed as heavy as stones in the deep pockets of her coat that Oma had helped her sew all those weeks ago. Beside her, pockets also bulging, crouched Wim. He carried the same, for a large amount was needed to cause enough damage to stop the train. Time was ticking by. She thought of Piet and hoped that he had the sense to keep well hidden. They would have to work quickly. The plan was to wait until the night-watchmen had retired to their hut, then climb up onto the bridge, find the halfway point, attach the explosives, set the timer for the fuses and run.

'I can't believe it. It's gone ten and the guards are still up there. If they don't stop patrolling soon, we'll have to abort the operation,' came Wim's urgent whisper. For the past fifteen minutes, he'd been obsessively checking the luminous hands on his wristwatch.

Trudi felt her anxiety rise. 'Stop doing that, Wim. They'll be able to see us from up there.'

'No they won't,' he said, checking the time again. 'Look... they're heading back to their base. It can't be long now.'

The two waited for what seemed like an age until the

bobbing lights of the patrolmen disappeared from view. More minutes passed before they saw the faint flash of light from the direction of where Jan was hiding, announcing it was time to get in position.

First, they needed to scramble up the embankment and find the gap in the barbed wire that one of the other men had cut earlier. They hadn't been able to practise this part of the operation and it only became apparent when they emerged onto the rail tracks that there was a problem; to their dismay, they saw there was no gap between the track and the side of the bridge. Reaching the middle to plant the explosives seemed an impossibility.

Trudi swallowed hard as she weighed up the situation. *Think! There must be a way.* Then she said out loud, 'Let me test it out and, if it holds with my weight, you come along behind me.'

Wim's face had a ghostly pallor as he held his watch up. 'I'm not sure we have time,' he said anxiously.

'Wim. I didn't come here tonight only for you to lose your nerve. I'm going, and if this is going to happen I need your support.' Her heart hammered in her chest as she waited for him to agree.

Wim gave a half-hearted nod and she turned to view the narrow train track leading to the centre of the bridge. Checking that the explosives were secure in her coat pockets, she dropped to her knees and began crawling forward slowly. She tried not to think about the inky cold blackness of the canal far below as she shuffled with painstaking slowness. After a few moments, she gained confidence, and called out to Wim that it was safe to follow. It wasn't far to where they needed to get to, but when they did, they would have to move fast. At 11 p.m. the freight train would be on its way. And this was the only way to stop it.

Once they reached the centre of the bridge, they got to work moulding the putty for each of the explosives till it held fast to the metal beam at their feet. Satisfied that their handiwork would hold, they checked to make sure the fuses were intact. All they needed to do now was to set the timer and get away fast.

'Stop! I can hear someone coming,' exclaimed Wim in a low whisper.

Just visible at the far end of the bridge, the light of a patrolman came bobbing along, growing steadily brighter as it bumped towards them. If they were to retreat back from where they'd come, he would be bound to spot them.

Trudi moved fractionally forward towards the broad metal girder and peered over the edge. It was scary, but she wasn't about to abandon her task.

She could just see what looked like a platform down below, but it seemed too big a drop for them to jump onto.

'What can you see?' whispered Wim, who had moved close to her side.

'The struts are sturdy enough. It's whether we can hold on. I can't be sure but I think there's a ledge down there that might break our fall. Unfortunately, I don't think we have any choice.'

They both eyed up the large beam that ran the length of the bridge, before clambering over and carefully lowering themselves down while gripping tightly to the metal supports. Trudi tentatively lowered one foot until the tips of her toes made contact with a hard surface.

'Can you feel something solid under your feet?' came Wim's voice.

'I... I think so. But it's too far down to put my weight on it. You should manage it if you stand on tiptoe. It's better than nothing.'

All Trudi could hear was Wim's laboured breathing, and she realised she too was panting. They whispered words of encouragement to one another, trying hard to ignore the growing numbness in their fingers against the cold metal. If it hadn't been for Wim beside her, Trudi wasn't sure she would have had the strength to keep holding on.

When she thought she couldn't bear it any longer, she looked up and saw a flash of light illuminate the struts of the bridge. Holding her breath, she watched as the light flicked back and forth, back and forth, until they were back in pitch darkness. The crunch of footsteps passed overhead... and finally she allowed herself to breathe out.

'I'm dying to see what the time is,' whispered Wim after a few moments.

'And if you do, that's one way to die,' said Trudi grimly. She heard what sounded like a gulping noise and realised that it was Wim trying to suppress a laugh. Realising the absurdity of their situation, she found herself giving in to the urge to laugh too, and bit down hard on her lip as she concentrated on maintaining her grip, her hands aching like never before. How much longer would they have to keep this up?

Minutes after they could be sure that the patrolman had gone, they somehow managed to haul themselves back onto the railway track, where they collapsed exhausted until their limbs stopped shaking and the adrenalin in their bodies began to ebb away.

'I don't know how we managed that,' gasped Trudi, trying to rub feeling back into her hands.

Wim didn't appear to be listening. He had been peering at his watch, and quickly got to his feet. 'It's not over yet. It's quarter to eleven and the train isn't due till eleven. I've just got time to set the timer. You keep watch and call me if you see the guards coming back.'

Wim was gone before Trudi could object. Could he really manage to set the time and get back within fifteen minutes?

Trembling, Trudi stared after him as he disappeared into the darkness. She strained for any sounds, but it was eerily quiet, apart from the occasional tap-tapping noise from where

Wim was working. From somewhere over the other side of the canal a dog barked. And then came the unmistakable rumble and squeal of wheels, starting up somewhere in the direction of the factory. Trudi's instincts were to run, but she knew she couldn't leave Wim behind.

'Wim! The train's coming... we need to get off this bridge quick,' she cried out, heedless of being overheard by the patrolmen.

'I've done it,' came his voice, before she could make out the shape of him moving towards her.

Trudi's breath came out in shaky gasps as she pulled him by the hand and ran.

With seconds to spare before the train came rumbling and rattling onto the bridge, they managed to hurl themselves down the embankment, and landed in a tangled heap in the muddy ditch. From somewhere close by Trudi thought she heard a voice cry, 'Keep down!' followed by a deafening explosion and an enormous flash of blue light.

Her head throbbed terribly. She was only dimly aware of the screams and pounding of feet above her as her eyes drifted shut.

TWENTY-SIX

'I think she's waking up. Can someone bring a blanket and some tea?'

She thought she recognised that voice, but was unable to place it. It was so deep and reassuring, the kind of voice that made her believe that everything would be fine. With a sigh of contentment, she felt herself drift off again.

'Trudi, you need to wake up.' The familiar voice sounded more urgent and succeeded in pulling her back to consciousness. At the mention of her name, her eyes flickered open and she looked up into Piet's face, which was pinched with worry.

'Where am I? What's going on?' She tried to sit up, but found she hadn't the strength, so let herself collapse back against a cushion. A moment later, Piet was handing her a cup of something hot.

'Drink this. You'll feel better. Then I'll tell you.' His voice was softer now, more calming.

Trudi took a sip of the warming liquid and realised that he'd handed her something stronger than tea. It felt so good as it slipped down. Gradually she began to take in her surroundings, and realised she was down in the bunker. Wim was sitting close by, hunched under a blanket draped round his shoulders. Jan crouched beside him and was whispering to him in a low voice.

Trudi frowned and turned her head back to Piet. 'He looks terrible. Will he be all right?' she asked.

'I think so. He has mainly cuts and bruises. It's you I'm worried about. That was a nasty knock to the head. Elco and Andries found you unconscious at the foot of the embankment. They were about to move in to assist the two of you when the explosion happened. We had to get you away before anyone discovered what we were up to. Elco and Andries helped me carry you back here.'

Trudi held her head in her hands as she tried to take it all in. How could she not remember this? She flinched as her fingers discovered a tender spot above her temple.

'How are you feeling now?'

'So-so. It's just a headache. I'll be fine.' Trudi smiled weakly. 'Where are Elco and Andries now? I should thank them.'

'They've gone home. I'll let them know.' Piet kept his eyes on her. 'Do you remember the explosion?'

It was all coming back to her now. 'We were the ones who caused it. Was the train hit?'

'No. It braked in time, but had it gone any further it would have tipped into the canal. Let's just say that no one will be able to go over that bridge any time soon.'

'We did blow it up though... didn't we?'

'Not exactly, but you caused enough damage to stop any more trains from crossing it.'

Trudi fell silent. She knew he was trying to encourage her, but from the sounds of it, their mission hadn't succeeded.

Piet lifted her chin and pushed a strand of hair back from her face. 'I saw it all. Jan and I were watching from the other side of the canal. I couldn't believe it when the two of you climbed over the side of the bridge. I knew it had to be serious for you to even attempt such a thing. I wanted Jan to flash his light as a warning for you to get away before the patrolmen spotted you, but he refused. He was right, of course. It would only have drawn attention to you. There was nothing we could do but let you carry on. I don't think I've ever been so scared.' He gazed intently at her, before going on more quietly, 'You did an incredible job in very difficult circumstances. Trudi, I'm so proud of you.'

But Trudi didn't want him to think it was all because of her. 'It was Wim's idea to go through with it after we climbed back on the bridge. There were only a few minutes to spare before the train came. If it had been up to me, I would have aborted,' she insisted.

Piet stroked her chin with his thumb as he looked into her eyes. 'But you didn't. Don't underestimate what you did. Wim did an incredibly risky thing by going back and it could have all gone horribly wrong. I'm so relieved you made it out alive.'

Trudi's head hurt as she tried to take in what he was saying... that he cared for her? And the way he was looking at her... what did it mean? She felt tired. So, so tired.

Sighing deeply, she said, 'I'm sorry, Piet, but I think I need to lie down again.'

Piet stayed by her side all through the night. She kept waking with a start and crying out, as she replayed the events on the bridge over and over in her mind. Each time it happened, she was aware that Piet was there to gather her in his arms until she fell asleep again. He stayed until Frans arrived in the morning, and promised to come and visit her as soon as she was settled back home.

Frans had come with a doctor friend, who confirmed she was suffering from concussion. Taking Frans aside, the doctor said she would need two weeks' bedrest. She heard Frans say that he felt responsible for what had happened to her. He insisted he take her back to his house where she could be looked after by Mevrouw de Wit until she was well enough to return home.

Trudi grew increasingly frustrated as she listened to Frans and the doctor discussing her condition in low voices as if she weren't present. Apart from a lingering headache, she was feeling so much better, so couldn't understand why she shouldn't be allowed back home.

'There's nothing wrong with me,' she protested, and attempted to get to her feet, but was overcome with dizziness and had to sit back down again.

'Concussion isn't something you should ignore,' said the doctor solemnly. 'You may think you're fine but your body needs time to recover. The time will fly by, but you need looking after.'

Trudi agreed reluctantly, though she hated being an invalid, and especially the idea of being attended to by Frans's house-keeper. She was unable to shake off the uneasy feeling she still had about the woman, though Frans clearly didn't share her concern; he had nothing but praise for her. But Trudi remembered that first conversation, when Mevrouw de Wit had casually asked, 'You're not one of *them*?' It had left Trudi wondering whether there had been real malice behind her comment, rather than thoughtlessness.

In any event, Trudi was surprised to be greeted so warmly by Mevrouw de Wit, who fussed over her from the moment she arrived. She installed Trudi in a sunny bedroom with a view of the garden, where the roses were in full bloom. Trudi would have been quite happy to doze peacefully throughout the day, had it not been for Mevrouw de Wit appearing at her door with drinks and things to eat, even though Trudi never asked for anything.

One afternoon, when Trudi was dozing, she started at the sound of humming and someone moving about the bedroom.

Opening her eyes, she saw Mevrouw come over and pull up a chair.

'Oh, good, you're awake. It's so nice to have someone to talk to. Frans is away so much these days, and it's just me rattling around in an empty house. He won't tell me where he goes, except to say it's business. But I have my suspicions.' She nodded knowingly, watching Trudi with beady eyes. 'Not that I mind, of course. He can do what he likes, but he really shouldn't involve young women in his activities. If you ask me, it's far too dangerous. Allowing women to carry guns and blow up bridges? It's not right.' She clicked her tongue in disapproval and shuffled her chair closer. 'Look what happened to you. Do you want to tell me about it?' Her black eyes shone with the anticipation of any juicy revelations.

'No. I don't,' said Trudi curtly and turned her head to the wall. What was she driving at? If only she'd leave her in peace.

Undeterred, Mevrouw de Wit kept on. 'I expect you're too tired. Maybe you'll feel like having a little chat later, hmm?' She sat back in her chair. She evidently had no intention of leaving Trudi alone. 'My nephew,' she started up again, now leaning forward in a confidential stance. 'He used to be quite taken in by the resistance and the things they get up to. If you ask me, his head was turned by the idea of learning to use a gun. He used to go along to meetings in Amsterdam, until one day the discussion turned to the cache of weapons the resistance were hoarding to pass on to the Allies for an attack against the Germans. It was the idea of the Allies provoking an all-out war that did it for him. That's when he saw the light, thank goodness. And he never went back.'

Trudi grew very still as she listened. She was perplexed that anyone could even think that the Allies were the ones provoking war, when everyone knew that the Germans had started it. It was obvious that Mevrouw de Wit agreed with her nephew.

She had no interest in any more of the woman's views, but she was curious to know what her nephew had done next.

'He got himself a proper job working as a clerk at the town hall. And we all know what that means,' she said, tapping the side of her nose.

'Oh, what's that?' said Trudi, who had a suspicion what she was alluding to, but wanted her to say it outright.

'Well, he hasn't told me as such, but I'd be surprised if he hasn't become a member of the NSB.'

Even though she'd been expecting it, Trudi gave an involuntary shiver at the mention of the name. NSB. She'd heard about the atrocious things the Dutch fascist party got up to in the name of protecting the country, including attacking and betraying Jews. She was on the verge of expressing her opinion, but didn't want to give Mevrouw de Wit the satisfaction of her hearing it. Instead she let it pass and closed her eyes, pretending to go to sleep, until she could be sure that Mevrouw de Wit had left the room. Then came the dawning realisation that she'd been right all along about the woman. She could not be trusted.

TWENTY-SEVEN

It was the day that Mevrouw de Wit always visited her sister, and Trudi enjoyed the feeling of being all alone in the house. She went to sit in the small sitting room, where she could catch the early-evening rays of sun, and to sit and read while waiting for Frans to return home. Feeling pleased that she was managing to concentrate on reading her book without dropping off, Trudi glanced up when she heard the scrape of Frans's key in the door. Closing her book, she laid it down on the table by her chair and called out to let him know she was there.

'I'll be with you in a moment,' he called back. She tilted her head and waited to hear the click of the front door shutting. Moments later he appeared. 'Well, well. It's good to see you're up and about. I must say, you're looking much better.'

'I feel it,' said Trudi, with a smile. 'I've obeyed doctor's orders, but two weeks is almost up. Don't you think it's time I went back to my lodgings?'

'Ah, I was going to speak to you about that,' said Frans, walking over and taking a chair next to hers.

'Don't tell me. You want me to move,' said Trudi, with a sigh.

Frans gave her a sheepish smile. 'I thought that, with every-thing that's happened to you recently, it would be for the best. I've managed to find you a bedsit near the centre of town. It's not permanent and I'm hoping to find you something better in a few days. No one will know you're there, so you'll be quite safe.'

Trudi smiled weakly. The idea of moving made her feel exhausted all over again, even though she had so few posses-sions to pack up. But Frans had been so kind to her and she knew she mustn't appear ungrateful. 'Thank you for arranging it, and for everything you've done for me.'

'It was the least I could do. But you should keep your thanks for Mevrouw de Wit. She's the one who's looked after you.'

'Yes. She's certainly been very attentive, perhaps a bit too much so,' she said, unable to stop herself from frowning. 'I wanted to talk to you about that. I woke yesterday to find her in my bedroom. It's not the first time. I think she comes in on the pretext of tidying up. But as soon as she saw I was awake, she came over to talk about her nephew who she thinks has signed up with the NSB. It was like she was waiting to tell me, and she seemed so keen to speak about him. As if I'd be inter-ested. But I was surprised at how pleased she was with the idea that he's joined them. Has she ever mentioned him to you?'

'I know she's fond of her nephew and she often tells me what he's up to. The last thing I knew was that he'd given up on his university studies to go back home and live with his parents.'

'Bloemendaal. I remember that's where she said her sister lives,' said Trudi, though it wasn't Mevrouw de Wit she was thinking of. It was Sem.

'Yes, that's right. And where she goes on Thursdays. Now, I'm rather hungry, so if you don't mind can we continue this conversation over supper?'

As she followed Frans into the kitchen, she mulled over what he had just told her. It seemed inconceivable that Sem was

Mevrouw de Wit's nephew. It just seemed too much of a coincidence. And yet, everything she'd heard seemed to fit.

'You're rather quiet,' said Frans, once they had taken a seat at the kitchen table. He was dishing up the supper of cold potato salad and hard-boiled eggs Mevrouw de Wit had prepared for them. 'What's going on?'

'I'm not sure.' Trudi speared a piece of potato on her fork, but wasn't in any hurry to eat it. 'I don't recall Mevrouw de Wit ever mentioning her nephew's name. Do you happen to know it?'

Frans was busy peeling his egg and dipping it into a small mound of salt he'd poured on the side of his plate. 'His name?' He paused for a moment, before raising his eyebrows. 'Seth, I think. Or was it Sem?'

'I thought as much,' said Trudi, laying down her fork on her plate with a clatter. 'My ex-boyfriend's name is Sem and his family live in Bloemendaal. The last time I saw him he was talking about quitting university because he wasn't getting tuition due to Jewish lecturers being forced to leave. But he was enthusiastic about the student meetings he'd been attending where they discussed building a new Netherlands within Europe. It sounded ominous to me, but when I asked him if it was anything to do with the NSB he denied it. Oh Frans. I don't know what to think.' She let out a long sigh. 'And to know he's Mevrouw de Wit's nephew... It doesn't seem possible. What more has she told you about him?'

'Let me think. She mentioned her sister is married to a fisherman.'

Trudi closed her eyes and sighed with resignation. 'Sem's father's a fisherman. It's him all right.' What could have induced him to get involved in the NSB? She remembered hearing about the rallies held across the country to boost the movement's membership and how hundreds of eager young Dutch men went along and were fired up by the pro-Nazi rhetoric and couldn't wait to sign up. She wondered if Sem had been to any rallies. Maybe that was what had caused him to change his opinion. Casting her mind back to their early conversations, she remembered how keen he'd been to spread anti-Nazi propaganda... could he really have changed his tune so much as to become a Nazi collaborator?

'It certainly is troubling. Have you seen him recently?' said Frans, interrupting her thoughts.

'Not since he told me all this. That was some weeks ago.'

Frans looked serious as he said, 'Has he tried to contact you since?'

'No. I didn't give him my address. But you're worrying me, Frans. Why do you ask?'

'It's probably nothing, but if he has joined the NSB and knows you're working for us...'

'No, he doesn't,' Trudi said firmly. 'I ended the conversation as soon as I heard what he was up to – but I never imagined he would go as far as joining them. What about Mevrouw de Wit... do you think she could be a collaborator too?'

Frans gave a dismissive laugh. 'She enjoys a gossip, but she has made it quite clear that she doesn't want anything to do with any organisation, either pro or anti the Nazis. But you're right to be cautious. To be on the safe side, you should move first thing tomorrow.'

TWENTY-EIGHT

All the time she'd been convalescing, Trudi had been looking forward to moving back to the pleasant house next to the Haarlemmerhout and seeing Oma again. Over cups of tea, Trudi had felt more settled there than anywhere else, and had been able to put her fears about the war aside. Now, she was returning only to let Oma know she would be leaving.

Trudi climbed the stairs and was greeted by Oma coming out of her room.

'You're back!' the old lady exclaimed, grinning broadly. 'Where have you been? I thought you'd disappeared, just like the last girl did.'

'It's good to see you, Oma.' Trudi put her bag down, slightly out of breath with the exertion of climbing up three flights of stairs.

'Are you quite well? Come in and I'll make you a cup of tea.' Oma didn't wait for Trudi to answer but just turned to go back into her room. Trudi smiled sadly to herself, knowing it would be for the last time, and followed her in.

How much to tell her, she thought, as she sat back in her familiar spot on the red velvet sofa surrounded by batik cushions. She fought her instincts to tell Oma all about the sabotage operation and how she'd been so close to losing her life. *Don't divulge what you do for the resistance. Assume you can't trust anyone*, Frans had repeatedly told her at every opportunity. Unfortunately, she knew he was right. As fond as she was of the old lady, and as alone as she often felt when Frida was busy at work, she knew she mustn't allow her feelings to cloud her judgement.

'So where were you all this time?' Oma placed the tray on the mahogany coffee table and busied herself pouring out the tea.

'I had to go away and then I wasn't well enough to return,' said Trudi, despising herself for not telling the truth.

'Nothing serious, I hope?' Oma settled into her armchair and gazed at her expectantly.

'No, I'm quite well now. Just a little tired.' Trudi stirred a spoonful of sugar into her tea. 'I'm really sorry, Oma, but I'm moving out. I only came back to pack my things.'

'Really? I thought you were so settled here.' Oma sounded shocked and sad.

'I am... I was, but my circumstances have changed and Frans, my... er... colleague, has found me a room closer to the centre of town.'

'Well, that is a shame, and I will miss you and our talks. It does me a lot of good finding out what young people like yourself get up to.' Oma put her cup down with a clatter and got up to go to her bureau. Opening the flap, she spent some minutes searching for what she was looking for.

'Ahh! Here it is,' she said, turning to Trudi. Her cheeks were quite pink from the effort of looking, She came back over carrying a small white box, which she presented to Trudi. 'A parting gift. It's only small, but I thought you might like it.'

'What is it?' said Trudi, intrigued.

'Go on, open it, and you'll see.'

Trudi prised off the lid with her finger to reveal a silver filigree brooch in the shape of a lotus flower lying on a soft pillow of cotton wool.

'I bought it on a whim the only time I went to Indonesia but I've never found a reason to wear it,' Oma said, gazing at the trinket with fondness. 'I have no use for it, but I think it will look nice on you. I want you to have it as a memento of our friendship.'

Trudi drew in a breath, overcome by her kindness and generosity, but the old lady refused to be sentimental. 'No need to thank me. You've given an old woman a lot of pleasure.'

Trudi was unable to stop herself from leaning over and giving her a hug. 'Of course I should thank you. It's beautiful. And thank you for being a good friend.'

Later, as Trudi left the house, she glanced up and saw Oma standing at the window. She blew Trudi a kiss and waved, as she had done in the past, except they both knew this would be for the last time.

Carrying two large bags containing all her possessions, Trudi gloomily eyed the three flights of stairs that she needed to climb to reach her new lodgings. It was a depressing prospect moving into a small attic room at the top of a run-down house of bedsits in the centre of town. Of course she was grateful for the financial support she'd received from Frans's group, but she wished she had some say in where she lived. Frans had assured her she would be safe here and it would only be for a few days until something better came up. She hoped he was right as she trod the first of the narrow uncarpeted staircases. At the top, there was just enough space on the small landing for her to put down her bags while she fumbled for the key in her coat pocket. The door stuck fast and she had to put her shoulder against it to push it open. The first thing that hit her was the musty smell, suggesting the room hadn't been used in a while. Depositing her bags on the faded blue threadbare rug that lay on the bare floorboards, she took in her surroundings, the narrow bed that took up nearly half the living space, the small wooden chest of drawers, chair and ancient washstand. She went straight over to the small-paned window and flung it open, letting in a welcome breeze.

Trudi turned her attention to unpacking her meagre possessions. Moving often was only to be expected, she knew that. But she was saddened that it meant she would no longer spend time with Oma. She felt sorry for the lonely old lady, and, as she traced her finger over the beautiful brooch, she reflected on how she had come to rely on their friendship.

A few days after moving in, Trudi had a visit from Frans. She took him up the three flights of stairs to her tiny room, where he was unable to stand without stooping.

'I'll sit on the bed. You'd better take the chair,' said Trudi, with a short laugh.

'I didn't realise it was quite so small,' said Frans, looking embarrassed. 'I'll have to see if I can find you something better.'

'It's fine. I can manage,' said Trudi. She had already grown used to her cramped conditions. She felt safe up here and no one bothered her. That was all that mattered right now.

Frans sat down, lit a cigarette and inhaled deeply. 'I've had some troubling news about the Friedmans. Their names are on a list of Jewish people who have been deported to Westerbork prison camp.'

'No,' gasped Trudi. Hearing the words 'prison camp' filled her with terror. After the Germans had taken over Westerbork from the Dutch a few years before, she'd heard rumours that they were turning it into a transit camp for prisoners before deporting them to labour camps in Germany and Poland.

Everyone knew that the conditions in these camps were brutal, and the outcome never good. As far as she knew, no one sent there had ever returned.

'I don't understand,' she said. 'They've done nothing wrong. Why have they been sent to such a terrible place?'

Frans paused to drag on his cigarette and looked around for an ashtray.

'You'll have to use this,' said Trudi, handing him her only saucer.

'I'm trying to find out more, but no one knows, or they won't let on. I've come straight from the town hall, where it's chaos. People have been streaming in all morning wanting to find out what's happened to their loved ones. There are tears and angry scenes, but nobody is prepared to give out any information. I suspect it's because most of the town hall officials are fascists and in the pay of the Germans. When I was there, I spoke to an elderly couple in the queue whose son and family are among those on the list – they're desperate to know if they are still at Westerbork. But they've been told there is no further news. No explanation, nothing. There's someone I can ask in Amsterdam who might know what's going on after deportation, but I'm not hopeful.'

'Poor Maria and Hans. They must be terrified and missing Rosy and Louisa terribly. Is there anything I can do to help?'

'There is actually,' said Frans, pulling one last time on his cigarette and stubbing it out. 'Many of those who've been transported to Westerbork have been separated from their children, who are being housed in villages near the Kennemer dunes. But we suspect someone in the network has been passing information about their whereabouts on to the Germans.'

Trudi's jaw dropped.

'No one I know,' Frans went on hastily, 'but still, it's unsettling to think that people you've worked with are prepared to betray you. Anyway, it's a matter of urgency to move these children as far away from Haarlem as possible before they are found.'

'The Kennemer dunes are where Louisa and Rosy are. All this time I've been convalescing they will have been in danger of being discovered too. I must go and find out.'

'No, you must stay here. It's all in hand and time is of the essence. As soon as I heard the news I made sure that the Friedman children were both included in the group leaving. They will be travelling to Dordrecht and I need someone with experience to accompany them by train. Will you take it on, Trudi?'

Trudi swallowed as she considered his request. 'You know I will, especially if it means I can help save Rosy and Louisa. If it's a large group, I assume there will be other adults in charge?'

'Yes of course. I can't tell you who just yet.'

Trudi frowned, wondering why he wasn't more certain on the facts of the operation. 'But you must know how many children I'll be taking?' she asked.

'No more than twelve. I can't be sure until I get firm numbers, but I'll know much more tomorrow. Come to my house at noon and I'll be able to give you more definite details.'

TWENTY-NINE

'The uniform is genuine. No one will think to ask.'

Frans stared at Trudi, who was regarding the stack of clothes on the desk, the blue and white pinstriped dress and white apron, neatly pressed and folded, with the white cap bearing the distinctive red cross lying on top. 'You want me to wear a German nurse's uniform?' she said.

'German Red Cross nurse's uniform,' Frans corrected, as if that made it any better. 'I'm afraid we don't have any Dutch uniforms in our supplies. Besides, people recognise that the Red Cross do a lot to help the sick and needy, especially children.' He frowned. 'You're not having second thoughts about this?'

Trudi shook her head, but she took the dress and held it against her. 'No, absolutely not. I gave you my word and I'll do whatever it takes. But I'm not sure the dress will fit,' she said with a grimace. Being above average height, it didn't matter how she positioned it, it didn't quite reach her knees. She had a moment of doubt about the task Frans had set her. A plan so precarious that any slip-up could mean the difference between life and death – not just her life, but Rosy's and Louisa's lives too. But as she stood holding the dress against her, she was determined to go through with it for their sake. She quickly reminded herself that she would be fine once she got going. The dress was a minor detail. 'No. I'm not having second thoughts,' she said, forcing a smile. 'I just don't want to give the *moffen* any additional reason to stop and question me. You know what they can be like. Now tell me what exactly the plan is,' she added brightly.

Frans began by describing the difficulty in finding safe hiding places for Jewish children where they could live without the threat of discovery. Naturally, those offering up their homes needed to be vetted, and there was always a possibility that someone might turn collaborator, though this hadn't happened yet. 'So I've been working out the details with resistance colleagues in the network – reliable colleagues – and everything is now in place for you to move the group of twelve children to foster homes in Dordrecht,' he said. 'It's not going to be easy, as the group is big and likely to attract the attention of the Germans. But you shouldn't worry – I've made sure you have all the documentation to get you through any awkward situation. The children are aged three to fourteen and your job is to get them onto the train, then a bus at Dordrecht, and you will have instructions on who will meet you at your destination. It's all been arranged.' Frans spoke briskly as he moved over to his desk and picked up a folder; he extracted two sheets of paper, one bearing an official stamp. 'This is as good as the real thing. Show this and I guarantee you won't have any trouble from the Gestapo. It states that the Jewish children in your care have an infectious disease and that you are bringing them to a hospital in Dordrecht, where they will be put in isolation.'

Trudi carefully examined the falsified documents, eager to commit the details to memory. 'Who will be coming along with me?' She lifted her head to look Frans in the eye.

Frans nodded, as if he'd been expecting her to ask. 'I've arranged for a reliable colleague from another group called Nils

Rutte, who will accompany you to the station and help you board the children onto the train. He'll be dressed in German officer's uniform and will accompany you to Dordrecht.'

'I see. And what happens then?'

'Once you reach Dordrecht, Nils will hand you over to Hans Timmerman – also very reliable – who knows the ropes and will escort you by bus to your destination. The children will of course not be going to any hospital. I've arranged everything personally, so there shouldn't be a problem. You'll be speaking German, of course. Are you happy about that?'

Trudi nodded. 'I can get by,' she said, unwilling to let on that she had basic schoolgirl German and had only the day before learnt a page of stock phrases off by heart in case she should be accosted. She knew she lacked the vocabulary to engage in a proper conversation with a native German speaker, but was determined not to let that deter her. If she was to play her part well, she would need to do so with conviction.

Turning her attention to the second sheet, she ran her eyes down the list of children's names. Twelve Jewish children entrusted to the care of a German Red Cross nurse. If the Gestapo decided to question her about what was written on this forged document, would she be able to convince them she was German and one of them? Pushing the thought away, she mouthed each name to herself. Each one believing they were on their way to a better life and unaware of the terrible alternative facing their parents. Bekkah, ten, Kees, eleven, Leo, fourteen... Trudi faltered when she came to Louisa and Rosy's names. Scanning the rest of the list, she discovered that at three years little Rosy was the youngest child by several years. Then came Louisa, aged seven. She simply couldn't allow herself to think how children this young would be able to cope with so much upheaval.

'When these children's parents found out they were being sent to Westerbork, they were desperate that their children shouldn't suffer the same fate. So they turned to us for help to get their children away from detection by the Germans and also out of harm's way should there be heavy bombing,' Frans explained. 'No one knows how bad the conditions are in the camp. What little information we do have is mixed. On arrival, it seems the prisoners are treated reasonably well and provided with food and medicines, but the worrying thing is the number who are not accounted for.'

Trudi felt an icy chill run through her as she thought about Maria and Hans travelling towards an uncertain future. Then she remembered something she had read. '*De Waarheid* has been reporting on what happens after Westerbork. It believes it's being turned into a transit camp for concentration camps in Germany, Poland and Czechoslovakia. Oh, Frans, we can only hope that Maria and Hans will be spared.' Pulling herself together, she asked when she would be meeting Nils.

'Tomorrow morning, go to Amsterdam Central Station at seven a.m. Nils will be waiting with the children under the clock. They have all been briefed that a German nurse will be accompanying them, so you must not give any indication that you know any of the children. Only the Friedman children know who you are and they have been asked not to interact with you. I know this is hard, but you must treat the children as if you've never met them before. Remember you are a German nurse, so you will need to be strict with them.'

Trudi blinked back tears as she thought of sweet, curly-haired, lively Rosy and solemn-faced yet tender-hearted Louisa, who took her responsibilities as an older sister so seriously. In their short lives, they had already suffered so much. It seemed so unfair that children so young should be expected to play this terrible game. Trudi dreaded having to pretend she didn't know them. Worse, she couldn't imagine ever having to discipline them.

Frans was waiting.

Biting down on her lip, she nodded. 'You can rely on me,' she said, knowing these were the words he wanted to hear. Maria's last words echoed in her head: *I know you will take good care of our babies. Please make sure they don't come to any harm.*

THIRTY

Trudi hurried towards the striking red-brick Gothic facade with its twin turrets bearing identical clocks that was the entrance to the imposing building housing Amsterdam Central Station. She glanced from one to the other clock and saw she was half an hour early. Relaxing her stride, she walked through the swing doors into the cavernous entrance hall surrounded by floor-to-ceiling arches under an ornately carved wooden ceiling. But Trudi was not in the mood for admiring this architectural gem as she made for the large clock suspended from the ceiling and positioned herself directly under it. It was ten minutes to seven.

In her right hand she clutched a small holdall containing the bare minimum for what was expected to be a short trip. Frans was confident that she would be back home within two to three days. He had also supplied her with a small medical kit whose contents she had studied carefully and committed to memory. She may not have been a nurse, but the responsibility of looking after such a large group of children weighed heavily upon her, especially if a medical emergency should arise. Plus, she wanted to be prepared to explain herself if she was interrogated. Everything Frida had told her about the hospital, her expertise and long evenings spent helping her study suddenly came in very useful. She thought of her sister, who had been so busy recently, and wondered how she was coping. How she longed to be with her, to go back to the old days before the war when they would cycle together along the canals with their mother, stopping to pick flowers and enjoying the warm sun on their faces. But Frida was occupied now with more important things, and she was sure her sister could take care of herself. She was relying on Frans to give Frida some resistance work of her own.

She smoothed her apron, and let her eyes dart back and forth, observing the growing number of people arriving to catch an early-morning train. A couple of German soldiers arrived and positioned themselves by the doors, but they seemed more interested in chatting to one another than the people milling around them.

Time dragged; Trudi kept glancing up at the clock to watch the second hand creep forward. Her palms grew damp as she considered possible doom-laden scenarios and what she would do if her charges failed to turn up.

Then, at two minutes to seven, the column of children trooped through the doors, some wearily dragging their feet, and all distinguished by a large yellow star stitched to their coats. At the head of the group was a fresh-faced young man in German uniform, holding Rosy by the hand. He saluted the soldiers at the door with a curt 'Heil Hitler,' before walking rapidly towards Trudi, who composed her features into a stern expression. She looked round the group and caught sight of Louisa halfway back. Louisa stared purposefully at her feet, biting her lip, before stealing a glance back at Trudi, who gave her a secret wink. Louisa quickly looked away, and Trudi was gladdened to see her smile. She longed to hug her, but it simply wasn't possible under the gaze of the German military close by.

'*Guten morgen*, Herr Rutte,' said Trudi in a clipped, no-nonsense voice, as he brought the line of children to a halt.

He returned her greeting and moved closer to whisper to her in Dutch. Rosy stood between them and Trudi sensed she was gazing up at her. She forced herself to remember Frans's instructions to play the part of the strict German nurse, but couldn't stop herself from glancing down at Rosy, who was clutching her toy rabbit. Trudi gave her the briefest of smiles.

'We've arranged for you to have a carriage to yourselves. I'll come as far as the platform and see you onto the train,' said Nils in an officious voice.

'But I thought you would be making this journey with us,' said Trudi, sudden panic rising up in her chest. 'That's what Frans told me.'

Nils didn't quite meet her eye as he replied. 'There's been a change of plan. I'm needed elsewhere. It's not far to Dordrecht and it's very early, so I'm sure you won't be bothered by anyone.'

'Mevrouw, can I please use the toilet?' A girl with short auburn hair and hazel eyes looked pleadingly up at Trudi.

'Can't you wait until we're on the train? It won't be long,' said Trudi, remembering to speak with a German accent.

'But I need to go now,' whined the girl. Another child piped up that she needed to go as well, then another.

'Quiet! Do you want to draw attention to yourselves? Now behave and stand in line while I check your names against my list.' Trudi's heart knocked against her ribs. Her instincts were to comfort these children, probable orphans, who knew as little about what the future held as she did. To her relief, they all did as they were told and she was able to call out their names without further ado.

Nils helped shepherd the children to the correct platform and their designated carriage. A sign had been attached to the outside that read: RESERVED FOR THE WEHRMACHT: TRANSPORT OF PATIENTS. Trudi was momentarily consoled, believing that once they were on board no German would want to come into contact with children carrying an infectious disease.

Nils seemed agitated as he walked down the line and shouted to the children to hurry up and get on the train. Several, including Rosy, began to cry. Trudi couldn't stop herself from going to Rosy and picking her up to console her. 'This one is too small to board by herself,' she said over her shoulder to Nils. He answered her with a disapproving stare.

They all embarked with moments to spare. As Trudi was ushering the children to their seats, she heard the march of boots along the platform and raised German voices outside the carriage window. 'Settle down, children,' she said as evenly as she could and went over to the window to see what the commotion was all about.

Several carriages along, Nils stood on the platform addressing a group of German officers who were making forceful hand gestures in the direction of Trudi's carriage. Trudi was relieved to see Nils stand his ground. She was unable to make out what they were saying, but she hoped that he could hold them off long enough for the train to depart. One of the children asked for the toilet again, but Trudi was distracted by a shrill whistle followed by a sudden jolt, which almost caused her to lose her balance.

Outside the window, plumes of black smoke billowed up, briefly obliterating the sight of Nils and the Germans. Trudi prayed the Germans hadn't boarded the train at the last moment. Then, as the train creaked and shuddered away from the station, the smoke cleared to reveal the shape of another man striding purposefully away from Nils, who was staring after him. Trudi peered more closely – the blond hair, a little longer than she remembered, now touching the upturned collar of his coat – surely it couldn't be Sem? She craned her head for a better view, but it was too late. The train had already cleared the platform and was snaking its way towards the suburbs.

Trudi couldn't afford to dwell on who the man might or might not have been, so she took her seat and turned to watch the carriage door, fully expecting a German soldier to appear at any minute to demand what she was up to with a group of children all prominently displaying the yellow star on their clothing. She reached down for her holdall, her hands shaking as she opened it and felt inside for the documents Frans had supplied her with. Although she'd checked it many times before leaving the house, she again scanned the details on the falsified certificate that would be her only possible escape from almost certain arrest.

The train rocked and squealed its way past tall, dingy-looking houses with narrow gardens that bordered the railway line. When it entered a tunnel everything went black and several of the children began to cry. Trudi put an arm round Rosy and felt her small body tremble against her chest.

No more than a few seconds could have passed before they were clear of the tunnel and the welcome sight of green fields signified that they were well clear of the city centre. Only then was Trudi able to calm her nerves.

But the children were growing restless. She accompanied several of them to the toilet and, when she returned, found the older boys were arguing over who should have the window seat. Louisa lifted Rosy on her lap; she was sniffing quietly, and several other children looked close to tears. Trudi's heart went out to these poor souls and she knew she could not keep up this pretence of the stern German nurse any longer. She decided then and there to tell the children who she really was and where she was taking them.

'Listen carefully to me, children,' she began, this time speaking without the fake German accent. 'I want you to know that I am Dutch, just like you, and that you will be safe with me. I'm not German, nor do I work for the Germans, so you can trust me. But what I have to say next is important. If anyone asks you where you are going you must tell them that you are ill and are going to a special hospital in Dordrecht. The truth is that I am taking you to a safe place. Before that can happen, I have to make the Germans believe that I'm in charge. I may have to shout at you or even raise my hand if any of you misbehave. But I want you to know that I don't mean it.'

No one spoke, and the older children were eyeing her suspiciously. Leo, the oldest boy, spoke up. 'Why should we believe you? We were told you're a *mof,* just like the one you who brought us to the station.' He sat with his arms folded across his chest. His eyes flashed defiantly at her.

The other children remained quiet. Trudi was dismayed to see distrust written over all their faces, and realised that she hadn't won them over. 'I can only tell you the truth, and I will do all I can to bring you to safety.' She looked down at Rosy, who refused to meet her eye and instead looked to Louisa for reassurance, before putting her thumb in her mouth and fingering her toy rabbit.

At that moment, there was a high-pitched squealing of brakes and the train slowed to a grinding halt. Trudi frowned, wondering what was going on, and saw that the train had stopped at a station she didn't recognise. The door to their carriage slid open and a guard in a hurry came walking through.

'Change here for Dordrecht. Opposite platform,' he said twice before disappearing through the door at the other end of the carriage.

'Gather your things together, children. We need to get off quickly,' said Trudi, trying hard to hide her confusion. Neither Frans nor Nils had mentioned anything about changing trains. She lifted Rosy onto her right hip and picked up her holdall. When everyone was off the train she counted heads, and was about to tell the group to start walking when she noticed the WEHRMACHT sign still attached to the side of the carriage. She quickly removed it and tucked it under her arm.

'Rosy, be a good girl, will you, and hold Louisa's hand.'

Rosy stiffened and clung more tightly to Trudi.

'Please Rosy. Do it for Tante Trudi,' she whispered. She had to prise the toddler's fingers from her arm, but at least she wasn't crying.

Turning to the others, she cried, 'Hurry up, children, or the train will leave without us. *Schnell!*'

They all trooped off after her, some dragging their feet. She turned to see that Rosy had fallen behind, unable to keep up with the others.

'Come on, hurry up!' said Trudi in German, hating herself for having to reprimand the little girl she knew so well. 'Take hold of Louisa's hand,' she whispered more kindly.

Finally, they boarded the train. Trudi was looking for somewhere to attach the sign just as the whistle blew and the train began to inch forward. She abandoned the idea and managed to jump onto the step just before it pulled away.

It was only when they were all settled into their seats that Trudi could breathe freely. Soon, the rocking motion of the train sent several children to sleep and even Leo sat with his eyes closed. Briefly, Trudi felt her eyelids droop, but moments later her eyes flew open at the sound of the carriage door sliding open. Two tall Germans in uniform and the standard shiny knee-length black boots stood staring directly at her. '*Heil Hitler!*' they barked in unison.

'Children, get up! All of you!' she yelled, rising to her feet. '*Heil Hitler!*' Her heart hammered in her chest as she raised her arm in a stiff salute. Never had she ever thought she would perform this vile gesture, let alone force innocent young children to follow suit.

All the children, bar Leo, shuffled to their feet, naked fear written all over their faces. One by one they saluted the soldiers, but Leo remained seated, his arms folded in defiance.

'Show some respect, will you?' Trudi spoke as calmly as she

could. Surely he could understand he was putting them all in danger by not saluting?

Still Leo sat with a smirk on his face and refused to move.

Her heart raced as she went to stand over him, willing him to comply. If he didn't, the Germans would be sure to question her authority and maybe even mete out their own worse punishment. She had to act quickly to defuse the situation. Before she could give it further thought, she slapped Leo on the cheek. The sound of the blow, like the crack of a whip, resonated through the whole carriage. There was a shocked silence. Instantly, she regretted her action, but she knew that if she were to get these Germans to leave them alone she had to keep up the pretence till they had gone. Inwardly cringing, she told herself that she was a German nurse with a job to do and Leo was a disrespectful Jewish boy.

'Now will you behave.'

Tears filled the boy's eyes as he got to his feet. Clutching the side of his face, he gave a half-hearted salute, but he refused to utter the words he was expected to say.

There was nothing more she could do, so she turned towards the two officers, who were waiting for her to hand over the papers. They passed them one to the other, before handing them back to her with a smile and a bow. 'All in order. Keep up the good work, *Fräulein*,' said the more senior of the two with a wink. He reached into his jacket pocket and, bringing out a cigarette case, handed her a cigarette. Trudi wanted to do nothing more than throw it in their faces, but she didn't. Instead, she accepted it and tucked it in the pocket of her apron. She didn't smoke, nor did she intend to start; she vowed never to even touch a cigarette again.

THIRTY-ONE

'I'm so very sorry. I hope you understand I had to do that,' said Trudi, as soon as the officers had gone. She noticed that the whole side of Leo's face had turned bright red. She wanted to comfort him by putting an arm round him, but desisted due to the waves of hostility she could feel rising off him. He stared back at her, hatred in his eyes, refusing to reply. But she persisted and took him to one side so she could better explain her actions.

'It may not seem like it, but the reason I hit you was that I was trying to protect you. I needed you to comply because if the Germans had found out I wasn't one of them and was helping you escape they would have shown no mercy. They would have turned the whole lot of us in. Now do you understand?'

Leo listened without saying anything, but she noticed his expression soften a little, and then he gave a small nod.

Fortunately, it was only a few minutes until the train arrived at Dordrecht station, where Trudi needed to have her wits about her for the next stage of their journey. *Please let Hans Timmerman be waiting for us*, she prayed silently to herself.

She led the group off the train and told them to wait until the rest of the passengers had disembarked and dispersed through the station. A few people looked in their direction, but most averted their gaze from the sight of the group congregating on the platform. Trudi wanted to call out to say that it wasn't what they thought and nor was she, but of course she didn't. She was terrified of drawing attention to them all. Lifting her chin, she looked over the heads of the children, and saw two men in German uniform striding towards her. For a split second she thought one of them was Sem, and her heart gave a painful jolt. Had he been on the same train after all? And what on earth was he doing here, dressed up in German uniform? But as the men drew closer she saw, to her immense relief, she'd been mistaken – the tall blond-haired man's features were more square, more solid than Sem's. He was also less attractive...

What's wrong with you? Pull yourself together, Trudi told herself sternly, bracing herself for an interrogation. In her head, she quickly ran through the German words she had learnt to say that she was charged with escorting infectious Jewish children to the hospital in Dordrecht.

'Hans Timmerman.' The man who didn't resemble Sem grinned broadly and held out his hand. 'And this is my brother, Gustaaf,' he said, with a nod to the blond man at his side. 'He's learning the ropes.'

'Thank goodness you came,' said Trudi, shaking his hand and glancing from Gustaaf back to Hans. 'Frans told me you'll be with me now for the rest of the journey and handover. Is that right?'

'Let's get out of the station, where I can talk to you about what happens next,' said Hans evasively.

Trudi felt a chill run through her as she turned to the children, some of whom were murmuring among themselves. She glanced at Leo, who was chatting to his friend Kees and seemed to have forgotten about the earlier incident, then turned her attention back to Hans. Surely he couldn't have come to the station just to tell her that she had to complete the journey alone?

Hans walked the group out onto the station concourse, where he told his brother to take up the rear, so he could walk with Trudi at the front. 'I'm taking you to the Park Merwestein. It's not far and the children can rest there while I give you your instructions about what happens next.'

Once they were in the park, the children visibly relaxed. They separated into small groups and sank down on the grass. The day had warmed up, and Trudi helped the young ones off with their thick coats. Hans brought out some apples from his ruck-sack and sat on the ground before carefully cutting each one into quarters and handing them round. Trudi wished she had thought of bringing food too. But how was she to know that what was meant to be a short train journey would be anything but?

Hans instructed his brother to keep watch over the group while he took Trudi over to a bench next to a deserted bandstand.

'I suggest we stay in the park and let the children rest before they move on. I'm afraid this next part of the journey is going to be anything but easy.' He brought out a map, unfolded it and spread it across his knees. 'This is where we are.' He placed his forefinger on a cross marked on the map, then ran it all the way down to the bottom, ending at a river. Trudi had no idea of the distance this represented, but she noticed a large area in the centre that had no marked paths or roads.

'What is that?' she asked, pointing at what looked like a wasteland. It was deep in the countryside. There were no build-ings around it, no houses or farms.

Hans gave her a quick glance and pursed his lips. 'You are

going to have to traverse a minefield. I'm afraid it's the only way you can reach the river from here. You'll find a boat, which you will need to row across to the other side. You can shelter on the riverbank and get some sleep. You'll need to wait until first light before attempting to cross. You'll find four oars, so I suggest you choose three older children to help you. Once across, you'll be met by Mr Janssen, the local farmer. He's bringing his tractor and trailer and will take you all to his farm. After that, I'm afraid I have no further instructions.'

Trudi heard only half of what he said. She shook her head vigorously. 'No. I'm not prepared to lead twelve children across anything as dangerous as a minefield. Who on earth decided that?'

'I can't say,' Hans said evasively. 'But there's no other way through. See here.' He pointed to a dotted line and said that it represented a barbed-wire fence and that the way was well marked. Some way along, a section of the fence had been cut by members of the resistance, he assured her. 'Around here,' he said, tracing a vague circle with his finger on the map, 'there is a gap for you to crawl through. I can't say exactly where, but I'm sure it will be obvious to you when you see it.'

Baffled, Trudi stared at him. 'And why aren't you coming to show us the way?'

Hans looked around him and leant towards her so he could whisper against her ear. 'There's a big operation tonight to blow up a stretch of railway south of here. Gustaaf and I are on our way there now and will meet the others at dusk. The plan is to sabotage a German goods train – if we get the timings right it should distract the Germans from your escape.' He folded the map along its creases and handed it to Trudi. 'All yours now. Oh, and here's a torch. You'll need it once it gets too dark – but use it sparingly. You don't want to attract *moffen's* attention, else they'll find you with their searchlights.'

Trudi had no choice but to accept the folded map and torch.

If she refused, she knew she would be putting the children's lives at more risk than they were already. She had no other plan, nowhere else to take them to. Hans gave her the remaining apples and a bar of chocolate 'for emergencies'. As she watched the two men walk away, she felt an overwhelming sense of abandonment. Was she really capable of carrying out such a perilous mission?

I knew I could rely on you. Words spoken by Frans after she had first saved Rosy and Louisa from almost certain capture by the Germans. She glanced over at Louisa, who was playing a quiet game with Rosy. Rosy was totally absorbed and the bubble of a giggle erupted from her. Trudi took a deep breath, knowing she would need to muster all her courage if she was to save these dear children again.

THIRTY-TWO

In a corner of the park was a water fountain and the children rushed towards it, pushing and shoving each other to get their turn. Trudi had to raise her voice to get them to behave, but felt she'd already lost her authority since admitting she wasn't the fierce German nurse she'd pretended to be. If this is how things were now, what would it be like once they were faced with crossing the minefield, she thought anxiously. How would she know which way to go? The very idea of twelve children and herself traversing a terrain littered with unexploded bombs terrified her, but she knew it was up to her to remain calm if she was to have any chance of keeping the children under control.

The children seemed a lot happier once they had all had their fill of water. Trudi led them over to a patch of grass where she got them all to sit down so she could tell them what would happen next.

'When we leave the park, we will walk a little way out of town into the countryside. We will come to a big field, which may take some time to get across, but on the other side we'll find somewhere to sleep for the night next to a river. In the morning, we will board a boat to take us to the other side. There we will be met by a kind gentleman who will drive us to the houses, where you can rest and enjoy a proper meal.'

The auburn-haired girl put her hand up. 'How far is it? I'm tired now,' she said.

'So am I. It's not fair. I want to go home,' another piped up in a whiny voice.

'Yeah, why should we do as you say? It sounds like a mad idea,' said Leo, looking to others for support.

'I agree it's a mad idea. If I had a better one, I would let you know.' Trudi was on the verge of losing her temper with him again, but this seemed to shut him up. 'This is what's been arranged and I suggest that we all help each other. The older ones can help the younger ones. Leo, when we leave, would you please bring up the rear and call out if anyone falls behind?' She waited, half-expecting him to object, but instead he jumped up with a broad grin on his face.

'C'mon! Let's get going,' he said, and went to pull his friend Kees to his feet. 'Kees, stay back with me... it'll be fun.'

'This isn't a game.' Trudi spoke sternly. 'We need to get to the river by nightfall or risk being caught by the Germans. It's a serious matter. Do you understand?'

Chastened, Leo and Kees both nodded.

'Good; now, everyone find a partner to walk with. No one is to be left out.'

At first, it was easy going walking through the streets of Dordrecht, although Trudi did worry how conspicuous a line of twelve children wearing yellow stars must look to any passers-by. Only one elderly man accosted her and asked her where she was going. When she replied in German, he spat on the ground and turned away, muttering to himself.

Once they were out of the built-up area and walking along an empty road between two ploughed fields, she was able to breathe again. She kept glancing at the children to make sure they were all right. They were so quiet; no one spoke a word as they concentrated on putting one foot in front of the other. She suspected they were too exhausted to complain.

Every so often, Trudi needed to stop to consult the map, but she could see no sign of the track that was meant to lead them to the field with the barbed wire. At one point, she thought they must have walked too far, and wished she had another adult with her to help work out where to go. Her relief was over-whelming when eventually she discovered the path, overgrown with weeds and snaking off to the left. It was then that some of the children began to cry.

'I promise it won't be long now,' she said in as bright a voice as she could muster, though she was aware that the journey had already taken them far longer than she'd anticipated. It would soon be dusk and they would be unable to see their way. She needed to keep their spirits up. 'All we need to do is get to the wire fence at the end of this path. I'll go first. If those right behind me trample down the weeds as we go it'll make it easier for the rest of us.'

Surprisingly, Leo offered to help, and brought out a small penknife to cut back the taller weeds. She decided to let him lead the way and went to the back to help the younger ones, who were feeling cold and scared and needed her reassurance.

Despite Leo's best efforts to hack back the undergrowth, they made slow progress. At one point the path petered out, but Trudi was able to get them back on track thanks to the map. She was grateful for the time her father had spent explaining maps to her and Frida on the long walks he liked to take them on in the summer holidays.

At last they arrived at the tangled barbed wire, which stretched as far as the eye could see. Its spikes stuck out in all directions, sharp and forbidding, and Trudi was faced with her next dilemma: which way should she turn in order to find where it had been cut? Aware that she needed to make a decision, she blindly chose to go left. It was the right choice – minutes later she saw a kink in the rolls of barbed wire.

'Stop here. I think I've found the way through.' She knelt down and saw where the wire had been severed and crudely put back to hide the gap. Carefully, she lifted a piece of wire to one side, revealing what looked like a narrow tunnel through into the field beyond. *The minefield*, she mouthed to herself, but she wasn't ready to tell the children this yet.

'Everyone get down on their hands and knees and stay as close to the ground as you can. Then wriggle through. It's only a few yards. Once you get to the other side, don't go anywhere until we've all made it through. Do you understand?'

No one replied, but she could tell from the resignation in their eyes that they would do anything she asked. They were beyond fear, beyond exhaustion, as was she, but they were still looking to her to get them out of this place.

'Leo, are you happy to go first?' she asked hopefully, knowing he was the only one she could rely on to give her any support.

Leo gave a single nod, but she could see his earlier bravado had left him.

'Good. I'll be right behind you and ready to tell each of you when it's safe to set off.'

Miraculously, they all managed to get through the frighteningly dark tunnel without any mishaps; but Trudi's relief was short-lived. Rosy started to cry and this set several others off. Trudi dug around in her holdall and found the chocolate; she unwrapped it and handed a square to each child. The crying stopped immediately and there were even a few smiles. Trudi hurriedly put the remains of the chocolate away, aware she might need to bribe them again before too long.

There was still just enough light left in the sky to see that they had arrived in what looked like a pleasant meadow covered in yellow flowers. It was alive with bees and insects and delicate blue butterflies. It was such a peaceful scene, but Trudi knew well enough what horrors lay beneath the surface.

She heaved in a breath, before telling them how dangerous the next part of their journey would be. 'We have to get across this field as carefully as possible. If you do exactly as I tell you, no one will come to any harm. That means crawling on your tummies the whole way to the other side. I will lead the way and each of you will follow behind me in single file. Louisa, have Rosy in front of you – I know you can do it. And Leo, I want you at the back this time. Make sure that everyone stays close together.' Trudi realised her heart was knocking painfully against her ribs, but she managed to keep calm in the face of this extreme danger.

But she hadn't appreciated how vast the field was. Progress was painfully slow as the group shuffled forward, inch by inch. Darkness set in quickly and Trudi soon needed to use her torch to show the way. Somehow she managed to hold it in her mouth, allowing her to keep her hands free. It wasn't much help, as the beam was weak and bobbed around so much that she was unable to see more than a few inches ahead of her. Slowly, slowly, she edged forward by putting first her left hand down, then her right, left knee, right and so on. It was painful going across the rough ground with all the small sharp stones and plants that grazed their arms and legs, but she moved as many as she could so the children wouldn't meet them, and if she missed any she didn't hear one complaint. She couldn't afford to look back, so had to rely on listening to the sounds of shuffling and breathing behind her, and hope that Leo was keeping up the rear.

They must have been no more than a third of the way across when it happened, the thing Trudi had dreaded the moment she set foot on the minefield. Not an explosion – she had managed to put that out of her mind – but a wide sweeping searchlight that appeared from somewhere over the town. To her dismay, she realised that in such a wide-open space as this there would be little chance of not being seen.

'Heads down and don't move!' she cried out, just as a beam bounced over the ground inches from where they lay. Her whole body went rigid as she watched it swoop in large arcs across the meadow, seeking out its target. Had someone seen them and reported them to the Germans? But who? The old man who'd spat his disgust at them, or even Hans, or Gustaaf, who looked so eerily like Sem? No, it must be pure coincidence that the Germans had started up right now. These thoughts and more swirled through her head, till she reasoned that it was probably nothing more than it was now nightfall, and this display probably happened every night. Even so, now was not the time for complacency. She raised her head and tried to see the way ahead across the black field – she didn't dare switch her torch back on.

Time passed, but she had no idea how long, as they lay flat on their stomachs, cold seeping through their clothing from the earth below them. Each time a bright beam came close, she held her breath, until gradually the searchlights moved away from their field and could be seen targeting another area to their left.

Trudi knew she had to act now, and fast. She turned to the children, silent dark shapes huddled behind her in a row, unmoving and barely visible to the naked eye.

'We should be safe to move off now,' she whispered urgently. 'We need to keep going just as we were, slowly and carefully. Is everyone all right to carry on?' She couldn't see their faces and worried about the fact that they all seemed so acquiescent. Was Rosy really fine back there with Louisa? Where was the fight she'd seen in Leo at the start of all this?

'Leo. Are you there?' she called.

'Yes, I'm here,' came his muffled voice.

'Good. Let's go.'

She began to move off slowly again, occasionally checking over her shoulder that the group was still with her.

One hand, one foot, and the next, and the next.

Occasionally she flashed the torch on briefly, and kept whispering words of encouragement.

All at once she caught a whiff of river water, and the gentle sound of water sloshing against the side of a boat. She raised her head and could just make out its dark shape right in front of her. Quickly snapping on her torch, she saw it more clearly, the large wooden rowing boat that would take them across the river to safety.

She let out a shuddery breath as she glanced back and saw that the children were right behind her.

They had traversed the minefield without incident. They had made it.

THIRTY-THREE

It was a short distance from the edge of the minefield across scrubland to the riverbank, where the drooping branches of a row of willow trees would provide safe cover for the night. It was the best Trudi could find, and she helped the children get comfortable by folding their scarves or sweaters for pillows and coats for makeshift blankets. Thankfully it was a calm, mild night. No one complained about the lack of food or drink, as they were all dog-tired after their exertions, though Trudi reiterated her promise that the morning would see them get to safety, warmth and a good meal.

For a long time, she sat clasping her knees in the shelter of a willow tree. The tension she'd been holding in her body gradually began to ebb away and tears trickled down her cheeks.

'Mevrouw, are you all right?'

Trudi turned her head to see Leo standing over her and staring at her with concern.

'Yes of course,' she said, quickly brushing away her tears. 'Aren't you able to sleep?' She glanced over at the other children, who lay in deep slumber. Rosy she could see, was curled into the crook of her sister's arm.

Leo came and sat beside Trudi and hugged his knees. She gave him a smile, grateful for his company. 'Thank you for what you did back there.' She spoke in a low voice so as not to disturb the others. 'I really couldn't have done it alone. It can't have been easy keeping calm under pressure. You've shown yourself to be more mature than your years.' She reached out to give him a consoling pat on the arm, but he flinched and turned his face away from her. 'If it's about me slapping you, I apologise.' She hated herself for upsetting this young boy who seemed so vulnerable.

He didn't respond, just pulled his knees more tightly to his chest. And then she heard him take several shaky sniffs. 'I miss my mum and dad,' he said at last, with tears in his voice.

Still sniffing, he turned to face her, but it was too dark to read his expression. 'Do you think I'll ever see them again?' he said, sounding like a little boy.

'I don't know,' she said truthfully and let out a long breath. 'Do you want to talk about it?'

She thought she saw him nod, but couldn't be sure, so she waited until he was ready.

'Today is my mum's birthday. We always have a big cele-bration with my aunt and uncle and cousins. The girls – Kitty and Lien are twins – are a year younger than me. We've always celebrated birthdays together for as long as I can remember. My Aunt Bibi bakes wonderful cakes and my Uncle Isaac is always telling jokes and getting the family to play games.' Trudi smiled at him and he smiled back happily, lost in his memories. 'And when it gets dark, Dad gets his guitar out and we all go out in the garden and sing songs around the bonfire. Not always Jewish songs. Mum knows lots of songs from the musicals. She and Dad used to go to the theatre a lot before the war.' Leo let out a weary sigh. 'I bought Mum a present just before I knew I'd be going away, but I don't expect I'll get to give it to her now.' He paused and the silence hung heavy between them, interrupted only by the occasional sniff. 'It was a tiny bluebird brooch with a sparkly eye and was all I could afford,' he said with tears in his voice. 'As soon as I saw it in the window of the jewellers I knew she'd love it. She and Dad were taken before I had a chance to give it to her.'

'And you... where were you and the girls?'

'Kitty and Lien have gone to Aunt Bibi and Uncle Isaac's, who live in the Veluwe. But they didn't have enough space for me, so I was sent to a family in the Kennemer dunes. They didn't tell me why I was going and that was wrong of them. I'm old enough to know and they treated me like a child.' He rested his elbows on his knees, so he could lean his head in his hands.

'They must have been so worried about you and wanted to act quickly to keep you safe.'

Leo made a scoffing sound. 'They could have told me. Anyway, nowhere's safe anymore. I can see that now.'

'No. I suppose you're right. But I do know that as long as we keep moving, we have a chance to avoid capture by the Germans.'

'Do you really believe that?' He huffed out a breath.

Trudi was dismayed to see him so deflated after he'd shown so much courage. She was determined to try to get him on her side again, not only for his sake but for hers. 'Can I ask you to help me one last time? We need to get the children onto the boat and row them to the opposite bank to safety. Have you ever rowed a boat?'

Leo didn't answer at first, and she dreaded hearing him refuse her request. For a while, they both gazed towards the dark shape of the boat. Briefly, a cloud moved away from the moon and they were able to see it more clearly. It was moored a little way away from where they sat – it looked large and solid enough. A chill ran through her as she considered whether it would hold all twelve children and herself.

'No, I've never rowed. But it can't be too hard, can it?' Leo turned his head and gave her the hint of a smile.

'Thank you,' said Trudi, sighing quietly to herself, though the thought of being in command of a rowing boat with so many children terrified her. She would simply have to do it. She switched her torch on so she could check the time on her watch, then off again. 'We should rest a while. Go and lie down with the others. I'll keep watch.'

She sat clasping her knees to her chest for a long while, listening for any sounds apart from the occasional splash of water against the boat, and pondered how they would manage to cross the river unnoticed. There were four oars, she remembered Hans telling her, and that meant she would need to ask two other children as well as Leo to row them across to safety.

THIRTY-FOUR

The sky was still dark when Trudi was dragged from sleep by the sudden crackle of gunfire. It came from far off, back in the direction they had come. Holding her breath in the silence that came after, she waited for the gunfire to start up again. When it did, she knew she couldn't afford to wait a moment longer or else they would be discovered. She had to take her chances to navigate the broad river. She switched on her torch and consulted the map, working out how far it was to the opposite bank and safety. Then she went over to the children and began to shake them gently awake, one by one.

'Wake up, children. It's time for us to get onto the boat.' Some were so deeply asleep that it took her several goes to rouse them. Several jerked awake as if from a nightmare and began to cry. She comforted them as best she could, and decided now was the time to hand out the last of the chocolate to give them a bit of energy before their last big push. Trying to ignore the loud bursts of gunfire, which appeared to be intensifying, she made them all go behind the bushes to relieve themselves before doing so herself.

'Listen carefully, while I tell you what is about to happen. I need three of you to help me row us across the water. Leo, come here beside me. Kees too – you're big and strong.' She gave them what she hoped was an encouraging smile. She looked round the group and her eyes came to rest on Bekah, who was only ten. A slight girl with spindly arms and legs.

But the other children were simply too young to ask such a thing of them. 'Bekah, come next to me so we can row together.'

Bekah looked close to tears, but she didn't object. At that moment, a searchlight swooped in a high arc in the sky and landed on the minefield behind them. It was accompanied by the rat-a-tat-tat of gunfire, making several children jerk and cry out in fright. Anxiously, she scanned the opposite bank for signs of where it had come from, but whoever was shooting was well hidden from view.

'All right. Let's go,' Trudi said, pretending that everything that was happening around them was perfectly normal. She stood by with a helping hand and waited till they had all scrambled on board before passing Rosy into Louisa's waiting arms. Untying the rope that was attached to a metal ring on the riverbank, she threw it to Leo, who caught it, and gave her a reassuring nod. The boat rocked back and forth as she climbed on board. With gritted teeth, she took her place beside Bekah.

The oars were massive, much larger than she had imagined and surely too big for a child as small as Bekah to handle. But it was too late to worry about that now. Trudi leant across to position Bekah's oar in the metal holder screwed into the side of the boat. She gave the girl a reassuring smile, then glanced over her shoulder. 'Are you boys ready?' She was rewarded by two grins, and was relieved to see Leo looking happier. If only she too could regard this whole episode as a big adventure.

She looked up at the still-dark sky and wished they had some light to row by. No sooner had she thought it than the searchlight snapped on again and came swooping closer and closer. Bracing herself, she pushed off from the grassy bank with her oar, and the boat gently glided out into the channel.

'Take it slowly. Push your oar away from you, then pull back.' She didn't know if this was the right instruction, but she had to say something to keep her mind away from the terror that threatened to overwhelm her.

The boat rocked alarmingly from side to side and Bekah's oar made a fearful squealing sound as she tried pulling it towards her. Several children began to shriek in fright.

'Stop rowing for a moment,' Trudi cried out, though it was hardly necessary; they were barely moving. A sudden wind had whipped up and sent the boat twisting round in a circle of its own accord. Trudi hurriedly pulled a handkerchief from her apron and leant over Bekah to stuff it in between the oar and the holder. 'That should help. Let's try again,' she said calmly. Bekah was shaking with fear.

This time the four of them managed to heave the oars in unison and the boat righted itself and edged forward in the direction of the opposite bank. Trudi called out, 'One... Two... One... Two.'

Everything happened so fast that Trudi would later have difficulty remembering exactly what had caused the boat to capsize. One minute they were moving through the water and the next they were in it, fighting to stay afloat as gunfire spattered all around them.

'Help! Help!' Bekah cried out, as her slight body hit the water with a splash and went under. Trudi struggled to reach her by stretching out one hand, while grasping onto the side of the boat with the other. Then, without warning, a sharp pain shot up her arm and she saw blood stream down her arm and disperse into the water. Dismayed, she saw she'd been shot; but right now that was the least of her worries. Trying hard to ignore the pain, she managed to grab hold of Bekah round the waist and tried to haul her back on board, but her wounded arm hampered her attempts and the girl slipped from her grasp. At the edge of her vision, she saw Leo, then Kees, jump in the water, followed by several others, as the boat listed dangerously and threatened to go under. Louisa hung on, cowering in one corner, her arm shielding Rosy, who clung to her sister's waist. Trudi was torn between staying and helping the others, but decided they were safer in the boat than in the water. Pain searing through her arm, she crawled nearer Louisa, whose dark eyes were wide with terror. Rosy had hidden her face against Louisa's chest.

'Louisa. Please listen carefully. I need to get to the others. Please hold tight to Rosy and don't let go. I'll come back as soon as I can.' She waited for the tiny nod from Louisa before turning away to save those who couldn't swim. Then, gasping in a breath, she glimpsed Leo, swimming strongly on his back, one arm securing one of the younger children. And just beyond him, at the far bank, the shapes of several people calling out to hold on, that help was on its way – all were waving frantically. In all the confusion she thought she heard German, but couldn't be sure.

Suddenly someone on the bank appeared with a rope and was preparing to throw it across to Leo.

'Leo, swim to the rope,' Trudi shouted with all her might as she lowered herself into the black water. She didn't care if she was overheard by the attacking Germans. All that mattered was getting the children out of the water, and fast.

The crackle of gunshot became more intense and when she looked back, she saw the boat had capsized. All around children were screaming, panicking and thrashing to keep afloat. Once one child screamed, then another started up, and the fast-moving current was sweeping them all downstream. Several were flailing so vigorously that it was impossible to make out who was who. Trudi was a good swimmer, but the searing pain in her arm slowed her down in her efforts to reach the others.

Panic overwhelmed her as she realised the boat must have sunk with Louisa and Rosy still on board.

'Louisa, Rosy, where are you?' she repeated in panicky gasps, before a wave broke over her head. Before she knew it, she found herself sinking below the surface of the water, unable to draw breath. She could do nothing more as her body was buffeted by the current. She gave in to it, entering a dreamlike state where images of her mother, father and Frida flashed through her mind. They were smiling and laughing. She was sure she heard Piet's voice too, urging her to hang on...

When she broke free of the water's surface, spluttering and gulping in great lungfuls of air, she realised to her dismay that she had ended up close to where she had started. On the opposite riverbank where she should have been, Germans in uniform were running and firing in the air. From far off, she could still hear the children crying. 'Please let them be saved,' she cried desperately to herself, knowing she had failed them all.

And then she became aware of a faint cry coming from a thick clump of bulrushes nearby. With a strength she didn't realise she had, she swam towards it and could just make out the pale shape of an arm. With a gasp of dread, she realised it was one of the children. Treading water, her feet made contact with the river bottom and sank into the mud, but she made herself take long strides forward. With a huge effort, she pushed the tall stems aside – and there in front of her was Rosy, wide-eyed and trembling, up to her waist in water.

'Mama,' Rosy wailed in a tiny voice and held her dripping arms out to Trudi.

Trudi winced as pain shot through her arm as she attempted to take hold of the child. She managed to hide her pain with a smile as she lifted Rosy out of the water and held her tight. She kissed the top of her wet head over and over. 'You're safe,' she said in a voice thick with emotion.

From across the water the cries, shouts and gunfire

continued and Trudi knew it wasn't safe to move yet. If she were to reveal herself now, they would be a certain target for German bullets. 'We have to stay in the water a little longer,' she told Rosy in a whisper.

The tall bulrushes stood sentry and provided good cover, enabling them to creep closer to the riverbank and above the freezing waterline. But it was small solace, as the other children's cries and the spattering of gunfire on the water hadn't let up. Trudi could feel Rosy trembling with cold and fear against her; she had to do something to distract her. Then she hit on the idea of whispering stories she remembered her mother telling her and Frida at bedtime. These seemed to soothe her, and also briefly helped take Trudi's mind off the wound to her arm that she feared was a lot worse than she'd first realised. But she needed to find out what had happened to Louisa, even if it meant upsetting Rosy again.

'Rosy, when did you last see Louisa? Can you remember?'

Rosy looked doubtful, then shook her head.

'Louisa was in the boat with you. Did you both fall in?'

Rosy nodded. 'Louisa held my hand, but the water...' She made a sweeping gesture in front of her face with her arms. 'Too much. I lost her.'

'We'll find Louisa, don't you worry. She'll be with the other children on the other side of the river.'

Her eyes filling with tears, Rosy stared at Trudi, who had parted the reeds and was peering out at the river, which appeared remarkably calm after the chaos earlier. One end of the capsized boat stuck up in the air and Trudi could just make out that it was riddled with bullets. There was no sign of the children. She told herself to remain calm; she could only hope that they had all been pulled from the water to safety.

Then, as she turned back to attend to Rosy, a wave of nausea swept over her, so great that she almost lost consciousness. She bit down hard on her lip and viewed the bank she needed to crawl up in order to get out of the cold water. How would she manage when her injured arm was as good as useless? Her strength was ebbing away and it seemed almost impossible, but she knew she couldn't let on. Forcing herself to put her worries aside, she smiled at Rosy.

'Now if I lift you up, do you think you can crawl up there where it's dry?' She spoke with forced brightness, and was relieved when Rosy obliged. The effort it took her to lift Rosy to safety was enormous, but they made it up onto dry land. They were both wet through and she knew they would catch their deaths if they didn't start moving soon. They simply couldn't hang around any longer. Where to, she had no idea, but if they kept to the riverbank they must surely reach a path or a road leading towards houses, where she could seek help.

We have to keep going, she told herself firmly, fighting against the desire to lie down and rest. 'Rosy. It's time to go now. I'm going to find somewhere for us to stay and get you some breakfast, but we need to walk along the river for a while.'

'Where's Louisa?' said Rosy, gazing up into Trudi's face, her eyes dark with worry.

Trudi spoke softly. It was vital she didn't upset Rosy any more than she was already. 'That's what we're going to find out. Let's go.'

THIRTY-FIVE

The sky was beginning to lighten as Trudi held Rosy by the hand and they trudged along an indistinct path by the side of the river. The little girl was clearly finding it hard going. She kept crying from time to time, however much Trudi tried to soothe her, but there was no alternative to what they were doing – it was either this or the unthinkable: going back into the treacherous minefield and through the coils of razor wire. Trudi had no idea where she was heading. Every so often, she lifted Rosy up with her good arm, but it made her more conscious of the pain from her injured arm and slowed them down even further. Then, a smudge of orange appeared on the horizon. She put Rosy down so she could briefly rest.

'See how pretty the sky looks,' she said, pointing upwards. 'That means it's morning and we'll soon find somewhere warm and dry and have some breakfast.'

Sniffing softly, Rosy looked up through tear-filled eyes, but at least she had stopped crying.

'Listen,' said Trudi. 'Do you hear the birds? They're singing for their breakfast.'

Rosy gave a watery smile.

'Do you think you can walk a bit more now? We'll get there quicker if you do.' Trudi stooped to kiss her wet cheek. She was beyond exhaustion herself, but had to believe this was the right thing to do.

Rosy looked doubtful, but allowed Trudi to hold her hand. Trudi sang nursery rhymes to encourage her to walk in step beside her. When Rosy began to lag and drag her feet, she felt herself run out of options to distract her. She was getting weaker and the thought that she might die here on this path began to occupy her mind. But somehow she managed to keep smiling and chatting normally for Rosy's sake, even after she realised that her sleeve was soaked with blood.

'Let's sit down a minute and rest,' she said, feeling shaky.

While Rosy sat picking at a blade of grass, she turned away from her and rolled up her sleeve to investigate, gasping when she saw the extent of the wound. It was impossible to tell for sure, but from the pain she was experiencing she surmised a bullet must still be lodged deep in her arm. At least the bleeding had subsided; but as she reached into her pocket for her hand-kerchief, she remembered she'd surrendered it to Bekah when she needed help rowing. Resignedly, she scanned the area, but could see no sign of the path leading away from the river. She had no choice but to carry on as before.

The sun came up and warmed their backs. Ahead, the path widened a little and Trudi could make out a lane up ahead. *If I could just get Rosy to safety...* The words stuck in her head as she concentrated on putting one foot in front of the other. Once they had moved away from the river she felt renewed hope. She made herself remember the route so that she could get back to Louisa and the other children later. This thought spurred her on as she lifted Rosy up onto her good arm. After a short while she rounded a corner, and gasped in relief at the sight of a farmhouse right in front of her. 'Please God, let there be someone willing to help us,' she muttered under her breath, as she realised how desperate she was.

They were about to pass through the gate when Trudi noticed a black and white dog chained up in the yard. As soon as it caught sight of them, it leapt to its feet and barked frantically. Rosy let out a piercing yell and threw her arms round Trudi's neck.

The front door flew open and a burly-looking man wearing blue overalls and muddy clogs came striding out. He was brandishing a rifle. 'Don't move,' he shouted as he took aim.

Trudi gasped. 'No... please don't shoot. We... we need help.'

'Gert, what on earth is going on out there?' came a woman's voice from behind him. He lowered his rifle and stood aside as a short stocky woman wearing a faded floral apron came bustling through the door. 'Oh dear God, what do we have here? Is the little one injured?' She rushed to Trudi to take Rosy, whose eyes had grown round in fear. 'You're a nurse, aren't you?' The woman glanced at Trudi's uniform and Trudi decided it would be best to agree.

'Yes. My name is Trudi. We've come from Dordrecht—'

The woman stopped her in mid-sentence. 'But what's this?' she said, staring at Trudi's blood-soaked sleeve.

'I... I...' Trudi couldn't bring herself to say the words in front of Rosy, so allowed herself to be led inside, through a hallway cluttered with all kinds of paraphernalia, into a large warm kitchen, where a kettle was whistling softly on top of the stove.

'Come inside and warm yourselves. My name's Nettie,' the woman said kindly. 'Now, let's get you out of those wet things.' She pulled a chair close to the source of heat and started unbuttoning Rosy's damp coat. 'Gert, warm some milk for them both, will you?'

She took a towel from a rack beside the stove and wrapped Rosy in it, gently patting her, while speaking soothing words.

Gert did as he was told and placed two cups of warmed milk on the table; he nodded to Trudi to take one.

'So what brings you here?' he said in a gruff voice. '*Moffen*, was it?'

Trudi nodded and wondered if it was so obvious – but then why else would she be running along a country road at dawn? She realised she was trembling and wasn't certain if it was from the cold or the loss of blood. She lowered herself onto a chair beside Rosy and spoke in a hushed voice. 'We've come from Amsterdam. I had charge of a group of young Jewish children who were on their way to foster homes after their parents were taken by the Germans. The plan was for me to dress up as a German nurse and pretend they were all infectious so we wouldn't get stopped or arrested. We had to cross a minefield and managed that, but the plan fell apart when we arrived at the river we were meant to cross. The Germans turned up and began shooting and the rowing boat sank. It was chaos, and I'm afraid I don't know what happened to the other children, all except Rosy here. Her sister, Louisa, I'm afraid...' She glanced at Rosy, expecting her to start crying again at the mention of Louisa's name, but the child was distracted by a pile of buttons Nettie had laid out on the table for her to play with.

'Where is the girl now?' said Nettie, turning to help Rosy drink her milk.

Trudi took a deep breath. The effort of talking had taken it out of her and her voice came out high and trembling as she said, 'I don't know. The only child I found was Rosy here, who must have been swept by the current into the reeds. I can only hope that her sister made it out of the water with the others onto the opposite bank. The place was swarming with Germans and I fear the worst. Mevrouw, would you please look after Rosy while I go back to look for Louisa? She'll be so frightened on her own.'

'Of course the little one can stay here. But you don't look to be in any fit state to go anywhere. We'll need to see to that arm of yours. Let Gert take a look at it, while I find you something dry to wear.'

Trudi acquiesced by nodding weakly.

Nettie went off into the scullery, where Trudi could hear her moving about. Trudi drank down her cup of milk and found it made her feel slightly better. When Rosy started to whimper, she lifted her onto her lap.

'If you can tell me whereabouts on the river the boat sank, I can drive you there in the van and we can make some enquiries,' said Gert.

'Would you?' said Trudi gratefully, then realised she had no idea how to describe the place. It had been so dark when she'd scrambled up onto the bank. All she could remember was the overgrown path leading to the minefield, so that's what she told him.

Gert remained silent for a bit, before saying, 'I know that minefield. When we were told about it, it caused an uproar in the community. We couldn't believe the Germans could be so callous, but there's not a thing anyone can do about it. Except avoid it. Fortunately, there have been no casualties. Frankly, you were very lucky you survived.'

'If I'd known how dangerous it would be, I'd never have taken all those children across. And I had no idea that the *moffen* would be waiting on the other side of the river. It all happened so quickly.' Trudi closed her eyes and remembered how Leo had overcome his resentment towards her and pulled his weight without any thought for his own safety. How trusting and brave he'd turned out to be, when he must have been hurting so much after losing his whole family. Where was he now? And what had happened to the rest of the children? It was small comfort that she had found Rosy in the rushes, knowing that the others might have perished.

She suddenly remembered something. 'The boat will still

be visible in the river where it sank. I found Rosy in the rushes right opposite the boat and at the side of the minefield.'

Gert looked thoughtful, and she realised he was looking with concern at her blood-soaked sleeve. 'Let me take a look at that now.'

Trudi put Rosy back on her chair and pulled up her sleeve to reveal the nasty wound running from her elbow to halfway down her arm. Her eyes met Gert's, and he shook his head. Without speaking, he went over to the dresser, rummaged around in a drawer and came back with a bandage, cotton wool, ointment and scissors. He filled a bowl of boiling water from the kettle.

'Sit still,' he ordered.

Trudi bit down on her lip as he carefully cleaned the wound and peered at it for a long moment.

'I'm afraid this might hurt, but I fear the bullet is lodged in there and has to come out.'

'All right,' she breathed, as she braced herself for more pain. Unable to watch him prod her wound, she turned her head away, but the pain proved too excruciating to bear. 'Please stop,' she moaned.

Gert's expression was set grim as he nodded. 'You'll need a doctor for this,' he said. 'I'll patch it up the best I can for now.' He applied strong-smelling ointment and wound a bandage round her arm with gentle care.

Nettie returned with an armful of clothes. 'My dear, you've gone quite white.' She deposited the clothes on the table and rushed over to help. Her words were the last thing Trudi heard before she lost consciousness.

THIRTY-SIX

Trudi became aware of the soft murmur of voices and the strong smell of disinfectant in her nostrils. Blinking open her eyes, she looked up at a high white ceiling and let her eyes drift down to a room lined with hospital beds, all of which were occupied. Hers was at the end of a row next to the doors, which at that moment swung open. A nurse came striding through, and beamed when she saw Trudi was awake.

'How are you feeling?' She came over and lifted Trudi's wrist to check her pulse while looking closely at the fob watch she held in her other hand. 'Your pulse is normal.' She recorded her findings in a report card at the end of the bed.

'Where am I?' asked Trudi, her voice coming out in a croak.

'The emergency hospital at Dordrecht,' said the nurse, still writing on Trudi's card.

Trudi watched, trying to work out why she knew of this place. Then it came to her and her spirits lifted. 'My sister works here. Frida Oversteegen. Does she know I'm here?'

The nurse looked up and frowned as she contemplated Trudi's question. 'I think she worked here up to a month ago, but I'm afraid once they've gone we're not told where to. Do you not have an address for her?'

'No,' said Trudi, slumping into her pillow. Where could Frida be? It wasn't like her not to be in touch. She hoped that her sister's absence was not a cause for concern, and wished the nurse could have been more helpful.

The nurse came over and examined Trudi's arm. 'That was a nasty wound you sustained and you lost a lot of blood. But the surgeon managed to remove the bullet. You'll have a scar, I'm afraid, but at least the movement in your arm will soon return to normal.'

Trudi looked at her arm, which lay swathed in a white bandage from wrist to above the elbow. It ached and felt like a dead weight when she tried to lift it, so she left it lying there.

'I wouldn't worry too much. It looks a lot worse than it is, and I'm confident you'll make a full recovery. Now, I will need to get some details from you. The gentleman who brought you in only gave me your first name. Trudi, is that right?' The nurse stood with her pen poised.

Trudi nodded wearily, then closed her eyes to gather her confused thoughts. The last thing she remembered was Gert's worried face as he tended to her arm. What had happened after that?

'Trudi. Can you hear me? I need to take your surname and address and next of kin,' urged the nurse.

Trudi opened her eyes and gave a little shake of her head. 'Yes of course. My name is Trudi Oversteegen, and I live in Haarlem. I can't give you my address because I'm in temporary lodgings.'

The nurse pursed her lips, but didn't query her reply as she entered the details on the record card. 'Next of kin?' she repeated.

She gave her mother's name and address and asked if the nurse would be contacting her. She didn't want to worry her mother, who had no idea that Trudi was in Dordrecht, let alone the serious nature of why she was there.

'Only if there's a medical reason to do so. I just need to check a few things with you.' She ticked off a list of health-related conditions, to which Trudi replied in the negative. All the time the nurse was asking questions, Trudi was watching the activity taking place behind her, the white-coated staff attending to patients, the low moans from the bed opposite, and a heavily bandaged patient being slowly escorted on foot the length of the ward and out through the swing doors. She felt groggy and was still trying to piece together what had happened since the river... she remembered a soft hand in hers... then it slipping from her grasp... the splash of water as she went overboard—

'You will need someone to take you home.' The nurse interrupted her thoughts. 'Will that be the gentleman who brought you in?'

In panic, she suddenly remembered Louisa. Where was she? She'd lost sight of her when the boat capsized. Did anyone go and search for her? Trudi caught her breath in a gasp and tried to sit up. 'How long have I been here?'

'Two nights. Would you like me to call the gentleman who brought you and ask him to come for you?'

'Erm...'

'Meneer Kuiper, he said his name was.'

Trudi didn't recognise the surname, but assumed she meant Gert. 'Please do call him, it's really urgent I speak to him.'

'You mustn't worry yourself. I will call him personally.' She put Trudi's notes in a folder and attached it to a clipboard at the foot of her bed.

'Thank you, but can you ask him to come straight away?' Trudi felt her chest tighten just thinking about Louisa, left cold and frightened for two whole nights out in the open on her own.

'As soon as I've finished my rounds on the ward. Now rest until I come back.'

Trudi hardly recognised Gert as he walked through the swing doors and over to her bed. He wasn't wearing his blue overalls but trousers and a dark jacket, with his fair hair combed back from his face. She sat on the edge of the bed, feeling slightly awkward. He must have seen her at her most vulnerable when she'd fainted. She barely knew him, yet she felt she owed him so much.

'Hello Trudi,' he said, taking a look at her bandaged arm. 'Looks like they've done a good job. Are you still in pain?'

'No. I'm feeling a little better. Thank you for all the trouble you've gone to.'

'It's nothing. I'm glad it wasn't anything more serious. The nurse says you're ready to go home.' He stood rubbing his calloused hands together, waiting for her to say something, when all she wanted was for him to tell her if he'd had any news.

It was easier to begin with Rosy. 'How's Rosy? Is she all right?' she said.

Gert let out a relieved sigh. 'Rosy is just fine and Nettie is doing a fine job caring for her. The first night she had a bad dream and woke up crying. It took an hour for Nettie to settle her. Last night was much better and she slept through until the morning. She seems to have taken to Nettie and has been following her round the house.'

Trudi noticed how the corners of his eyes crinkled at the mention of Rosy, which made her glad. 'That's a relief. But has Rosy been talking about Louisa?' Her heart filled with dread, for she didn't dare ask the question she really needed to.

'She has, and Nettie keeps telling her Louisa will be coming back soon. It's what we're all hoping.'

'It's two days since the boat capsized. There must be some news about the children. What have you heard?' she said, willing him to say something that would give her hope. But Gert's face gave nothing away as he said how he went looking for Louisa after dropping her at the hospital. 'From how you described the area, I was sure I'd find her. I took the dog with me and we spent at least two hours searching the whole length of the riverbank, especially in among the reeds. I saw the boat in the river and knew this had to be where the children had fallen in. I'm afraid there was no sign of any girl, or any of the children for that matter. I'm sorry.'

It was a terrible blow. She must have been deluded to expect Gert to find Louisa and bring her back. 'What time were you searching?' she asked, reasoning that the earlier he had got there, the quicker he might have found evidence that Louisa and the children had been there.

'Early afternoon. When it was obvious she wasn't there, I knocked on a few doors of the nearby houses, but no one said they'd seen or heard anything. I'm not sure they were being entirely truthful. I wonder whether it's because the locals simply didn't want to get involved. With all the German activity in the area that morning, people were probably suspicious of strangers calling round. But it doesn't mean it's bad news. It's still early days, and I'm sure we'll hear something soon. Nettie wanted me to say that you're very welcome to come back and stay with us till you feel better.'

Trudi knew Gert was being kind and didn't know what else to say about this terrible situation in which eleven children had gone missing. Her mind raced as she tried to work out what would be best for Rosy. She was safe with Nettie and Gert, but Trudi couldn't rely on their continuing generosity. At the same time, she had to find out what had happened to Louisa and the others, who could all be in mortal danger. 'I'm grateful for all you've done,' she began. 'But I must get back to Haarlem today and speak to Frans, who organised this whole mission. He must have knowledge of what's happened and will have the contacts to organise a proper search. Gert – can I please ask you one last favour?'

He nodded, and she went on, 'I can't take Rosy back to Haarlem – it's not safe. Would you be prepared to let Rosy stay with you for a few days until I can come back?'

Gert's face softened. 'Of course. We have a big house and no one bothers us out here. I'll keep making enquiries and contact you as soon as I hear anything. And if her sister turns up, we'll keep her safe too. I'm sure we'll get to the bottom of this quickly.'

THIRTY-SEVEN

Trudi hurried straight from Haarlem train station to tell Frans the whole story. It had been a wrench leaving Rosy in Nettie and Gert's care, but she knew that the remote farm was the best place for the little girl. And if by some miracle Louisa were to turn up safe and well, she was confident that the kindly couple would look after her until she could return.

It was late afternoon when she arrived at the tall town house in the quiet tree-lined street. As she raised her hand to ring the bell, she remembered the last time she had been there and the feeling of unease she'd had about Frans's housekeeper. But she was in no mood to explain to her why she'd come, and decided there and then to keep quiet about where she'd been. Her qualms were confirmed when Mevrouw de Wit opened the door with a suspicious look on her face, before recognising Trudi and welcoming her in.

'This is a surprise. I've been wondering what you've been getting up to since your incident on the railway bridge. Are you quite recovered?' Her eyes roamed over Trudi and came to rest on her bandaged arm. 'My word.' She let out a gasp. 'Been in the wars again, have you?'

Trudi felt herself blush and told her it was nothing, just a light sprain. 'Is Frans at home? I need to speak to him urgently.'

Mevrouw de Wit tipped her head on one side. 'Let me see. He went out at ten and didn't say when he'd be back, but he's usually home by six. Why don't you come into the kitchen and have a cup of tea?'

It wasn't long before she began to talk about her favourite subject of her nephew and how he had got caught up in riots in Amsterdam a week ago and only just avoided getting badly injured himself.

'Did you not hear about this? It's a scandal.' Her voice rose in indignation as she recounted her story. 'Hundreds of Jews targeted a paint shop belonging to a member of the NSB and beat down the door with hammers and axes. They attacked the owner, who luckily escaped with his life. Then the mob ran down towards Dam Square attacking anyone who crossed their path. My nephew was just leaving the town hall at the time and got caught up in the brawl, but managed to fight them off. He was lucky to get away with a few cuts and grazes. Such a tragedy that things have come to this, don't you think, Trudi?'

'I-I didn't hear about this. How did it end?' Trudi asked, fearing the worst.

'Well,' Mevrouw de Wit huffed. 'The German police turned up with batons and dogs and put a swift end to it. They chased the perpetrators back to the *Jodenbuurt* and closed off the main streets, then imposed a curfew from seven p.m. till eight in the morning, which is a nuisance for all law-abiding citizens.'

Their conversation was cut short by the sound of a key turning in the lock. Trudi jumped to her feet and excused herself.

'Thank goodness you're back,' she said, seeing it was Frans.

'What happened?' He stared at her heavily bandaged arm.

'I'll explain, but not here. I need to talk to you. Somewhere quiet,' she whispered, glancing over her shoulder to see if Mevrouw de Wit was listening, but from the clatter of pans it seemed she was occupied in the kitchen.

'Right. We'll go out,' he said briskly, retrieving his hat from the hatstand where he'd deposited it moments earlier.

They walked away from the house quickly. 'I've been so worried,' he began, and waited till they had turned down a quiet street where they couldn't be overheard. 'When I still didn't hear from you, I went into town to make enquiries. But the only information was that the farmer who was due to meet the boat arrived too late and found the whole place in chaos, and there was no sign of you or the children.'

'The plan failed,' Trudi said bluntly. 'The plan was doomed as soon as I met Nils at the train station. He had no intention of accompanying us on the train. I could accept it if Hans hadn't also left me to my own devices with twelve children to look after. He brought his brother along and said they couldn't stay to help as they were off on a sabotage mission. Did you know anything about that?'

Frans looked mystified as he turned to her. 'No, that definitely was not part of the plan. Nils was meant to give Hans maps of the area and detailed instructions on how to cross the minefield with you. Are you telling me that he didn't go along with you?'

'It was terrifying. Hans gave me only the sketchiest of instructions and they weren't much help. Nor was the map. You must have known the plan was to lead the children across a minefield in the pitch dark with searchlights swooping all around us.'

Frans shook his head. 'That should never have happened, Trudi. You were never meant to be alone. I'm truly sorry.'

Trudi let out a sob and wiped away a tear. 'I managed to get the children across the minefield, despite the searchlights and the very real possibility that we'd be blown up. Then when we

got to the river, I discovered the boat had four oars. I needed
three of the children to row us across. It was a disaster,' she said,
the words catching in her throat. 'The boat sank, we all fell in
and meanwhile the Germans were shooting at us. As you can
see, they got me in the arm. It almost put me out of action. I
hope I was the only one they shot, but I wasn't able to find out –
when I tried to help the children the current swept me away. By
some stroke of good fortune I found Rosy had been swept
downstream too and was cowering in the reeds on the opposite
bank. But she was on her own and there was no sign of Louisa. I
didn't know what to do, except that I had to get help, even
though it meant leaving the scene without knowing the fate of
the children. I was getting weak and I wasn't sure I'd make it,
but I had to make sure that Rosy was safe. It was miles to the
first farmhouse we came across, in the middle of nowhere. But
fortunately, the couple who lived there were so kind. I wanted
to go straight back to look for Louisa, but my wound was serious. I lost so much blood that I ended up in the emergency
hospital in Dordrecht. And when I came out two days later I
discovered that Louisa and all the children had gone.' Trudi
shook her head in an attempt to blank out the awful memory.

'This is terrible news.' Frans's face fell. 'And you never saw
the farmer.'

'No. I didn't see any farmer,' said Trudi in frustration. 'I
didn't see anyone, but I could tell there were Germans from
their shouts and the gunshots. I pray none of the children were
shot. I dread that the Germans caught up with them and took
them away.'

They turned back into Frans's street and arrived back at the
house. 'Come inside while I make a telephone call,' he said.

She waited in the sitting room off the hallway. He took so
long that she thought it could only be bad news. When he eventually returned, he gave her a small smile. 'I managed to speak
to the farmer. Earlier today he heard a knock on the door and he

was amazed to see the children standing there. At their head was the oldest one, who said they'd been hiding in the reeds all this time. Apart from being very cold and hungry, they seem no worse for wear, and will be moving to their foster homes in the next day or two. But Trudi, when I asked him how many children were accounted for, he said ten. I'm afraid that means that Louisa is missing.'

In one short moment, Trudi's mood swooped from total elation to complete despair. 'It can't be true. Why would she be the only one not found? What did the farmer say about it?'

'That he's sending a search party out as soon as it's safe to do so. I'll be keeping in close contact and will go myself if necessary.'

Trudi felt a lurch in her chest as a terrible thought came to her. 'If the Germans took Louisa, they'll be looking for the other children. But what if someone who knew of our plan informed on us?'

'But who? The only people apart from us two who knew about the plan were Nils and Hans.'

'And Gustaaf, Hans's brother, who didn't talk much and I thought nothing of it. Hans told me they were on their way that evening to blow up a stretch of railway used by German goods trains. That sounds more like the work of the resistance than collaborators, so it's unlikely that it would have been either of them. Unless they weren't telling the truth. Frans, did you tell anyone else about our plan?'

'No. Of course not,' he said sharply. 'I'm always careful who I take into my confidence. But we can't take anything for granted. I know I can trust Nils. We've been good friends since school and he's always been trustworthy. He introduced me to Hans through the friend of a friend. It never occurred to me that Hans would involve his brother. I should have kept a closer eye on him.'

'Are you saying that both brothers were informers?'

'I'm afraid we have to work on that assumption. I'll see what I can find out about them. At this stage, we can't rule out any information.'

'I knew I should have stayed—'

'No, Trudi.' Frans interrupted her. 'You did what you believed was right. If you'd stayed, you'd have run the risk of being arrested. You saved a little girl's life.'

'But I didn't save Louisa,' said Trudi despairingly.

'You mustn't think that. Until we know anything to the contrary, we must assume that Louisa has survived. Listen to me. If it's true that someone was following you, it's also possible that they know about you and where you are staying. I know of a room that has become vacant at 149, Herensingel. I think you should move there straight away.'

Trudi nodded, knowing she should be grateful for his help, but feeling more miserable than scared. Could things possibly get any worse?

THIRTY-EIGHT

The house was one in a row along a quiet tree-lined street on the canal, and belonged to a resistance member and minister of the Reformed Church. As an itinerant preacher, he travelled across the Netherlands giving sermons against the occupation. He let out rooms to *onderduikers* who needed a safe place to hide from the Germans, as well as a steady stream of resisters in search of a temporary place to stay. Trudi's own room was at the back of the house overlooking an untended garden that had seen better days. Just visible at the far end was a bench beneath a cherry tree. She found it sad that no one ever sat out in the garden, and wondered if the people upstairs gazed wistfully out of their windows, wishing that they could wander outside without fear of being seen. She knew little about who they were or how many people were living above her, only that there was a secret room that had been constructed behind one of the top bedrooms, big enough to hide six people at one time.

It was always so quiet that sometimes she found it hard to believe there was anyone else living in the house apart from her, let alone the large number she knew to be true. Occasionally she passed someone on the stairs – a resister like herself, she guessed – and they would quickly exchange a greeting before hurrying about their business. She remembered with nostalgia the short friendship she'd struck up with Hannie when they were both living in the same house as Oma. Would she ever be settled enough in one place to put down roots and make lasting friendships, she wondered?

The only constant was Ida, the kindly preacher's wife, who could usually be found at work in the kitchen preparing meals for the family kept hidden on the top floor.

Trudi was passing the kitchen door one afternoon when she heard Ida call out to her.

'Is that you, Trudi? I almost forgot – a letter came for you.'

Trudi went into the kitchen and found Ida standing at the stove prodding a long wooden spoon into a huge pan. Plumes of steam rose into the air. She was flushed from the exertion and strands of hair that had escaped from her bun were sticking to her face. 'I was busy folding the laundry when I heard a knock at the back door. I went to see who it was but I realised I could smell burning. I only just managed to save the pot of porridge from boiling dry.' She peered at the contents of her pot and gave it another prod, then noted the look of surprise on Trudi's face. 'No, this isn't the porridge pot. These are bed sheets,' she said with a laugh. 'Why don't you come and sit down? I'll be with you in a moment.'

'Let me help with that,' said Trudi. She didn't feel she could sit by idly while Ida was so hard at work.

Ida stopped her stirring and switched off the stove. 'I've done as much as I can. Would you mind helping me lift this pot down?'

'Where do you want it?' said Trudi, coming over to help. She took one of the wooden handles in her good hand and was surprised at the weight of it.

'By the sink,' instructed Ida, heaving the black pot from the stove. They shuffled a few steps together before putting it down on the flagstones.

'I'll deal with it later,' she said, stretching out and placing her hands in the small of her back. 'Now, let me get you your letter.' She went over to the sideboard and picked up a slim brown envelope with Trudi's name written on it in black ink. 'Here you are. I hope it's from someone nice.'

'Did you see who delivered it?'

'I'm afraid not. Whoever it was pushed it under the door and was gone by the time I could get there.'

Trudi took the envelope and stared at the handwriting, puzzling over who it could be from. As far as she knew, the only people who knew her whereabouts were Frans – and Piet, who had begged Frans to let him have her address so he could visit her. It had been such a nice surprise when he'd come from Amsterdam bearing a bunch of big blowsy pink peonies that he'd picked from his mother's garden. No one had ever given Trudi flowers before and she'd been unbelievably touched by his gesture and concern for her well-being.

He promised to visit her again the next time he was free, saying it might be a while as he was working on a confidential assignment in Amsterdam. Trudi knew better than to ask for details, suspecting that he would have been sworn to secrecy.

No, this ordinary-looking letter couldn't be from Piet, she concluded.

'I don't think it's anything important. I'll open it later.' She was reluctant to open it in front of Ida in case it was bad news concerning the Friedmans, or Louisa, who was still unaccounted for.

'Will you stay and have a cup of tea?' said Ida.

'That would be very nice. But let me make it while you sit down.' Trudi put the letter on the kitchen table and went to fill the kettle from the tap.

Ida sat on the nearest chair and let out a sigh. 'Thank you. I haven't stopped all morning. The Cohen family left late last night and I'm getting the room ready for the next couple, who will be arriving at any time.'

'Who arranges it?' asked Trudi, as she measured out a scoop of tea from the metal tin into the teapot.

'My husband, Willem. He does it all through his contacts in the network. We're both keen to help the Jewish community, but we find we can only do so much. It's a sad situation to see so many Jewish families being hounded from their homes. Whatever we do never seems to be enough. You'll find the cups are in the cupboard above the sink.'

Trudi finished making the tea and talked about her own experience. She told Ida about the plight of the Friedmans, the children she'd been in charge of ferrying, and Louisa's disappearance.

'You mustn't blame yourself. It sounds like you were in an incredibly dangerous situation. I doubt you could have done any more than you did.'

'I wish you were right, but the fact is that a seven-year-old girl is missing and may have been taken by the Germans. The farmer has been making enquiries, but no one admits to knowing anything about the situation. If anyone is hiding the children, they're hardly going to admit to it.'

As she talked, she kept looking at the letter lying on the table, and became increasingly convinced that it must contain news of Louisa. She reached for it and stood up abruptly. 'I'm sorry, I must go. In case this is important.'

Ida rose to her feet at the same time. 'Of course. And if there's anything I can do to help, you only have to ask.'

Not until she'd arrived breathless in her room, having taken the stairs two at a time, did Trudi pause to consider who might have delivered the letter and how they even knew where she lived.

Apart from Frans and Piet, she'd shared her change of address with no one. Closing the door behind her, she took a deep breath to steady her nerves. At first she wondered if there was even a letter inside the envelope, it was so thin; she had to peer inside to see the small sheet of paper, folded twice over. Her fingers trembled as she eased it out.

Bold black letters were written large across the top of the page. Four stark words that caused Trudi's heart to jolt. They could only refer to Louisa.

I HAVE THE GIRL.

Trudi gasped and dropped the letter as if it had burned her fingers. Louisa was still alive! Torn between hope that Louisa had been found and heart-clutching dread that someone was holding her hostage, she searched her mind for who might want to do her harm. Could it be Nils, Hans or Gustaaf – or all three, who might all be resisters turned collaborators with a motive to snatch a Jewish child and hand her over in exchange for a reward? But if that were the case, were they holding Louisa in order to blackmail her?

Trudi quickly bent down and picked up the letter. Without properly reading the rest of the message, she flipped it over to read the signature.

'Sem?' She spoke his name in disbelief. It seemed incomprehensible that he could have anything to do with Louisa's disappearance. She was certain she hadn't mentioned Louisa and Rosy to him the one and only time she'd met him for coffee in the centre of Haarlem. And yet... but no, how could he have known about her assignment? With a stab of realisation, she remembered thinking she saw him from the window of the train to Dordrecht just as it was pulling away. An image so fleeting that she hadn't managed to catch sight of his face, and had convinced herself that she was mistaken. But what if he had been there, and had known all along that she was on the train with all those Jewish children?

Her heart pounded as she turned the letter back over and began to read the scrawl that appeared to have been written in a hurry.

You may wonder why the girl is with me. If you come and meet me you will find out. All I can say is that she's safe for the moment, but my circumstances make it difficult to keep her any longer.

I could just hand her over to the Germans. I know they'd be more than happy if I did. I've thought long about this, but that would be too easy. There is another way, that is if you agree to my proposition, but I don't want to write it in this letter. I want you to come and speak face to face with me alone. Please understand that under no circumstances must you bring anyone with you. If you do I can't be held responsible for what happens to the girl.

Meet me tonight at five o'clock at the south entrance to the Haarlemmerhout.

And so you know... if you don't turn up, I will have no choice but to get rid of her.

Sem

Stunned, Trudi could barely take in what she was reading. He said he had a proposition, but it sounded more like a threat – and how could she comply when she didn't know what he was intending?

She paced up and down, unsure what she should do next. Louisa was bound to be distressed, but the idea that he was mistreating her in some way and was planning to harm her was totally abhorrent. Did he really have it in him to be so callous?

Glancing at her watch, she saw it was four o'clock. Her

instincts told her that she must speak straight away to Frans. He lived a short walk from the Haarlemmerhout, which gave her just enough time to get over there and bring him up to date on the situation.

All that mattered right now was persuading Sem to hand over Louisa. Even if it meant putting her own life in danger.

Trudi arrived at Frans's house less than half an hour later, having run all the way from the bus stop without stopping. She pressed the bell and moments later Frans opened the door.

'Can I come in?' She didn't wait for his reply as she pushed past him. 'Is Mevrouw de Wit in?' she added in a nervous whisper, as a thought struck her that she might be the one who had come with the letter.

'No, she went out an hour ago on an errand. Please tell me what's going on.'

Trudi thrust the letter into his hand. 'It's about Louisa. Sem has got her.'

Frans took in a sharp breath. 'Did you see who delivered it?'

'No. Neither did Ida. Frans, you don't think it could have been Mevrouw de Wit?'

'She doesn't know where you live, so no.' Frans frowned as he turned his attention to reading the letter, just as the clock in the hallway struck the half-hour, its sonorous chime giving Trudi a shock.

'I think you need to sit down,' he said, looking grave. Holding the letter, he led the way into the small sitting room. Trudi went over to her usual chair.

Frans pushed the door shut behind them. 'I don't like the threatening tone he uses towards you. I think I had better come with you.'

'No! He means it when he says I must come alone. I can't risk Louisa coming to any harm. This is between me and Sem.'

'I understand. But you must go prepared in case he turns nasty.' Frans took a bunch of keys out of his trouser pocket and went over to the bureau under the window. With his back to Trudi, he opened the flap and unlocked one of the inner drawers. When he turned round, she saw he was removing a small silver pistol from a black leather holster.

He must have read the expression on her face, for he said, 'Don't look so scared. You know perfectly well how to handle one of these.'

'I'm not scared,' she said, trying to ignore her heart thumping in her chest. 'But I can't imagine pulling a gun on Sem. He's the man I used to love.'

Frans's expression hardened into a frown. 'You must put any sentimental thoughts like that out of your head. He's holding an innocent girl hostage and he's dangerous. I've seen you shoot a gun with confidence and you're as good as the next man. Now take it.' He held the gun out, keeping his eyes fixed on hers.

Trudi nodded uncertainly, then looked nervously at the pistol.

'I'm not saying you have to use it, but you will be in a far stronger position if you're armed. Go on – take it.'

The weight of it was reassuring and fitted exactly into the palm of her hand, and she noticed how cool the metal felt against her skin. She studied it carefully, checking that the safety catch was on and confirming with Frans that it was loaded. When she was satisfied with the workings of it, she carefully tucked it back in its holster and slipped it into her secret coat pocket, the one Oma had helped her sew all those weeks ago.

When it was time to leave, he gave her a hug, something he'd never done before, even after her accident.

'Bring Louisa back safely,' Frans said to her, and watched from the door as she left.

THIRTY-NINE

As Trudi approached the entrance to the park, she could see that Sem hadn't arrived. Perhaps he'd been held up, she thought anxiously, or maybe there was some other reason that had prevented him from coming. She looked around, half-expecting to see him come pelting down the street full of smiles and apologies for being late, and thought briefly of the old Sem she'd known and loved. Could he really have changed so much from the sweet boy who stole her heart? With a shiver, she realised she barely knew him; she had no idea who he'd become nor what to expect.

She went and stood by the gates as instructed, and waited. It was turning chilly and she thrust her hands into her coat pockets for warmth. Her right hand found the smooth leather of the holster and she let her fingers curl round it. She envisaged pulling out the gun and firing it, but the thought was only briefly consoling.

She checked her watch. It was already past five o'clock. Where was he? Perhaps he'd lost his nerve... but what about Louisa? She cast a desperate look about her, willing Louisa to appear, unharmed.

A woman came out of the park pushing a large pram, caught Trudi's eye and quickly looked away. An elderly gentleman walked slowly towards her with the aid of a stick. He doffed his hat as he passed her by. When her watch showed that another few minutes had passed, she took a deep breath and a last look around before deciding to turn back the way she had come. But no sooner had she set off than she heard her name being called.

'Trudi, wait!'

She swung round to see Sem crossing the road by himself and striding quickly towards her. It gave her the opportunity to take in his appearance, which, quite frankly, shocked her. If she hadn't been expecting him, she wasn't sure she would even have recognised him. It wasn't just his fair hair, no longer flopping over his forehead but cropped so short that she was sure she could see his scalp. His face was so much thinner, gaunt even, and the corners of his mouth sloped down in an expression of what could only be described as disapproval... or was it anger? Even his blue eyes, the first thing that had beguiled her all those months ago, seemed different. They no longer twinkled with amusement but held a cold hardness that frightened her. Even so, she forced herself to smile a greeting. She was relieved to see him return it, and fleetingly wished she'd been mistaken about all this.

'So you got my letter. I thought you might not come,' he said with an icy stare that made her look away.

'How could I not? You said you had Louisa. It's my priority to make sure she is safe. But where is she?' she said nervously.

'Later,' he said abruptly, and roughly grabbed her elbow so he could steer her through the park gates.

She was terrified she'd said something to rile him, but didn't dare ask what it was. 'Sem, please tell me where you're taking me.' Wincing under his grip, she glanced anxiously at his severe profile.

'You'll see soon enough.' He shot her an unreadable look and kept marching towards a fork in the path that she knew would take them away from the one they were on, where most people walked. While there were still people out for a late-afternoon stroll or taking a short-cut across the park she felt reasonably safe, but she quailed at how empty the path looked, the one he was walking towards so determinedly.

'Can't we stop here and talk?' Panic gripped her as she tried to extract her arm from his grasp, but he only held on more tightly.

'Not here. It's too public,' he said tersely.

She looked along the path disappearing into tall trees that formed a thick green canopy, and realised she no longer knew where she was. She wanted to run back the way they'd come, but he wouldn't let go of her. 'Where are you taking me?' she cried out.

Sem didn't answer, nor did he release her arm. Resignedly, she decided it was best to remain silent to avoid inciting his anger any more than she had already seemed to.

On they marched, deeper into the deserted woods. Trudi calculated they must have gone at least a mile when they reached a wooden gate bearing the sign PRIVATE. On the other side was a low wooden building – it was more of a hut – set well back from the path. It could have been a shed or storage facility of some sort, she couldn't be sure.

Sem led her round the back, where he finally let go of her arm and took a key from his pocket. He unlocked the door and kept his hand on it.

From where she stood, it was so dark that she couldn't make out anything inside. 'You want me to go in there?' she whispered nervously.

'If you want to see the girl.' Sem spoke impatiently.

Of course she did. But Sem was blocking her way. She

thought how easy it would have been for him to push her inside and lock the door.

She took a tentative step back. Hesitating between her longing to be reunited with Louisa and fearing that this was all a trick, she forced herself to remain calm and tried to appeal to his sense of reason. 'Sem, I don't know what you want from me, but I'm willing to talk if that's what you want. But I'd rather we talked out here.' She waited for him to answer, certain he could hear her heart thudding painfully in her chest. In the silence that followed, she strained for any sound that suggested Louisa was inside the hut, but there was none.

'Please tell me what's going on, Sem,' Trudi said, her voice trembling.

FORTY

Sem's eyes followed hers to the open door and he shoved it shut. Trudi wasn't sure whether to be alarmed or relieved. If Louisa was inside, she would surely recognise her voice. Wouldn't she call out if she was? Trudi concluded that either Sem was bluffing or Louisa was too frightened to make a sound. She needed to keep him talking, that was all that mattered right now. She gave a slight nod for him to speak.

Frowning, Sem dropped his eyes to his feet and kicked at an imaginary stone. When he was ready, he fixed her with a stare. 'Ever since the day we met at the market, I've been turning over the things you said, and it's been getting to me.'

'What things?' Trudi said in a small voice, trying to remember what it was exactly she might have said to rile him so.

'The resistance, of course. And your belief in what they stand for. Then I heard you'd actually joined up. When I was told what you've been getting up to, I knew I had to keep an eye on you. There aren't that many resistance groups in Haarlem and I have enough contacts of my own who've been keeping me informed, but I didn't like what I was hearing. I wasn't happy when I heard you've been cycling around with ammunition, but

I was prepared to let that go. It was when I heard you were planning to dress incognito as a German nurse and move Jewish children across the country that I simply couldn't believe you'd be foolish enough to put yourself in such danger. Did you honestly think that you wouldn't get caught?'

Trudi knew that to say anything now could make him more angry than he was already. To her relief, he didn't wait for her to answer.

'I had to make you see sense,' he went on. 'But you're stubborn and I knew you wouldn't listen to me, so I had to find another way. By pure chance I bumped into Hans, an old friend from way back. He said he was meeting you in Dordrecht and was briefed to accompany you on the most dangerous leg of the journey. All it took was a bribe of a few hundred guilders to get him to agree to take the group off you and hand them over to my contacts, who I briefed. I even bought a return train ticket, which he was meant to give to you. I was waiting for you to reappear at the train station, but when you didn't turn up I knew something had gone wrong. It appears that Hans had other plans and hadn't bothered to tell me. And then told my contacts the whole thing was off. Shows how you can't trust anyone,' he said with a short laugh. 'And all this time you carried on regardless, heading straight into danger.'

Trudi felt herself grow hot with anger. She couldn't let this lie. 'What was I supposed to do? I was responsible for twelve vulnerable children who were in danger from the Nazis and there was no one around to help me. I had no choice but to take them across that minefield. If you were so concerned about me, why didn't you come and help?'

He gave her a pitying look. 'By the time I got to the park you'd already left and were heading towards the minefield. There was no way I was going to go across that. The only way to reach you was by taking a detour along the road, which would have taken twice as long. It was getting dark, so I found shelter and waited until daybreak before setting off, but when I got to the river I was already too late. The boat was in the water and everyone had gone. I had this idea that you would still be around somewhere, so I began to search through the reeds. Imagine my shock when I heard crying and found the girl. She was shivering and soaked through. But still all I could think of was finding you. Saving you from your stupidity. I began to walk away, but all I could hear were her pitiful cries coming from the reeds. I couldn't just leave her, could I? So I went back and got her.' For a moment, his hard expression dropped and he let slip a smile.

Trudi exhaled quietly, hoping against hope that he wasn't all bad. If he was prepared to save Louisa then, surely, he wouldn't be about to harm her now?

'You saved Louisa...' But her momentary pang of sympathy for him vanished when she remembered he'd kidnapped an innocent girl. 'Where have you been keeping her all this time?'

'To be honest, once I decided I couldn't leave her, I didn't know what to do with her. The Germans would have made it worth my while to hand her over, but I had to get her away from that place first. I knew if I was caught with a Jew, they'd jump to the wrong conclusion, so I took her back home till I could work out what to do next.'

'To Bloemendaal?'

Sem nodded.

'What did your parents think about that?'

'My mother was happy to comply. She's been helping people hide for some time. Not that I agree with it. It provided me with a short-term solution, although the place was getting crowded with *onderduikers*. She said the girl could stay temporarily, but that I had to find somewhere else for her. I got talking to one of the *onderduikers*, who knew about this place and said he could get a key. Said it was safe enough in the woods. That's when it came to me. All I had to do was get you to come and take her off my hands. And here you are.' He smiled, but it wasn't a pleasant smile.

'What is it you want from me, Sem?' she said with a sense of foreboding that he was holding something back.

Sem frowned. 'I would have thought that was obvious.' He paused, and, when she didn't answer, he gave a derisive laugh. 'I want you back. But only if you promise to give up working for the resistance. I can show you a way to a better future, if only you'd let me. You must have seen the posters urging thinking women to join in the fight. Soon as I saw them, I thought of you. Come on, Trudi. We can do this together.'

A sudden chill went over her. *So that's what this is all about*, she realised. *He's never got over the break-up and it's been eating away at him ever since.* She considered carefully how to reply. 'I can see with my own eyes what's happening to our country thanks to the Germans. Their vision is terrifying and bleak. The future you believe in is not something I share, or ever will.'

He stared at her, then, almost spitting out the words, he said, 'Don't I mean anything to you anymore? I still care for you.'

She looked at him warily, unable to reconcile his words with his cold, calculating expression. It would have been easy for her to say that he had a strange way of showing it, but the way he stared at her frightened her. She knew she had to avoid antagonising him further; he was holding Louisa hostage. But the words were out before she realised her mistake. 'It's over, Sem. It has been for some time. How do you think I could love someone who would put anything above helping poor innocent children?'

Suddenly, he grabbed hold of her wrists and pushed his face up close to hers. 'Be quiet! I don't want to hear any more from you. Now listen carefully to what I have to say.'

She kept very still, hardly daring to breathe. He abruptly

released his grip and roughly pulled her into a clumsy hug. Almost as quickly, he broke away, and she saw he had tears in his eyes.

'I don't want to lose you, Trudi. We belong together. I've known it from the first day I set eyes on you. I'm not going to give up on you now, despite all the mistakes you've made. I brought you here to make you see reason. To come over to our cause and to get you back. Say you'll do it, Trudi, and then I'll hand over the girl.' He took her hand, more gently now, and gazed pleadingly into her eyes.

Trudi didn't dare pull away, but neither was she prepared to give in to him. It was inconceivable that he could consider bartering an innocent girl in exchange for her beliefs. Clearly, he thought he should get his way whatever the cost. Just like the Nazis, he wanted power. And maybe that was what he'd become, she thought with a feeling of cold dread – a Nazi who expected to have power over her, power over everyone, the power to feel good about himself. What he failed to grasp was that true power came from helping those who need you. He would never understand that.

Sem was standing with his back to the building, so didn't see the door opening slowly behind him.

Trudi glanced over his shoulder and saw Louisa appear from inside, wide-eyed and tiny. She was wearing the same dirty dress she'd had on the last time Trudi had seen her that fateful day. Trudi tried to warn her with a look to stay quiet, but the girl let out a tiny mewling sound, which became a panicky cry the moment Sem swung round.

'Get back inside!' he roared and, with his arms raised, started moving towards her.

The young girl crossed her arms across her face as if she expected to be struck.

With her heart in her mouth, Trudi quickly reached inside her coat pocket for the small silver pistol. She felt it slip easily out of the holster into her hand. Gripping it tightly, she raised the pistol and pointed it directly at Sem.

'Leave her alone!' she yelled.

Sem swivelled round and, when he saw the gun, his expression changed to one of panic. 'Don't be stupid, Trudi,' he said, raising his hands in a gesture of surrender. 'You know you wouldn't dare.'

'Wouldn't I?' Her voice was steady, belying the crashing of her heart against her ribs. Louisa was in her line of vision, standing right behind Sem. Taking shallow breaths, she willed Louisa to move out of harm's way, but she appeared to be rooted to the spot.

'Have you lost your mind?' Sem's voice seemed to come from far away.

Trudi snapped her attention back to Sem and the threat he posed to her and Louisa. He took a stumbling step towards her. He raised his arm as if to knock the gun from her hand, but Trudi was ready. She squeezed the trigger and Louisa let out a high-pitched scream.

For a long sickening moment, Trudi thought her aim had missed and that she'd shot Louisa. Then, as it became apparent what she had done, she let the pistol fall from her hand to the ground and held out her arms to catch the terrified girl who came running barefoot towards her.

FORTY-ONE

The sun had dipped below the tops of the trees as Trudi retraced her steps along the path that would take them back through the woods and into the park. She had to get out before the gates were locked for the night. She needed to remain calm. She would have run if she'd been alone, but with Louisa at her side, clinging tightly to her hand, she had to go more slowly. There was nothing to be done about Louisa's lack of shoes, but Trudi had thought to warm her up by taking off her own cardigan and wrapping it round the girl's slight body and fastening all the buttons. The cardigan reached almost to her ankles and she was sure it would draw suspicious glances should they encounter anyone, but it would have to do.

They were on the main path and the park gates were in view when Louisa stopped suddenly and began crying loudly.

'What's the matter?' said Trudi, crouching beside her. She tried to soothe her, but the child was unable to answer through her sobs as the tears streamed down her face. Trudi could only think that it was because she was overwhelmed by hunger and exhaustion, but they couldn't stop now. 'We're nearly home... it's just a little bit further,' she said, and gave her a hug.

She stood up – and came face to face with a man who had stopped to see what the matter was.

'Is everything all right?' the man said, gazing at Louisa with concern. He looked harmless enough. Trudi considered asking him for help, but decided against it. After all that had just happened she dared trust no one. Her priority was to get Louisa to safety.

'Everything's fine. She's just a little upset.' Trudi lifted Louisa into her arms. Louisa stopped crying and stared at the man through tear-filled eyes. Trudi smiled at him as if to say, 'See, there's nothing wrong.'

'I couldn't help noticing that she has no shoes,' the man persisted. His eyes travelled from Louisa's bare feet and rested on Trudi's hands. Trudi felt her cheeks grow hot, realising he must have noticed they were spattered with blood. He tipped his head to one side and gave her a questioning look. 'Are you sure she's fine?' he said.

Trudi felt herself tense up. 'Perfectly. But thank you for your concern.'

As she hurried away, she was certain the man's eyes were boring into her back. She would have to carry Louisa all the way if she was to avoid attracting anyone else's attention.

It had been Sem, not Trudi, who had ended up being locked inside the wooden building. She told herself she'd done it for her safety and for Louisa's – what else could she have done?

The idea of moving him inside came to her because she was petrified it wasn't over yet. Wounded, he'd staggered to his feet, and she'd been terrified he was about to come for her, even though she could see he was gravely hurt. The easiest thing would have been to shoot him again but she just couldn't. She could only watch as he clutched his side and slumped to the ground, where he'd lain unmoving, inches from the doorway.

Trudi would never have been able to get him inside on her own, but he had inadvertently helped her by falling so close to the entrance. She'd had no idea how badly injured he was, but she'd known she couldn't just leave him outside. It had taken a great deal of effort on her part and there had been more blood on his clothes than she could ever have imagined. Somehow, she'd managed to roll him over the threshold, and quickly slammed the door shut. Luck was on her side; she'd found that he'd left the key on the outside. Moving swiftly, she'd turned the key in the lock and pocketed it.

With fast shallow breaths, she'd twisted round to see where Louisa had got to, feeling sick to the stomach at what she'd just done. All the time she'd been pushing and shoving him, he hadn't stirred. There was a strong possibility that he was dead, but she hadn't dared check.

Louisa's white face had peered out from behind a tree. Trudi had walked over to her, and seen that the girl was trembling. 'Don't be frightened. He can't hurt you now.'

Louisa had shaken her head. 'How do you know he won't come after me again? He said I could trust him, but he brought me here and locked me in and didn't say when he was coming back.'

'Did he hurt you?' Trudi had hardly dared ask.

'I don't know.' Louisa had hung her head.

Trudi had waited for her to carry on. After a moment, Louisa had begun rubbing her arm and Trudi had noticed she had four small yellow-blue bruises. It must have happened some days ago, perhaps when he'd manhandled her inside and squeezed her arm too tightly. She hoped there were no other bruises.

'He didn't hit me,' Louisa had said, as if reading Trudi's thoughts.

'Good,' Trudi had said carefully, as she'd tried to imagine what this poor child had been suffering. She'd held out a hand.

She needed to regain her trust. 'I'm going to take you home with me,' she'd said, deciding on the spur of the moment, 'but we need to walk. Do you think you can do that for me?'

Louisa had stared down at her feet. 'I've lost my shoes,' she'd said.

'I know, but we'll just have to manage.'

'I'm cold.' Louisa had begun to shiver.

'Here, let me warm you up.' Trudi had opened her coat wide and gently pulled Louisa against her for warmth. After a while, a smile had come to Louisa's face. She'd even giggled.

'That's better.' Trudi had unbuttoned her cardigan and discovered a forgotten sweet in one of the pockets. 'Look what I brought you,' she'd said brightly as she'd unwrapped it and popped it into Louisa's mouth. After she'd dressed her in her own cardigan, she'd kissed her cheek and said, 'Now, let's go home.'

FORTY-TWO

Before leaving the park, Trudi stopped by a water fountain and held Louisa up so she could lean forward and reach the water spout with her hands.

'Have you had enough?' she asked. Her arms were starting to ache from the strain of holding the girl steady. But Louisa kept slurping greedily, using her hands to scoop the water into her mouth. How long was it since she'd had a drink, wondered Trudi, when at last Louisa had finished and dropped back to the ground. The girl looked down at the front of her cardigan, which was wet through, but she didn't seem to mind. She giggled and said, 'Aren't you going to have a drink, Tante Trudi?'

'I am,' Trudi said, but first she rubbed her hands briskly under the flowing water, watching it turn pink. Only when she was satisfied that all traces of blood were gone from between her fingers and under her nails did she cup her hands to drink the cool refreshing water.

They were among the last to leave the park. Understandably, Louisa wasn't keen on walking barefoot in the street, so Trudi had to carry her again. The park attendant was calling out for people to exit the park as he was about to lock the gates, and Trudi noticed him staring at Louisa's bare feet. She smiled sweetly and hoisted Louisa to the opposite side of her body as she walked past him and out of the park.

The bus was waiting across the road and, still holding Louisa, she ran to catch it. Several people who were waiting to board turned to stare, but she made a point of not meeting anyone's eye, for fear of being drawn into a conversation she had no desire to engage in.

She found a seat at the back and sat Louisa on her lap, and in no time at all the child's head lolled heavily against Trudi's chest. Trudi felt exhausted herself, but she needed to keep alert. Every time the bus stopped, she peered anxiously at the passengers boarding, in case any of them were in uniform. She had an uncomfortable memory of the time she'd been escorting the Jewish boy, Aaron, and how German Wehrmacht officers had boarded the tram and demanded to see their papers. She'd been prepared then, with false papers that were accepted without question. This time, not only had she forgotten her own papers but she had none for Louisa. If ordinary people in the street were giving Louisa suspicious glances, she was certain she'd be found out if asked for identification. Yet, despite her worry, she found herself dozing to the soothing rumble of the engine. *It's over, it's over—* She came to with a start when the driver announced her stop with a shrill ring of the bell. She jumped to her feet, anxious not to miss the stop.

'Excuse me, is this yours?' asked a young woman about Trudi's age in the seat opposite. Trudi turned to look and saw the woman lean down to retrieve something at her feet. To her horror she saw it was her silver pistol. How on earth had it fallen out of her pocket, she thought in a panic. Their eyes met and the woman smiled sympathetically as she handed it to Trudi.

'Best you put it away before someone else sees it,' she whispered.

'Thank you,' said Trudi, shoving it in her pocket. She was grateful the woman didn't stare, or comment on Louisa's wet clothes and lack of shoes. 'Come on, Louisa,' she urged, and held her firmly by the hand in her rush to the doors before they closed.

She felt a surge of relief to be outside again, though her heart hammered in her chest. Glancing up as the bus began to move away, she glimpsed the woman looking out and giving a small wave through the window. 'Thank you,' Trudi mouthed gratefully, but she berated herself for having been so careless, and prayed that no one had seen their exchange.

Trudi let herself in by the back door and heard Ida humming to herself in the kitchen. She pushed open the door dividing the kitchen from the scullery and was greeted by the warm comforting smell of soup, which instantly reminded her of home.

'Hello, Ida. I'm back,' she said.

'My goodness, what have we here?' said Ida, who was attending to a pot on the stove. 'Is this the girl you were talking about?' She gave Trudi a tentative smile and wiped her hands on a cloth before coming over.

'Yes. This is Louisa,' said Trudi, and found herself choking up. She couldn't quite believe it herself after all that had happened these last weeks. But the feeling was bitter-sweet, knowing that this whole terrible saga wasn't over yet.

With a sniff, she crouched down and held Louisa by the shoulders. 'I need you to get out of these wet clothes. Ida, you wouldn't have something more suitable for her to wear?'

'I'll go and see if there's anything in the airing cupboard. There are all sorts of items of clothing that get left behind when my lodgers leave. They rarely come back for them, but I always keep them, just in case.'

After Ida had left the kitchen, Louisa glanced nervously at Trudi. 'Am I going to stay here with you?' she said uncertainly.

Trudi hadn't thought through what would happen to Louisa after tonight, but staying here seemed to be the safest option until she had a chance to discuss things with Frans. She knew she should have gone straight to him, but was nervous of having to tell Mevrouw de Wit the whole sorry story about her nephew. Not tonight, she thought; but sooner or later she would have to know.

'Yes, you'll be staying with me for a little while,' she said, unwilling to say any more.

'And where will I go then? I'm scared.' Tears welled up in Louisa's large eyes and splashed over onto her cheeks.

Trudi steadied her chin so she could look her in the eyes. 'Now listen, Louisa. You're safe here and I won't let anything bad happen to you.'

'Promise?' asked Louisa, her voice a sob.

'Look what I have for you,' said Ida brightly, returning to the kitchen carrying a small pile of clothes with a pair of brown sandals on top. She must have seen Louisa's tears, and pretended not to notice them. Instead she got to work washing the dirt from Louisa's feet with warm water and drying them before trying the sandals on her for size. They were only slightly too big and she was able to pull the straps through the buckles to the last hole to secure them in place. The pink and white striped gingham dress and matching white cardigan were a better fit and brought a smile to Louisa's face. Trudi was glad, though she refused to allow herself to think of what lay behind these clothes that must have once belonged to a child long gone from here.

Ida's soup was even more of a success. As soon as Ida had put it in front of Louisa, she began to eat ravenously, and finished her bowl before Trudi was even halfway through her own. She gave a sigh of pleasure that made Ida and Trudi smile, but shook her head when Ida offered her a second helping.

'No, thank you,' she said solemnly, unable to suppress a long yawn.

'It's time you went to bed.' Trudi stood up and took Louisa by the hand. 'She can sleep in my bed tonight. I'll sleep in the chair,' she said, before Ida could object.

Ida agreed. 'Good idea, and we can work out what to do in the morning.'

FORTY-THREE

'I've done a terrible thing.' Trudi stood hesitating in the kitchen doorway. 'Can I tell you about it?'

'Shut the door and come and sit down. You look as if you could do with a drop of brandy.' Ida went to the dresser and brought out a bottle and two glasses. 'I could do with one too,' she said, pouring out a generous amount into each and handing one to Trudi. 'Before you say anything, drink it down. You'll feel better for it.'

It was as if Ida knew. Trudi was relieved that she wasn't thrown by her words; she was dreading going into detail about the scene in the woods and how she had left Sem for dead. It was far easier to sit in Ida's comforting kitchen letting the brandy slip down and warm her insides while the clock ticked peacefully over the stove. She kept sipping the amber liquid until her glass was empty. Ida insisted on topping up their glasses, and appeared in no hurry to hear what Trudi had to say.

Eventually Trudi took a deep breath, and began with the letter that Ida had given her only that afternoon. 'All this time that Louisa was missing I never actually suspected that Sem had taken her. We split up months ago. I knew he wasn't happy about it, but I never thought he had it in him to want to punish me. So it was a shock to get his letter that he was holding Louisa hostage. I believed I could persuade him to give her back without resorting to violence.' She shook her head, just as there came a sharp rap on the back door.

In a flash, she thought that it must be Sem who had come searching for her, however irrational that thought might be. She rose to her feet so fast that her chair tipped backwards, crashing to the floor. Wincing, she reached down to pick it up.

There was another rap, louder this time.

Ida remained calm and said, 'Don't worry. You'd know if it were the Germans.' She patted Trudi on the arm before going to investigate.

Breathing fast, Trudi listened to the murmur of voices, but couldn't make out the words. She gripped tightly to the back of her chair as if it would offer her some kind of protection. It was a relief when Ida returned with Frans. He was red in the face, as if he'd been running.

'Thank goodness you're safe. And Ida tells me you brought Louisa back,' he said, removing his hat and twisting it between his hands. 'I've been out of my mind with worry ever since you left to meet Sem. I realised straight away I'd made a mistake in letting you go by yourself. I should have come with you.'

Trudi was surprised at his comment. 'No, it wasn't a mistake. You were right to let me do this alone. Sem was dangerous and you turning up would only have jeopardised the whole situation.'

Frans nodded, but didn't look convinced.

She told him what had happened: what Sem believed, his preposterous plans, and what she did, wishing she could undo her actions.

'Well,' said Frans, looking thoughtful. 'You were right not to leave him where he might be found. But I need to ask you – are you absolutely sure he's dead?'

'I can't believe he isn't. There was too much blood.' She examined her hands briefly as if expecting to see the evidence still there, before burying her face in them. 'What have I done?' she wept.

FORTY-FOUR

Trudi strode purposefully towards the entrance to the train station, which was guarded by two uniformed German soldiers. She was smartly dressed, wearing a tweed coat and navy-blue hat, and carried a small cream suitcase. Beside her walked Louisa, clinging tightly to her hand. The soldiers let their eyes linger on the couple for a moment before losing interest and turning their attention to a family group who were approaching.

Trudi held on to Louisa's hand tightly as they passed the soldiers and entered the busy entrance hall, which echoed to the sound of voices. It was full of people hurriedly criss-crossing the vast polished marble floor, or standing staring up at the departures board, trying to make out what was being said every time an announcement crackled into life over the tannoy. She glanced briefly up at the board to check, before hurrying off in the direction of their platform.

No one took any notice of the woman and child mingling with other passengers, but Trudi wasn't prepared to take any chances. The memory and fear of the last time she'd been here were too strong for her to ignore, so when the train drew alongside the platform she made sure they were among the first to board, taking their seats in an empty compartment. She slid the door shut.

'There, that wasn't so bad, was it?' said Trudi, lifting the suitcase onto the luggage rack and taking her seat by the window. She patted the seat next to her and noticed how pale Louisa looked.

Louisa took her seat and stared out of the window, then turned her head to Trudi. 'It won't be like last time, will it? I mean, when we had to crawl across that horrible field in the dark.' She shivered at the memory.

Trudi put a consoling arm round her shoulders, wishing there was something she could say to reassure her. She knew she could never fully comprehend the terror Louisa and all the other children had experienced, and suspected it would take Louisa a long time to get over her ordeal. 'No, I can assure you it won't be anything like that. There'll be no walking miles into the countryside. I know which way we're going this time. We'll be met at the station and the rest of the journey we'll go by car.'

Just then, the door of their compartment slid open and a curly-haired young man stuck his head in, before swivelling round to tell his companions this was their compartment. Three more young men trooped in after him and sat down on the remaining seats.

Trudi sensed Louisa's nervousness as she felt her push up close against her.

'Nice morning, isn't it?' said the curly-haired one, with an inquisitive stare.

Trudi smiled and nodded non-committally. They had an hour's journey ahead of them, and she was in no mood to talk to strangers.

'Is she your daughter?' the man said, leaning a little forward in his seat.

'No, she's not.' Trudi thought his question impertinent, but wasn't prepared to say more. She opened her bag, took out a

book and handed it to Louisa, then took out one for herself,
hoping that would put an end to the conversation. Out of the
corner of her eye, she saw the man shrug and whisper to his
companions. Whatever he said appeared to cause them much
merriment.

After the train had pulled out of the station, one of the men
brought out a bottle of jenever and passed it round. Soon the
group were chatting and laughing noisily.

It could be so much worse, Trudi told herself, and turned to
speak quietly to Louisa about what she was reading.

It was a relief when the conductor opened the carriage door
and laid eyes on the rowdy group. 'You should know that
drinking on the train is forbidden,' he said, raising his voice. 'All
of you must get off at the next stop. Now go and stand in the
corridor and leave this woman and child in peace.' He insisted
they hand over the bottle, even though it was almost empty, and
waited for them to file past him with sheepish expressions on
their faces.

'My apologies for not spotting those troublemakers earlier,'
he said, turning back to address Trudi. 'I hope they didn't
disturb you.' He furrowed his brow.

'No, they were no trouble.' She gave him a smile and
thanked him for his concern.

'May I please see your tickets?' he asked.

Trudi opened her bag to retrieve her purse and handed over
the tickets. A return for herself and one-way for Louisa. As he
examined them, he lifted his eyebrows with only the faintest
expression of surprise, but he made no comment. She waited for
him to ask for their papers.

'Thank you,' he said, after he'd punched the tickets and
handed them back to her. 'I hope you have a pleasant journey.'

Trudi carefully put the tickets away next to the fake ID
cards she'd been expecting to produce, and snapped her purse
shut in relief.

. . .

Gert was waiting for them under the station clock, looking around anxiously. When Trudi called his name and waved, his face broke into a smile and he came rapidly towards them.

'I hope we haven't kept you waiting,' she said, and shook his hand.

'Not at all. How was your journey?' He reached to take Louisa's suitcase from Trudi's hand.

'Trouble free,' she said with a wry smile.

Gert beamed at Louisa, who peered out, half hidden, from behind Trudi. 'Hello, young lady. I've heard your name is Louisa. Do you like dogs?' he said.

Louisa looked up at Trudi, who shrugged. 'Do you?' Trudi said gently.

Louisa nodded. 'We used to have a spaniel called Fifi,' she said, speaking softly. 'Papa let me hold her lead when we took her for walks.'

'Well, then I'm sure you'll like Fido. He's not a spaniel, mind, just a bit of this and a bit of that, but he's very friendly.'

Gert carried on chatting as they left the station and went over to his van parked a little way down the road. Trudi glanced at the two of them, Louisa happily listening to Gert's doggy stories, and was pleased about the effort he was making with her.

'You can sit up front between us,' Gert said, unlocking the passenger door. 'Unless you'd prefer to be in the back with Fido.'

From the back of the van came a series of barks and the scrabbling sound of claws on metal.

Louisa, who had visibly relaxed as she'd listened to Gert, now looked worried.

'I was only joking. You can meet him properly when we're back,' he said cheerfully, and ushered them both inside. He went round to his side and got in. Before he started the engine he turned to Louisa and said, 'I'd better warn you, it can get bumpy in this old van, but it shouldn't be long till we're home.'

Home, Trudi repeated the word in her head, and stole a glance at Louisa, wondering how she would adapt to yet another change in her life. It hadn't been easy telling her that she would be going to live with a couple she'd never met before, and many miles from her former home. When Louisa had asked if it meant she wouldn't be seeing her mama and papa, Trudi decided to be honest with her and said she'd had no news, but that she would let her know as soon as she heard anything. The truth was that things had become so chaotic that no one was able to offer any clarity over what happened to the Jews who had been rounded up and transported away. Most people were led to believe that they were sent to work for the Germans, but rumours had begun circulating that a more sinister fate awaited them on arrival at the camps. Naturally, Trudi didn't say any of this to Louisa, who had taken her explanation well – at least Trudi thought she had, though it was hard to tell as the girl was always so quiet. At least she had cheered up at the news that she was to be reunited with Rosy.

The van turned into the lane leading to the farm and Trudi was reminded of the first time she'd run along it with Rosy in her desperate search for help. Instinctively, she rubbed her arm where the bullet had penetrated. It no longer hurt, though it had left a deep red scar, which she suspected she would always have. The memory of the pain came back to her as if it had been yesterday, along with the panic she'd felt after losing Louisa when the boat had sunk. Even now, it made her shiver with guilt to think that she could ever have considered leaving Louisa to fend for herself in such perilous circumstances. She laid a hand on Louisa's and squeezed tight.

Gert drove the van into the yard and Fido began yapping frantically. 'Keep your hair on,' he said in a jovial voice and jumped down to let the dog out of the back. Panting enthusiastically, Fido immediately scurried round to the passenger door, where Louisa was gingerly stepping out. He circled round her wagging his tail, his long tongue lolling out of the side of his mouth. Louisa patted the dog on the head and he nuzzled his snout into her hand, making her giggle.

'You soppy thing,' said Gert, casting a look at the dog. 'Come on. Inside.'

Rosy was kneeling on the carpet, chatting to herself as she arranged a pile of wooden bricks into a tower. She glanced up and smiled as Louisa entered the room with Trudi, and accidentally knocked her tower flying. 'Bother!' she said and went back to her play.

Louisa went straight over and crouched down beside her. 'Let me,' she said, and picked up several bricks and began rebuilding the tower. 'If you do it like this,' she said, 'you can make it higher.' She patiently handed Rosy a brick. Together, they stacked all the bricks into a tall column until the last one on top made the whole thing wobble and tumble down. Both girls shrieked with laughter.

'I never thought I'd see the two of them back together,' said Trudi, after she'd followed Nettie into the kitchen.

'I never doubted it,' said Nettie, putting the kettle on for tea. 'Well, perhaps I did after you came out of hospital and had gone home. But I didn't allow myself to think the worst. Besides, I've had Rosy's welfare to think of.'

'Yes. She looks as if she's settled in happily. I can't thank you enough... but are you absolutely sure you want to look after both girls?'

Nettie held up a hand. 'No question of it. Rosy and Louisa belong together and will be safe with us. I hope you brought new ID cards for them?'

Trudi nodded and fetched them from her bag. 'They'll stay as Rosy and Louisa but will take yours and Gert's surname for now. I've explained things to Louisa – she understands – but Rosy's too young for it to matter yet.' She showed Nettie the cards, which were indistinguishable from the real thing. Most important of all was that they did not have J for Jew stamped on them. Trudi went back to her bag and brought out an envelope. She opened it and took out several ten-guilder notes and booklets of food and clothing coupons.

'This is too much,' said Nettie, shaking her head, and tried to push them away.

'No, Nettie. You'll need these – and there will be more every three months. Frans insists. The local group has raised the money and had extra coupons printed.' She placed them firmly in Nettie's hand. 'And it gives me an excuse to come back and visit the girls often.'

From the living room, Gert could be heard playing with the children. He appeared in the hallway carrying Rosy on his back, Louisa beside him, shrieking with laughter as she tried to climb up herself.

Nettie gave an indulgent smile. 'He's a changed man since Rosy came to live with us. We never could have children, so these two are the best gift we could ever have wished for.'

EPILOGUE

It was late afternoon. The setting sun shone straight into Trudi's eyes, and at first she didn't notice the hunched figure dressed in black who was tending the flowers on the newly dug grave. Trudi hung back, believing it to be Sem's mother and not wanting to intrude on her grief. Taking a detour around some gravestones, she went to sit on a wooden bench in the sunshine at the far corner of the cemetery. She watched the woman, who was taking her time arranging the floral wreaths and potted plants, and found herself growing impatient. Should she go over and say something, she wondered, then thought better of it. What could she possibly say? That she was responsible for her son's death because she'd feared for her life and the child he'd been holding hostage? The story Frans had put about was that Sem had been unlucky and was caught by a stray bullet when out minding his own business. It was a plausible enough explanation, as German soldiers were ever-present on the streets these days and accounts of tragic shootings weren't uncommon. But Trudi felt uncomfortable with this version of events, knowing the truth to be so different.

The woman had finished what she was doing and was now

standing beside the grave with her head bowed. Trudi narrowed her eyes and to her surprise realised she was looking at Mevrouw de Wit, who had come to pay her respects to her deceased nephew. She decided she should go and speak to her.

The woman turned her head to see who was walking towards her. Trudi noticed her eyes were red-rimmed from crying.

'Ah, Trudi,' she sighed out in a resigned voice, as if she'd known all along that Trudi had been waiting to speak to her.

'Don't let me disturb you.' Trudi glanced down and caught her breath. The grave was so new that it was still a mound of soil strewn with flowers from well-wishers. At one end, a small wooden cross had been planted in the dug earth. Trudi stooped to read it: SEM SCHIPPER 5.5.22–17.9.41, scratched in black ink. It was a stark reminder that Sem was here, buried right beneath her feet; she found the notion that he was no longer alive almost impossible to accept.

As she made to move away, Mevrouw de Wit held a hand out to stop her.

'Stay a moment,' she said. 'I don't want to be here on my own. Tell me, did you know Sem? Is that why you're here?'

Trudi observed her face, trying to work out if she was pretending not to know anything about her history with Sem. But she was so taken up by grief, it was hard to believe she was putting it on. She hesitated, wondering whether to tell her she'd once been close to Sem, but what good would it do? It was too late for that. 'I knew him a little. I was passing, so thought I'd come and see where he was...' She couldn't bring herself to say the word.

For a long while they stood in silence, each lost in their own thoughts.

Trudi was about to leave when something occurred to her. 'Mevrouw, can I ask you something?'

'Hmm?' The older woman blinked rapidly. She seemed to

have forgotten that Trudi was beside her. 'What is it?' she said, now attentive.

'It's just something you once told me about Sem. That you expected him to join the NSB because he worked at the town hall. Do you know if he ever did? I mean, join the NSB.'

'Not that I know of. He never mentioned it. You don't think —?' She halted mid-sentence.

'Think what?'

'That someone shot him for being a collaborator.' Mevrouw de Wit took in a sharp breath and covered her mouth with her hand.

Then Trudi remembered something in the letter Sem had written to her. Something she hadn't understood. He'd said that if she didn't come to meet him by herself he couldn't be held responsible for what happened to Louisa. So, if it were true that he'd switched sides and actually become a collaborator, was he intending to betray Louisa all along because she was Jewish?

Mevrouw de Wit was watching, waiting for her to say something.

'I don't think we'll ever know,' Trudi said, preferring not to acknowledge the unpleasant truth.

'Sem was always good to me. He didn't deserve to die.' Mevrouw de Wit took out a handkerchief and buried her nose in it.

'No,' murmured Trudi, unwilling to say any more. She gave an involuntary shudder and noticed how the sun had sunk behind the tall trees that encircled the cemetery. The air had turned chilly. She needed to get away. 'If you don't mind, I must go,' she said.

'Yes, of course,' said Mevrouw de Wit, regaining her composure. 'I must go too. I don't want to miss the bus to Bloemendaal.'

'To stay with your sister,' confirmed Trudi.

'She's taken it very hard. It was a relief when Frans told me to go and stay with her. He said I should take as long as I need. Anyway, I've decided it's time I moved on. I've been working for Frans and his family for twenty-five years.' She gave a pinched smile.

So Frans had seen sense and found a way to get rid of her, Trudi realised. Despite her misgivings, Trudi still had some sympathy for the woman's position. She'd clearly been fond of her nephew and would have accepted him whatever his beliefs. 'Frans has always spoken highly of you.'

'Has he really?' said Mevrouw de Wit, looking pleased.

Trudi nodded, for it was true.

'Shall I take those from you?' Mevrouw de Wit said after a moment.

Trudi had forgotten she was carrying a bunch of pink and white wildflowers that she'd picked that morning down by the canal. It had seemed like a good idea at the time, but the flowers were now wilting in her hand.

'Thank you,' She handed them over, glad to be rid of them. She made her excuses and hurried away without a backward glance.

Trudi's mood was gloomy as she packed her bags for the umpteenth time that autumn. Frans hadn't told her where she'd be moving to next and she'd grown tired of the constant upheaval. If only she could stay put for more than a couple of weeks in one place, maybe put down roots and find a job offering purpose and security. She longed to see Frida and found it hard to accept her absence. It had been so long since she'd had word from her, that she was starting to be worried for her safety. Where could she have got to? Trudi knew that her sister was probably doing what she loved best – working in emergency hospitals and saving the lives of war victims, but that was small consolation. Trudi missed her strong, capable sister dreadfully.

Feeling sorry for herself, Trudi was emptying a drawer and dumping the contents into her suitcase any old how when there was a soft knock at her bedroom door. Glancing at her watch, she sighed, thinking it must be Frans arriving early to help her with the move.

'Just a minute,' she called out, and hurriedly tidied a few things before going to see who it was.

'Hello, Trudi. May I come in?'

Trudi's heart skipped a beat. Piet was the last person she had expected to find on her doorstep. They hadn't seen one another in weeks, since he'd gone back to work for his old resistance cell in Amsterdam. They'd promised to keep in touch, but nothing had come of it. They were both too busy and she hadn't honestly expected anything to come of their friendship... and yet, Piet had never been far from her mind.

Trudi looked into his kind brown eyes, and became aware of her face growing warm. 'Have you come with Frans?' she blurted out for want of something better to say, for she couldn't imagine why he would come by himself.

'No, it's just me. If that's all right.' His smile was warm and genuine.

Trudi shook her curls. 'You'll have to excuse the mess. Frans will be coming any minute and I haven't finished packing,' she said, feeling flustered. She went over to the bed and lifted her open suitcase onto the floor. 'Do you want to sit down?'

'Actually, Frans won't be coming. If it's all right with you, I'll be helping you with your move.'

'Really? Is there something you're not telling me?'

Piet lowered himself down beside her with a laugh. 'I'm taking you to Amsterdam – but only if you want to. It's an idea I've had for a while, but I didn't want to tell you until I was certain I could arrange it.'

'Piet Menger, are you going to tell me what this is all about?' Trudi said, unable to keep the smile off her face.

He took her hands in his and kept hold of them. 'I've found you a job,' he began. 'My boss has been secretly working with the head of a Jewish school in the centre of Amsterdam. The situation with the Nazis is getting worse by the day and he's had parents begging him to take their children into hiding, so he started smuggling young children in his care out of the city and away from the Nazis. The operation started out small but it's got to the point that he is having to turn away desperate families simply because he doesn't have enough people prepared to help bring their children to safety. You see, it's dangerous work and some of the children are barely toddlers. It means taking them across town hidden in baskets or bags right under the noses of the Nazis. As soon as my boss told me about his predicament, I thought of you and what a natural you are with children. And how brave and fearless you are. I thought the position would suit you down to the ground.'

'I would love to, but... do you really think I can do it?'

'I wouldn't say it if I didn't believe it. So does Frans, actually.'

'You've been discussing my future with Frans before even asking me?' She wanted to be annoyed with him, but how could she when he was giving her such a tender look? Before she knew it, he moved closer and kissed her softly on the lips.

'You don't mind then?' he said, before kissing her again.

'Not at all,' she said, slightly confused as to what he was referring to, but either way it felt right to be here with Piet with the prospect of more to come.

Eventually, she said, 'When am I to start?'

'Tomorrow, if that's not too soon. If we leave now, we can get the bus and be in Amsterdam before midday.' He pulled her to his feet. 'I think you'll like your room. It's at the top of the house with a nice view over the Rozengracht. And it's walking distance from the school.'

'You organised all this for me?' Trudi said, laughing, as he squeezed her into a hug.

'A room came up in the house I'm sharing with four others. I hope you don't mind...'

'Why would I mind?' said Trudi, her heart feeling lighter than it had in months. There was nothing to keep her here in Haarlem and every reason to start afresh in Amsterdam. And she'd be living at an address on the Rozengracht – the very name reminded her of Rosy, whose life she had saved. It felt like a good omen.

'I'd love to come,' she said, and was delighted to see Piet's face light up.

She was under no illusion about how difficult, dangerous and potentially heartbreaking her new job would be; but, if she could save even just one young person's life, it would all be worthwhile.

A LETTER FROM IMOGEN

I want to say a huge thank you for choosing to read *The Girl from the Resistance*. If you did enjoy it, and want to keep up to date with all my latest releases, just sign up at the following link. Your email address will never be shared and you can unsubscribe at any time.

www.bookouture.com/imogen-matthews

I think it's fitting that I am writing this letter on 4 May, the Dutch national day of remembrance, when the Dutch observe a two-minute silence to commemorate victims who died during and have died since the Second World War. For me, it's a day to reflect on the lives of the Dutch citizens who refused to give in to the Nazis after they had taken over their country and sent three-quarters of the Dutch Jewish population to their deaths. These intrepid people came together to resist the oppression of their occupiers and help those less fortunate than themselves by undertaking acts of immense bravery. Among them were three young women: Truus Oversteegen, her sister Freddie Oversteegen and Hannie Schaft. It is these three women who inspired me to write a new series of three novels based on their lives.

My interest in the Netherlands comes from my own Dutch heritage. My mother was a teenager when her country was occupied by Nazi Germany, and her incredible stories of resistance and survival have shaped my four novels, before this, my latest novel: *The Girl from the Resistance*.

History tells us that sisters Truus and Freddie Oversteegen, and Hannie Schaft, joined a small resistance group based in Haarlem, the town where they lived, which lies to the west of Amsterdam close to the North Sea coast. When war broke out, they were ordinary teenage girls, aged between fourteen and nineteen, and should in normal times have been experimenting with hairstyles and make-up and giggling about boys. Instead, they joined the resistance; they became proficient in using firearms and were not afraid to use them against the enemy. This wasn't bravado, for they took their assignments very seriously and would only draw a gun on someone they believed to be intent on harming others – in some cases, people who were responsible for sending hundreds, even thousands of innocent victims to their deaths.

What made Truus, Freddie and Hannie's actions all the more extraordinary was that few, if any, women were involved in such active resistance in the Netherlands. These three must have been all too aware that their youth and femininity put them at an advantage, for no one suspected young women to be engaged in such fearless and dangerous acts.

My main source of research were two books written about these three remarkable women:

- *Three Ordinary Girls* by Tim Brady
- *Seducing and Killing the Nazis: Hannie, Truus and Freddie: Dutch Resistance Heroines of WWII* by Sophie Poldermans.

These books give breathtaking accounts of these young women's actions, such as sheltering fleeing Jews, ferrying young Jewish children from probable deportation to concentration camps to safe houses, covertly transporting weapons to help the Allies, sabotaging bridges and railways, and the assassination of German SS officers and Dutch collaborators.

Many of the events that take place in *The Girl from the Resistance* were true. Trudi's heart-stopping dash across a minefield at the dead of night with a group of Jewish children, the youngest just three, was true. So was the daring plot to blow up a bridge over the wide Haarlem River, the training Trudi was given in how to handle explosives and the meeting of the resistance group down in the bunker to discuss tactics.

At all times I have tried to remain faithful to the true story of Truus, but because this is a work of fiction I have changed people's names and relationships and imagined some events that perhaps didn't happen in exactly the way I describe them.

I hope you loved *The Girl from the Resistance* and if you did I would be very grateful if you could write a review. I'd love to hear what you think, and it makes such a difference in helping new readers to discover one of my books for the first time.

I love hearing from my readers – you can get in touch on my Facebook page, through Twitter, Goodreads or my website.

Thanks,

Imogen

www.imogenmatthewsbooks.com

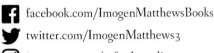

facebook.com/ImogenMatthewsBooks

twitter.com/ImogenMatthews3

instagram.com/oxfordnovelist

ACKNOWLEDGEMENTS

Every book is a team effort and I'm grateful to everyone at Bookouture who has made this one happen. It started over a lunch in the shadow of St Paul's, London with my editor Susannah Hamilton, who listened to my ideas for a new series based on three remarkable Dutch women resistance fighters, and enthusiastically encouraged me to write a three-book series based on these resistance women.

Thank you, Susannah, for helping me shape the first book in this series, and to Jennifer Hunt, who came back from maternity leave and jumped straight in with her excellent guidance and suggestions to make it a much better book than I could have imagined.

Thanks also to all the amazing professionals in the editorial, marketing, digital, publicity and sales teams at Bookouture, who have all played an important part in bringing my book to you, my valued reader.